Bad Decisions

BY: G.M. PARRILLO

Dedication

To my Inkbound Society crew, love your faces!

To Jojo and Wendy thank you for being my Denise!

To my Harley, thanks for being my puddin'!

For those who were told you couldn't do it, don't listen to them.
Because you can!

PROLOGUE

Denise

Labor Day Weekend, September 2008

This was not a Monday. Only awful, terrible, bad decisions were made on Mondays - but here she was making one on a Saturday. Sometimes, Denise found herself making bad decisions on a Tuesday, carrying over from her Mondays. But Saturdays were reserved for Shenanigan Saturdays. Which was why she found herself high and drunk, in a dirty hotel room with the lovely couple she had just met at the concert… shenanigans.

Summers in New Jersey meant that all the concerts had officially been underway and they were getting closer to the end of the season. Which also meant tickets were in high demand for most big-name headliners. These were not easy to come by. Negotiating for the past two weeks with one of her old Navy buddies whose brother worked at the Art Center to get her two tickets for her and Nick - Denise had said she would take anything. Hell, she was happy with the steeply pitched ground lawn seats that had no more grass growing on it, because of all the people who had trod on it since the season began back in May. She would bring her own blanket for her and Nick to sit on, just as long as she could get to see the opening band, The Dirty Mucks. No one had heard of them, but she caught them once at a bar off-base back when she was in the service and she fell in love with their sound.

Nick had never appreciated her taste in music. Truthfully, he also never appreciated her. Despite him knowing that she was a former Navy ammunitions expert (one of only two women in her division) and her high school class valedictorian, he still looked down on her because she didn't have a regular job like he did. What was supposed to be a late one-night stand had somehow turned into a relationship.

It had been four months of listening to Nick droning on about landing a bunch of really large companies as his clients for the accounting firm he had been working at since he graduated college. Finally getting the promotion he had been working towards Denise had praised him over and over again for all his dedication. But she just wished that he would have been as supportive, especially since she had just been signed on by a large company to provide her yoga classes for their employee wellness program. But that wasn't what Nick Dupree was like. He was unsupportive, self-centered, entitled, money driven and constantly gaslighting her. Worst of all - he was a cheater.

Which was why the day before the concert Denise had had enough and kicked him out. Never one to let perfectly good seats go to waste, she figured she would make the best of the situation and not miss out on a chance of seeing the Mucks!

Shuffling along with the crowd, in the excruciating humid heat of a typical New Jersey summer, packed like a bunch of sardines in a can with other sweaty, beer soaked, high as a kite Jerseyans she climbed the dirt hill to find a bare spot to sit and considering that she was only one person she thought to herself, *how hard could it be to find a single spot.*

Bumping into people in the crowd was par for the course in an event like this one. She could deal with the sweaty flesh of others, but it was the fear that she was going to step on someone who had already found a spot. Being tall was a bit of a blessing, you could scope out locations before everyone else. Her towering frame at five feet and eleven inches tall made it much easier indeed - but her large feet were a bit cumbersome when needing to navigate these tight spaces.

Stopping to survey the landscape she noticed that there was a tiny enough spot for herself and her blanket. The only issue was the couple sitting to the right of it practically dry humping right there in front of everyone. She was there for a concert, not to watch a live action porno. Heavily resigning herself to the idea of dealing with these two, Denise nimbly made her way through the dense crowd, struggling to make her way to the spot without stepping on another patron. It served her right for getting there late.

Spreading her multicolored waterproof blanket on the ground, Denise did her very best to avoid being a voyeur to the amorous couple groping each other to her right. The slurping of their kisses was actually making her nauseous. Being fresh out of a relationship and suddenly surrounded by this energetic couple was not in her plans for the evening, or it could be that she hadn't even bothered to eat something since breakfast and that beer in the parking lot may not have been a wise choice. Bad decision number one. If only Nick hadn't been a jerk, she would have had someone to enjoy the concert with. But with him now in her rear view, all she was left to contend with was the two wanna-be porn stars.

"Jersey! Are you ready?" The lead singer of the Mucks had yelled out over the mic and received a lukewarm response, but it had drawn Denise's attention away from the pair until the red headed woman pried herself away from her succubus of a partner to pay attention.

"Babe, Babe, they're on!" Scrambling to her feet the voluptuous redhead bounced like a child being handed their favorite toy and Denise couldn't get over two things. One that someone else knew the band, and two, that the woman in the pale-yellow shirt and booty hugging jean shorts with the massive breasts was not wearing a bra and impressively was not giving herself a black eye every time she jumped.

As beautiful as Denise thought this one was, she herself was no shrinking violet. Blessed with a statuesque height, people seemed drawn to her. Her father had called her, his "ma belle crème caramel". Deep caramel colored skin with the faintest sprinkling of freckles that danced across her nose and cheeks, complimented many times over for having bewitching hazel-green eyes that always seemed to stop men and women alike in their tracks. But if someone asked Denise what her favorite feature about herself was, it would be the long, pin straight jet-black hair that she had inherited from her mother. Her svelte curves with her height had many people thinking that she was in modeling and would never have guessed that she had been in the Navy specializing in ammunition.

As 'Babe' lumbered up from his dirt spot on the lawn at the same time as Denise, he caught her looking at him. Returning her glance with a quick wink, she flashed him a quick curt polite smile. 'Babe' was very handsome for sure but definitely too short and lanky for her taste. As for her women, she liked someone like 'Red', but 'Babe' could take a walk unless he was packing something surprising in those dirt-stained khaki cargo shorts.

"Woooo, Tommy! Woooooo!" 'Red' carried on as the lead singer scanned the crowd to find them and it must have worked - stopping mid-chord to point up to her which only sent 'Red' into a tizzy. Denise looked around and it seemed that they were the only ones in this sea of people who were excited to be listening to them and she turned back to her fellow Muck fans to her right.

"Do you know them?" yelling over the music to 'Babe' who was singing along with the band. He had heard Denise and smiled.

"Yeah, the lead singer is her brother."

The shrilly scream-singing by 'Red' mixed with the reverb of the mics was pinging a part of her inner ear she was sure had been damaged from years of ammo use, but this seemed to be cutting right through her head. With the heat drunk crowd now up on their feet, Denise decided that despite the choking humidity and crush of people surrounding her, she would enjoy herself; especially if 'Red' bounced her breasts a little closer to Denise, it would at least give her some form of action tonight even if unintentional.

BAD DECISIONS

Despite the stretching ache in her feet and calves from the incline of the ground Denise was dancing on, she was enjoying herself. The Dirty Mucks had closed their set and by the end, the crowd was cheering them on, which made her neighbor overly exhilarated resulting in Denise's favorite part of the show, 'Red's' Gogo routine of leaping up and down. Her large boobs just kept grazing against Denise's arm and as she turned to apologize for being so close, Denise caught a glint of desire in 'Red's' eye. Smirking down at her new friend, Denise then fixed her eyes to 'Babe' who just gave her a knowing gleam.

And now here she was in this tiny stale smelling, tan and maroon covered hotel room with 'Babe' and 'Red', completely drunk and high on Ecstasy. Denise was not one to indulge in narcotics, a joint or a cigarette here or there, definitely alcohol, but never anything heavier. Another bad decision. It dawned on her that she seemed to be making a lot of them lately. Bad decisions always lead to one thing, trouble. However, this was her kind of trouble.

'Babe' despite his scrawny appearance, was indeed blessed with a gorgeous thick dick that angled ever so slightly to the right. Slowly licking along the thick vein that ran from the base to the crown of his dick, Denise gasped as 'Red's' lips sucked down hard on her swollen clit urging her to take his shaft deep into her already salivating mouth. This was not how she imagined the night going. She figured she would crawl into her cold soft bed after the concert with her ears ringing and eventually fall asleep with all her pillows surrounding her, not be deep throating some random guys cock while his girlfriend sucked hard on her overly stimulated bundle of nerves while finger fucking her dripping quim.

As tears collected in her eyes, she strained against her gag reflex at his girth as the tip hit the back of her throat. Closing her eyes, Denise took deep breaths as he grabbed the back of her head and began mouth fucking her slowly allowing her to accommodate for his size. On the other end, her thighs were starting to quiver, as the sensation of 'Red's' tiny fingers drove in and out of her. If that wasn't enough, 'Red' was still keeping up her relentless pace of swirling her tongue over and over Denise's clit driving her closer to climax. Her moans against 'Babe's' dick letting him know that she was going to cum stopped him mid stroke.

"Honey, I think you have had enough of her, it's my turn." 'Babe' said dislodging his dick from Denise's mouth. Gasping for air, Denise wasn't sure she was ready for that, but at this point she would rather have one of those delicious breasts in her mouth than be choked by his cock.

"But she is close, I can feel it." 'Red' pouted as she scooted out from underneath Denise. The warmth of 'Red' leaving suddenly left a chill running through her.

"I'll make you both cum at the same time, okay Honey? Will that make it all better?" he teased as he gathered the redhead up against him, kissing her deeply so that he could also get the taste of Denise in his own mouth. Her head fuzzy, Denise took this moment of brief respite and finally allowed herself to collapse back against the bed. Every part of her tingled more than normal, and despite the air conditioning set at the highest it would go, she felt like she was dripping in sweat.

"I don't care what happens, but someone needs to fuck me now." Denise remarked as she looked on to her bad friends who were keeping themselves entertained. 'Babe' pulled away from the tempting red-head and turned his attention back to Denise. Climbing up onto the bed, he stroked his hands over Denise's legs and the sensation sent an electric ripple through her whole body as her pussy pulsated at the sensation of his hands on her. Sliding himself between her long legs, he ran the pad of his thumbs along the inside of her thighs as he scratched his nails along the outer edge of them and it felt as if she would dissolve into the starchy maroon comforter she was laying on.

A warmth settled next to her, and it felt like the sun had risen on her right side, as 'Red' joined her and Denise couldn't quite seem to stop herself from grasping those juicy breasts she had been eyeing all day. As the tip of 'Babe's' cock poised its way into her dripping pussy, Denise pulled 'Red' up to her and finally got to stuff one of her beautiful tits into her mouth. It was soft, salty and perfect as she danced her tongue over her pert pink nipple, grazing it with her teeth causing a squeal from 'Red' just as 'Babe' drove deep into her dripping core.

Moaning against the breast she was feasting on, Denise closed her eyes to the overwhelming sensation. She was seeing stars and feeling colors, if that was possible. The moans and grunting from her partners just kept escalating. Denise wasn't sure what was going on, but whatever it was felt amazing and as quickly as it all started, it exploded and ended all around them. The only rationale that she had in her foggy mind was that the drug had made it all so quick because these feelings were all incredibly intense. Out of breath, she looked at the clock on the nightstand and it appeared that they had actually been at this for longer than she thought, three a.m. had rolled around and they had finally all came. Laying in the embrace of her new friends Denise couldn't quite pull herself away. So, she decided to stay and rest, and in the morning she would thank them by grabbing breakfast with them at the local diner.

As she sat there in the cold medicinal smelling waiting room, Denise was kicking herself. The room had a soft gray wallpaper with some kind of late 80's metallic print on it, but it had been thankfully hidden behind all the picture frames with countless baby pictures or Christmas cards that had gaggles of kids poised on from previous and current patients. Looking around the room, there were pamphlets about STDs, menopause, birth control, baby formula and pregnancy. She was only here to get tested for an STD since her stupid evening at the concert a month ago.

Denise knew something was off, she had been having weird spotting, but it was par for the course for her. As someone with Polycystic Ovarian Syndrome (PCOS), she had irregular periods and would often have random spotting, but lately something was not right.

With all the odd symptoms she had been having, Denise felt it best to get tested. There was that odd metallic taste in her mouth, her temperature was up and there was a bit of discomfort in her pelvis, so she thought it best to get in to make sure it wasn't something more serious. *It's probably just a yeast infection*, she thought. The only good thing about being here was that she was going to talk to Dr. Jean about getting a different birth control. Considering how she had been on the lowest dosage for years, and still having irregular cycles, it was best to up the dosage. However, she would need the doctor to approve of it.

As Denise eyed the birth control pamphlets, two of the tiniest women she had ever seen walked into the office through the oak front door. They looked like they were probably separated at birth and by different fathers. The blonde had a round baby bump and was breathing rather laboriously as she pushed the heavy door open. The plus sized brunette with her was scolding her for trying to open the door.

"For the love of God, I could have opened that for you." She reprimanded her tiny associate as she held the door. "Anyway, all I did was ask him if he could stop and get me sour patch watermelons and you would think I asked him for the entire candy store." The brunette struggled through the door behind her friend and grabbed a bag of said candies out of her bag as they walked up to the reception window signing their names in on the clipboard.

"Fuck him, I say you kick him out and raise this baby by yourself, you know you are gonna be doing all of it anyway. I knew I should've kidnapped you the night before the wedding and held you hostage, your parents would have thanked me." Quipped the blonde, whoever the brunette's husband was seemed to be a dick. Denise wondered if he was related to Nick. He still hadn't gotten his last box out of her apartment and she was tired of looking at his old crap. Gaslighting, dickhead. A wave of nausea came over her at the thought of him, it seemed that it was happening a lot lately, probably a bug from one of her yoga clients or whatever this was she was dealing with.

The receptionist opened the frosted glass window and looked at Denise. "Ms. Gagnon, you can come in." Getting up from her seat, she stood for a second and felt a wave of dizziness hit her as she held her head. Out of the corner of her eye, Denise saw the two other women look over to her with a bit of concern.

"Ugh, dizzy spells? They were the worst in the first couple of months." The blonde said to her and Denise arched her brow not understanding what the Hell she was talking about. Did she think she was pregnant? "They go away eventually."

Denise just smiled, not sure exactly how to respond and walked into the back of the doctor's office. As she sat there getting her blood pressure taken, the nurse went through the standard questions. This normally didn't bother Denise, but when the nurse told her the reading was up and they would need to do it again, she was now starting to get really worried. Nurse Betty just smiled as she handed her a specimen cup.

"Here, go fill this up and come back, I'm sure it's fine. We will do it before you leave, white coat syndrome is a real thing." The older woman winked. As Denise walked into the bathroom, she thought to herself that she never had an issue going to the doctors before, so she couldn't imagine why her blood pressure would be up. Filling the cup and returning back to Betty, Denise followed her into one of the exam rooms and grimaced at the terrible paper gown she was handing her.

The exam room was another cold room and she didn't understand why it was always so cold in these offices. *Probably for all those menopausal patients that must come in,* Denise thought to herself. Looking around she felt a bit sick at the bubble gum pink and tan striped wallpaper with a bunch of posters depicting a woman's body and what it looked like when they were pregnant. As she sat with the ridiculous gown on, there was a knock on the door and the nurse poked her head in.

"Denise, the doctor asked if you don't mind moving to a different room, I'm so sorry about this, I'm gonna get you a second gown so you can fully cover-up, it's the room at the end of the hall." Too exhausted to argue, Denise grabbed her stuff, not even waiting for the second gown and followed the nurse down the hall. This was a much larger room with an ultrasound machine and a couple of chairs, it was yet another pink and tan room, however, these walls were covered with pictures of all the babies the doctor had delivered and now she was starting to get concerned.

Dizzy spells, metallic taste, weight gain, nausea and the irregular spotting… *it couldn't be*. Her heart pounding in her chest, she walked over and placed her pile of clothes down on a chair, she wasn't sure why she was so nervous it wasn't possible that she was pregnant. But while she tried figuring out the percentages of the possibilities, she let the nurse help her up onto the cold paper-lined exam table just in time for the older female doctor to walk in.

"Denise, this is a pleasant surprise, how are you feeling?"

That seemed like a loaded question. *How was she feeling*? Scared. Nervous. Unsure.

"Um, I'm just here to get tested to see if I have a yeast infection or an STD. Not sure why I'm back in this room." Denise looked between the nurse and her doctor searching for one of the two women to say something. Turning to her, Dr. Jean clicked a couple of buttons on the ultrasound machine and then walked over to stand in front of her as Denise brought her feet up into the stirrups.

"Well, we are gonna do a scraping and send it out for testing. But, sweetie, we just did a rapid pregnancy test and it's positive. I'm guessing you didn't realize that was a possibility?"

Pregnant!?!?! Denise's brain exploded and all she could think was that this couldn't happen.

"No, I'm on birth control and I haven't had sex with anyone in a month."

"Okay well you are on the lowest dosage, were you taking any antibiotics at all? Sometimes that can affect the effectiveness of the birth control." Dr. Jean explained, looking through Denise's chart.

Denise couldn't believe this; she had had a sinus infection a month and half ago almost two weeks before the concert. And then it hit her, bad decisions had been made. A wave of fear and self-loathing rolled over her. She hadn't been careful. She had given into the booze and drugs and had forgotten to make sure that that asshole 'Babe' had wrapped his damned dick. All because of those pretty titties 'Red' had. Scanning her clouded memory of that night to try and remember if she had seen a condom wrapper or not she realized that wasn't even the biggest concern. Just a few days before she and Nick had had sex before she kicked him out. So now she'd had unprotected sex twice and with two different men. As she laid there on the cold hard table she felt the sting of tears starting in her eyes and Dr. Jean took her hand.

"Denise, let's just take a look and make sure everything is okay and if you don't want to keep this pregnancy we can make arrangements if this is not in your plan."

Perhaps it wasn't a good idea, she was just starting to get her life together. Things were going so well and having to go through an unplanned pregnancy by herself seemed incredibly daunting. She had wanted to eventually find someone and settled down. Her parents' marriage was abysmal and despite all the chaos from that, there was still the tiniest part of her that wanted someone that she could share her life with. Someone who would love her and accept her for all of her bad choices in life. However, adding a baby to the mix left her realizing that the hope of finding that person was completely out of reach.

As she wiped away the tear that had escaped, she nodded and Dr. Jean gave a quick warning that the wand needed to be inserted to get an accurate reading. As she carefully guided the ultrasound wand through her vaginal canal and up past her cervix she winced at the pressure and tightened her fists. Betty walked over and held her left hand comforting her as the doctor clicked the keyboard and moved the wand. Suddenly stopping Dr. Jean bit back, a small smile and clicked the keyboard again and gave a quick sliding glance to Denise. *She must have found the baby.*

"It looks like everything is normal. Now, I am going to ask you a very difficult question and if the answer is no, I will move on and proceed with the exam. But I have to ask, would you like to see?"

That was the question of a lifetime, did she? Did she want to see, what if it was not what she wanted? Maybe it would be okay, maybe it would be awful, maybe… Taking a deep breath in, all Denise could do was nod. Craning her neck to look at the screen there it was a minuscule bean-like thing on the screen with some weird fluttering going on.

"Is that the heart fluttering?" Denise asked and then immediately regretted saying it because it made her sound incredibly stupid.

Of course it was; this tiny creature with a fluttering heart beating away was real. She wasn't sure whose heart was going faster, hers or this creature's. And then two clicks on the machine there was a rapid whooshing sound coming from the speaker. Blinking back tears, there was the sound of her baby, this teeny fluttering speck on the screen, was hers.

Denise had never even thought it was possible to get pregnant, in fact she was sure that because of her PCOS that it would never happen. She figured that she would be living on birth control to regulate her cycles for life. Never get pregnant, never to know the joy of being a mom but those damned antibiotics and fucking Nick or 'Babe'; here she was.

And then it hit her, she never expected to have kids. They were supposed to be forever out of reach. The joy of the unconditional love that her father had given to her would never be and the realization hit her like a freight train. The unconditional, no judgment love she had hoped for; had craved was right here. Someone who would possibly accept her for who she truly was. How could she give that up? Denise had always been an independent resourceful person. She could do this. That fast-beating heart would forever know that they were loved and cared for, that they would want for nothing and that they would be accepted for who they were.

Dr. Jean smiled at Denise knowing that she was going through everything in her brain and gave a wink towards Betty. Making another adjustment with the wand she took a couple more snapshots on the screen taking measurements and then hit a button prompting the machine to make a printout of the sonogram which was being ripped off and placed in the file.

"Okay let's do one final thing and you can go home and think about it."

Denise just shook her head.

"I don't need to think about it." She said as a lone tear escaped her eye. Smiling down at her Dr. Jean clicked a few more buttons and printed out another copy of the sonogram handing it to Denise before she moved to do her physical exam.

"Okay, well let me just do a quick scraping, then get dressed and we will set you up with prenatal appointments. Congratulations Mommy."

The word stole her breath away and the dam that had been holding back the tears finally broke. Mommy, she was going to be a mom, and for the first time in her life she made a great decision on a Monday.

CHAPTER ONE

Denise

September, 2024

Alright, easy out!" Hank stood up from his spot as catcher as Denise was taking her time to stride up to home plate, the loudspeaker playing *Jessie J, Ariana Grande and Nicki Minaj's 'Bang Bang'*. Gripping the metal bat in her hand she contemplated a number of things. How much time would she get in jail if she pounded him into a pulp with the bat? How quickly could she run once she did and would George actually bother to arrest her considering how he was standing right there watching Hank instigating a fight with her?

"Stop being an ass, dickhead!" Nikki screamed from behind the dugout fence as she rattled it with her bat. The raucous crowd in the stands yelling and screaming as Denise squared up to the plate, staring at the pitcher. Fundraising season had started for the marching band and the Parents Softball Game was always a big favorite as the kids got to play some of the music they were starting to practice for the upcoming season.

Historically, they had the color guard parents play against the band parents. Which meant that Denise was playing against Grace's team, and unfortunately Hank had decided to be a good dad and play as well.

"Can you shut it, you are gonna get a bat to the head Hank!" Grace screamed from right field. "Don't worry girl, just remember you don't look good in prison orange."

Grinning, she looked down at Hank, taking a few practice swings. *It's too bad they weren't using wooden bats, wouldn't it be grand if it splintered and a shard got in his eye*, she thought to herself snickering.

"What are you laughing at?" Hank questioned.

"Well, I was just looking at you, so I guess I'm laughing at your dumb ass." It wasn't her best, but that should at least rile him up. The umpire behind Hank just laughed and shot Denise a wink through his mask causing her to blush. George didn't have kids, so he offered to be the umpire for the game. His laughter had gotten Hank pissed as he grabbed the catcher's mask and pulled it over his face.

"Just because you two are screwing doesn't mean you can go easy on her, that last at bat you knew that was a strike." Fumed Hank, she had been walked and Hank had argued that it should have been called a strike, but George said it was high and out of the strike zone. Hank had thrown a hissy fit and Jim had actually had to intervene before George threw him out.

The size difference between the two men wasn't all that much, Hank was an inch shorter than Denise and to his credit did have a very good physique, while George on the other hand was six foot two and built like a tank, just how Denise enjoyed her men. The night of Grace and Jim's wedding George had finally summoned up the courage to ask her to dance. The storm that had rolled in just as they had said their 'I do's' had created a very humid atmosphere despite being on the beach. Coupled with her perimenopause kicking into high gear that night, her gauzy heather purple dress had clung to her body, making her feel a little self-conscious, but despite the fact that she felt like a drowned rat, George had asked her to dance at every opportunity.

"You're just jealous that we are getting laid and you are a sad lonely man, who screwed it all up and now you have to watch your ex-wife and her new husband live their best lives. That must suck big hairy moose balls, huh?" Denise couldn't seem to help herself; she hated him and needed to goad him at any and every opportunity she could. He reminded her too much of Nick. Narcissistic assholes the both of them. She could hear him taking deep breaths in and out, probably trying to calm down before he said something he would regret later.

She did need to give him some credit; Grace had told her that he had continued going to therapy even after he had fulfilled his legal obligations to the court order, and that it helped. The boys had been much happier and Hank had been actively working on co-parenting with Grace and getting along with Jim, which she found shocking. But he was still an asshole, it's hard to forgive the torment that he subjected on her best friend for years. Grace may have forgiven but she wasn't ready to no matter how much time had passed.

The first pitch had flown right past her and she was caught looking, strike one. Taking a deep breath in, she closed her eyes and let it out calming herself before the second pitch and that one she caught a piece of but it went foul, for strike two.

"You know if you just rest the bat on your shoulder and let the next one go, then you can go sit with Nikki and drink your 'diet coke'." He must have smelt the vodka on her breath. Nikki, Grace and Denise would add alcohol to their sodas in their insulated water cups so they could enjoy an adult beverage at events like these and try and pass it off as just soda. They weren't alcoholics or anything, it was just to relax and have a good time, and they would never be the ones behind the wheel at the end of the night. Besides, organizing these events was stressful, sometimes you just needed a little something to get through.

Denise lowered her head, her hazel-green eyes laser focused on the pitcher determined to prove Hank wrong. The pitcher wound up and released the ball; Denise took a swing and caught it at just the right time as it flew deep into the outfield. Grace and one of the other moms, Sheila, both ran trying to get under the ball. Grace was calling off Sheila, who didn't seem to care what Grace said as the ball arched in the air and was coming closer to her. Denise took off to first base and just kept watching Sheila running over toward Grace resulting in the two colliding with each other, tumbling down onto the ground.

As the crowd roared, Mike, who had been on second base, made his way to third and Denise just kept running as the two women in the outfield kept scrambling and laughing as they searched for the ball. Looking over her shoulder at Grace, Denise waved to Mike to keep going and he scored as Grace finally managed to pick up the ball just as Denise got to third base. Hearing Jim calling to Grace to throw him the ball, Denise locked eyes with Grace whose cocky smile just spurred Denise on wanting to score for home.

They weren't playing by the standard rules of baseball, all they were trying to do was score runs, otherwise she would have had to hold up back at second and the other team would have gotten an error. No errors, no holding up, just play ball, score, win. This was why this event was always one of the big fundraisers for the marching band.

As she took the first two steps off third base, Grace lobbed the ball towards Hank, setting Denise into a sprint. She was sure she had plenty of time, but then she remembered Grace mentioning before the game that she had played softball as a kid and specifically outfield. Which meant that she could very easily make that throw to home plate and it would be close.

Focused on scoring, Denise took her eyes off the ball and back to home. And there positioned partially blocking the plate was Hank. With renewed determination, Denise slid headfirst with her arms stretched, praying she would get to the plate before the ball got to Hank. As the tip of her fingers dusted across the plate, her head collided with Hank's groin sending him back with a yelp.

"SAFE!" George proclaimed, and the crowd in the stands erupted as the band started playing. Denise's head and neck hurt from the impact to Hank, but it was well worth it. Hank didn't seem as thrilled by her actions as he lay on the red clay field - grasping his nether regions - gasping for air while he let out a string of inarticulate mumbles about her being a bitch. As she got up, Denise walked over to Hank, pulled her hat off to dust the field clay from her shirt, and smirked as she towered over him.

"Easy out, huh? How'd that work out for ya? You might want to have your doctor check and make sure your balls aren't in your ass now." She teased, holding her hand out to offer him help up.

Glaring up at her hand, Hank grimaced and rolled onto his stomach as he gingerly made his way upright, wincing when he straightened to his full height. Stalking over to her, they stood practically nose to nose - and before either could do or say anything George was right next to them.

"Back up, both of you. I don't want to have to eject you both. It was an accident. Let's just remember this is a charity event and your kids are here. Hm?" George stepped in trying to diffuse the situation, Denise knew he was right, it was for the kids, but damn it felt great that she had proved him wrong and literally busted his balls at the same time. Taking a tiny step back Denise held out her hand again and continued her gaze into Hank's piercing blue eyes. He did have gorgeous eyes, *no wonder why Grace had married him all those years ago*, probably one of the reasons she had allowed him to stay married to her for so long. That and he was stupidly handsome with his chiseled jaw, and well-built olive-skinned physique - gifted to him by his Greek genes.

Denise couldn't understand why she felt a rising heat blooming across her cheeks as his narrowing gaze skimmed over her body. She had known him for years, had fought with him time and time again, so what was it about him sizing her up *this* time that had her feeling off? Not one to be intimidated by him, she puffed out her chest and shoved her hand closer to him so that he would be forced to look like a sore loser if he didn't take it. He stared at her hand, as George cleared his throat, inclining his head for him to take it and walked towards the backstop to get out a new ball and check the line-up.

As Hank took her hand into his, an electric shock stung them, it ran right up her arm making the hair on the back of her neck stand on end. After the ten years they had known each other, this was the very first time they had ever touched. Hank and Denise had never once hugged or shook hands before like most mutual acquaintances do. They had, however, spent the last ten years arguing and making insults at each other.

Which was why she was puzzled was this unease in her belly as he tightened his grip on her hand, his thumb tenderly padding over her knuckles in a very intimate manner. Her lovers had done that in her past, even George had done it when they went for walks, but why was Hank doing this? They had a mutual loathing for each other, and this tiny, gentle caress was off-putting to her. Her eyes widened as he pulled her close to get her nose to nose with him, his body was more solid than she had thought and she could feel his muscular form underneath his sweat and clay covered shirt, stealing her breath for a moment as he smiled at her.

"Next time Gagnon, you won't be so lucky to have your big boyfriend to call you safe. Now be a good girl and smile and wave for the crowd." He had said through gritted teeth, and a smile on his face as he waved to the crowd. Heat rose as she stared at him, the *audacity* of him telling her what to do. No one except a commanding officer had ever given her an order. As his eyes darted down to her lips, he had done it again – he'd stolen her breath away with another quiet order.

"I said," pausing only to pull her even closer as she stared at his lips, watching as the words formed across them, the warmth of his breath mingling with hers.

"Be a *good girl*. Smile and wave." This time, although he had that cocky fake smile on his face, his stern tone sent a chill down her spine causing her brain to short circuit. Never one to take orders from anyone, she couldn't help but wonder, why the Hell she felt compelled to obey? Eyes fluttering to regain her senses, his gaze never straying and she felt herself moving involuntarily as she placed a smile on her lips and waved. *Wake up Denise, don't let this asshat tell you what to do*, she thought. Regaining her composure, her grin widened into a smirk as she looked at him.

"I'm not a good girl, Nereid, you should know that by now and I will make you pay for that comment, mark my words. No one tells me what to do."

Squeezing her hand tighter, a dark laugh bubbled up his throat, "Oh I know you're not, but I bet I can get you to do what I tell you to, when I tell you to."

The flashy grin disappeared off her face as she turned to him, a scowl tightening her features. *What was it with this man, always knowing which buttons to push*, she questioned. *Always challenging her, constantly picking fights and now he was issuing a bet?*

"Fat chance." She spat and out of the corner of her eye she saw Grace moving in from the outfield, she must have noticed that this exchange was going on too long, and if anyone knows what Hank was like it was *her*. Always astute, George had finally noticed and was at her side just seconds later.

"Everything okay here?" The concern in George's voice was a comfort to her. Being this close to Hank and the exchange between them made her feel far too hot. But it wasn't the heat of the day that was making her feel so hot and bothered. It was the asshole catching. Fucking Hank, breaking her grip from his hand, she smiled turning to George and kissed him right in front of everyone, especially Hank. *But why did she feel so drawn to show such a display of affection right in front of him.* Denise knew she had nothing to prove to him, she and George had been dating now for two months and everyone knew it.

"Yeah, everything is great." Denise said and sauntered off, walking back to the bench. Sitting on the warm metal she took a deep breath again taking a sip of water from her insulated water bottle thankful that she had packed it with ice, no "diet coke" for her right now. Denise felt Nikki's glance over to her as another dad stepped up to bat, and she must have known something was up.

"You want to tell me what happened up there or I am just gonna sit here in suspense?"

"Nothing." Denise spluttered; she didn't want to talk about it. *Be a good girl?* Who the Hell did this guy think he was? He was a narcissistic, hot tempered, jerkoff that she wanted nothing more than to pummel his face into the field. Denise felt Nikki's inquisitive gaze on her as she sat there in the dugout fuming.

"What? He's a dick who knows how to push my buttons, that is it. Wish Liz had run him over and not Grace!" Denise smirked.

"Wow, tell me how you really feel." Nikki choked out after spitting out her water. "Listen you know I'm not a fan, but honestly - and I'm not defending him - but he has gotten a bit better." Denise couldn't believe what she was hearing. She thought that Nikki was public enemy number one to Hank, and now she is sitting there saying that Hank had changed so much that she was openly giving him credit for changing. Slowly turning to the petite blonde, Denise placed her hand on her forehead to check and make sure Nikki wasn't running some kind of crazed fever.

"What are ya new? He hasn't changed!" she exclaimed. "He just told me to be a good girl and to smile and wave like I'm supposed to do whatever he says, that isn't normal or him getting better. That is some bullshit!" Grimacing at Nikki whose eyes were bugging out at the mention of being a '*good girl*'. Nikki curled her lips inward to keep from laughing.

"But you WERE a good girl, because you did what he said. Sounds like someone got to you this time." Denise had done what he said, didn't she. Like a fool she had done exactly what he had commanded and now she was sitting there feeling like a complete ass. Once again, Hank had gotten to her - normally he would only piss her off - but this time it was different.

"I was doing it to save face and not get everyone worked up. The last thing I need is to catch a charge because I threw a punch and my boyfriend had to arrest me for it while I was at a fundraiser for my kid." Denise pouted and then took another sip of her water, swished it around her mouth and spat it out onto the ground. She could feel Nikki's judging glare and she knew if she kept this conversation going Nikki would just say something else and then she would be pissed at her friend and not the idiot behind the plate. Furious with herself, Denise got up from her spot on the bench and walked out of the dugout, starting for the parking lot. She needed to get away and stop thinking about what had happened, because no one tells her what to do, *ever*.

"Congrats everyone, we made $4,789 from today's game!" Mike exclaimed as the group clinked their glasses to a great game. The marching band parents had won by one run, thanks to Hank who had smashed a walk-off home run much to Denise's dismay. She had been hoping he would have been struck out with her curveball; she had been throwing sinkers and was sure he was going to chase one, but then she had changed it to a curve ball and he must have noticed the change up. Staring daggers at him while he rounded the bases with his snarky sneer, it took everything in her not to storm off the mound and throttle him right there on the field. Now she was stuck having drinks with him.

Nikki must have filled Grace in on what had happened because she stayed glued to Denise right after the game and was sitting next to her probably to make sure that she wasn't gonna lunge over the table to the man across from her. Placing her hand on Denise's shaking leg, Grace arched her brow and leaned in to whisper in Denise's ear, "No killing, you don't look good in orange and there are no gin and tonics in prison. Good choices only, it's not a Monday." Leave it to Grace to show sympathy to the idiot across the table but at least it got Denise to smile.

"Aw you are no fun, fine I'll be a -" she stopped, sucking in the final words not willing to utter them out loud. Closing her eyes she turned her head to Grace and flashed her best *Cheshire Cat* smile. Squeezing her thigh, Grace bumped her shoulder to let her know that she understood.

What really was bothering Denise was *why*, why was this whole interaction bothering her so much? Maybe it might be best to leave, say she didn't feel well and that she just wanted to go to sleep, but she was never one to run from something difficult.

As Grace got up, she motioned to Denise to follow her as they walked outside with their drinks onto the patio. Lighting a cigarette and passing it over to Denise, Grace took a sip of her water. "Alright, we are outside, so get it out. I'll start; he's an ass."

"Oh my God, I want to throat punch him right now! Who the fuck does he think he is? I'll tell you who he is, just some lonely miserable mother fucker who needs to have his head pulled out of his perfect ass."

Denise could feel her blood pressure skyrocket as she spewed all her vitriol out as she felt spittle actually come out on the last comment. The heat in her cheeks seemed to grow as her mind raced over the last comment, *his perfect ass*. Why did she say that? She didn't mean it, she hated him.

Clearing her throat Grace quirked an eyebrow at Denise, "He is a miserable mother fucker; you are not wrong. A giant dick, well" Grace started and then screwed up her face in regret to what she was going to say next. "He does have a large dick and a perfect ass, but we hate him for that too right?" her tone dripping with sarcasm.

"Are you trying to trap me or something? You and that clever brain of yours. And ew I didn't need details about his dick." Denise knew Grace was poking fun at her, probably to lighten the mood. Taking the cigarette out of Denise's hand, Grace took a drag and Denise could see her mind working, which for Denise was never a good thing.

"Listen, I get it, you loathe each other. This is not news, but he is trying to be a better dad which is what is far more important to me right now. So, if we can table World War Three for another time that would be great." Fanning herself as she turned to Grace, Denise knew that she would have to put this aside, for today at least. "I'm not here to defend him, just if you can please not attack him when he is actually trying to put in the work as a *perfect assed* dad that would be stellar."

And there it was back to haunt her, Grace capitalizing on that comment with a snarky wink as she stuck that zinger back in her face. Crushing out the last of the cigarette, she hugged Denise and headed back inside leaving her to sit there with her gin and tonic.

Grace had a point, he was trying, but at the same time Denise was still holding onto the fact that he had cheated on her friend and caused so much emotional abuse to her for years all because he was a terrible person. He had neglected his wife and cheated on her, if he hadn't been so blinded by that blonde psychopath, then *maybe* he could have been a better person a whole lot sooner. He had followed his dick, and now there Denise stood, for no reason whatsoever, imagining just how large his dick was because of Grace's unnecessary comment.

A different type of fever was creeping up in her, something deeper than her hatred, something primal and hungry. *Did his dick curve, or perhaps it was just perfectly long and thick?* Her loins tingled with the illicit pondering of just how big he was. Her head had careened into his groin, so was it the fact that it was the top of her head that was throwing off her perception. Perhaps if her hands had plowed into him first she could have gotten an idea, but now she was standing there in the heat - thinking of the one person in the whole world she hated the most - suddenly wanting to find out just how big his dick was. Eyes widening and pulse rushing, Denise knew that no good would come from this thought process. Downing her gin and tonic, she poured the ice down the inside of her shirt. But she realized that she should have dumped it in her pants, because only bad decisions were coming from there. And this wasn't even a Monday.

CHAPTER TWO

Hank

What d'ya mean you can't come in? It's only nine, just hop on a train and get your ass in here." Hank looked out his window as the dusky hue of the sunset cast a crimson light across the drab living room.

He had forgotten all about hanging out with Nick after the game. He had been shocked when the whole group had invited him to go out to The Sun Porch. Not wanting to pass up time he could spend with the boys Hank had agreed, completely forgetting about his plans.

"The game was a bit intense and some bitch plowed into me," Hank said wincing. "She smashed my nuts, so there is no way I'm gonna make it." Hank said shifting the ice pack on his groin trying to get any sort of relief from the awful ache and pulsating pain he had.

"Well, that is your fault for not wearing a cup." Nick said.

"How was I supposed to know that some behemoth was gonna barrel into me while playing a simple softball game!" Hank groaned, adjusting the ice pack again on his lap.

"Fuck that bitch. Come on man, pull your balls back down and get in here. You can just crash here tonight, let's get drunk and maybe enjoy something recreational and you can tell me all about the beast who busted your nuts. Was it Grace, I can see that frigid bitch pulling something like that." Nick said clinking ice into his glass on the other end of the phone and Hank knew he was already drinking. The idea of even getting up out of his recliner was not something that Hank was willing to do right now.

"It wasn't Grace and please don't speak about her that way, I'm the one that-" he paused reflecting back on his own faults.

Nick had totally encouraged the affair, so it wasn't worth talking to him about it, but Hank just wished that he could act like a mature adult sometimes. Hank wasn't into partying or doing drugs, it wasn't thrilling. However, Hank noticed more and more every time he talked or hung out with Nick just how messed up of an individual he was. There were parts of him that wanted to stay close because of the fact that they had been college buddies, and his family had practically taken him in after his mom died. But lately the appeal to hang out with Nick just seemed like a chore rather than something he actually wanted to do.

Shifting in his chair a sharp shooting, electric pain rippled through his body and he could tell there was zero chance of leaving his current location.

"Another time, actually next time just come here. That way if I get hurt there is no excuse for us to hang out." Hank was trying to placate him as he listened to his friend pour himself another drink on the other end of the line.

"Fine, be a bitch. Go ice your nuts, I'll go and get mine sucked. Later dick!" Nick hadn't even bothered for a response before he hung up the phone on Hank. Rolling his eyes he put down the phone and just tried to relax.

He hadn't been this sore in years, if only Denise hadn't barreled her way home, and if Grace had just thrown it to Jim like she was supposed to, Denise would have been out! It seemed that any opportunity to stick it to him brought Denise joy, but now that he thought about it, there was a level of joy he seemed to crave as he gave it right back to her. The first time he had ever met her, he knew she was going to be awful.

It wasn't that late when he had gotten home, and he just needed to rest for a few moments before he would make the tiny, yet arduous walk from his boring white walled living room to his even more boring unpainted basic bedroom. Sitting there in the oversized red velour covered recliner with his legs up and an ice pack on his groin, he looked around the room noting just how unattractive his place was. Not bothering to decorate the two bedrooms other than making sure that he and the boys had some place to sleep, watch TV and eat at, he had decided to get the most uncomplicated furniture around knowing that he would eventually find his own home.

Grace had offered to help him with decorating, which was beyond nice of her, however, he knew it might have had an ulterior motive. It had come up in family therapy, which was a once-a-month staple for the four of them and if he was being honest, it was actually helping. Those words would never come out of his mouth mind you, that would only encourage Grace's thrill of being right. That if they had been to therapy years ago perhaps none of this would have happened. But deep inside he knew that wasn't true. Grace would always be in love with Jim, and after spending time with him, Hank understood why. To his utter dismay, Jim was exactly what Grace had needed.

Hank had asked his therapist; what exactly was wrong with him, why was he always attracted to women who were emotionally unavailable or in love with someone else. Dr. Mahoney let him know that they really needed to do a deep dive into himself before he could even gauge where the issues lie. However, there had to be something in his past that spurred this pattern of self-abuse. Hank had gone over his family history, what it was like growing up and the more he went, he was starting to get a clearer idea of where this all stemmed from. His mother. She had not exactly been a woman that was very loving, in fact, it was her lack of love that seemed to be the biggest issue.

Closing his eyes, trying very hard not to recount the last session; he chose to clear his thoughts instead. But then a surge of pain from his balls again brought his mind right back to his current issue. *Fucking Denise*, he thought. *What was her problem?* You would think getting laid on a regular basis by someone like George would have made her less, *her*. Why couldn't she just take one day off from trying to poke fun or instigate something with him? Unable to remember what the Hell had actually started this whole feud that she seemed to have against him.

Since starting therapy, he would take time to reflect on his past, something he had never done before. He thought about how he had met Grace and all the people she had introduced him to over the years. Nikki had been in Grace's life since high school and they were inseparable, which made her hatred of him the longest. Yet recently, her icy demeanor seemed to thaw and he attributed it to Grace probably keeping her in the loop of all his work that he was doing.

Denise, however, he had met when Grace was in the PTA for Cal's class, kindergarten or first grade, he was pretty sure it was kindergarten but the details were a bit fuzzy. Not because it was ages ago, but because his job had always been his top priority instead of his own family. Always working, he knew Grace had everything taken care of, so why should he bother, he would only be getting in the way. He could work, numbers didn't have feelings to hurt, numbers were concrete and cold. There was something about how devoid of emotions numbers were that he found comfort in, it was an odd feeling and yet familiar.

Taking in a deep cleansing breath, he cleared his thoughts and it hit him when he had first met Denise. Back to School Night when the kids were in kindergarten. They were now sophomores in high school, and all he could seem to remember was that after their first meeting, Denise hated him ever since.

He remembered not wanting to be there, he and Nick had been forced into attending a retirement party for one of the managing partners at the firm, and Nick stuffing one drink after another in his hand which had been disastrous. Grace had reminded him earlier in the day that she needed him to attend Back to School Night, so he wound up leaving the party early. Stuck sitting in those stupidly tiny chairs, listening to some teacher drone on about kindergarten curriculum, Hank sat there utterly annoyed and slightly buzzed from the party. That was when he had been introduced to Denise. Probably because of all the vodka he had consumed before showing up to the school, he couldn't remember saying anything or doing something that would cause her to hate him so much.

The nagging pain in his balls pulsed again, pulling his thoughts to his present, as he cursed under his breath taking a swig of the cold water and ibuprofen sitting on the side table next to him. Plastering on a brave face since the game, he didn't want Denise or anyone else to know that she had hurt him. Looming over him, menacingly as she taunted him, it was almost like she enjoyed getting him so angry all the time. But after all these years, he knew right where to hit her ego, telling her to do something and forcing her to do it.

Denise's rotation of sexual partners was dizzying, he had felt really bad for that one guy, Nate, Ned, some N named dude. They had been seriously dating for seven months, one month longer than any of her other relationships and the poor sap had fallen in love with the untamable beast of a woman. She was a shrew, but at least she was a good mother. Her only redeeming quality, he guessed. Denise dedicated herself to Jodi, nothing and no one could come between them, unlike himself. So, as a parent, she was by far a better person than he was for sure.

As sleep started lingering over him like a cloud, he found his thoughts drifting in and out of different things. The pain, therapy, Grace, the boys, but one thing kept sneaking in. What was it about this damnable woman who hated him so much? His mind swirled with the image of her standing over him at home plate, her long legs, her delicious caramel colored skin that looked like a piece of candy good enough to eat. And those hazel green eyes. They reminded him of a fresh field of wheat right before it was ready for harvesting. She had antagonized him about that comment he had made about her at-bat being an easy out, in fairness he had been an ass, but she didn't need to smash his balls in.

He felt bad for George, the poor fool was stuck dating her and it was only a matter of months before she would toss him aside. Hank liked George, not initially, but now that he has had the chance to get to know him - he really did like him. So, the fact that he was dating Denise made him upset. He was a good guy and deserved to find someone who would take him seriously and not slap an expiration date on him.

If there was anything he had learned about Denise over the years, it was that things needed to be done on her timeline and in her own way. Lounging there in his thoughts, it dawned on him, he knew more about her than he realized. He knew for sure that Denise loved only one person in the whole world, and that was her daughter, Jodi, and she would probably never allow someone to out rank her. It was something that he was starting to grasp with himself. He loved his boys, but before the divorce he had never truly appreciated them or loved them as much as they deserved.

Needing to get up and out of the chair, he knew he would sleep better in his bed, but sleep had other plans as he finally succumbed to her sweet embrace and passed out in his recliner.

The thumping sound of the heavy-handed knocking at his door, jarred him from his restless sleep. The cool dampness in his crotch area had Hank grimacing, reminding him that he had forgotten to take the ice pack off before falling to sleep. Fortunately, the ache in his balls from the previous night was not as bad, as he gingerly pushed his recliner back into the sitting position and made his way to the door. With his stiff achy muscles, the door seemed a bit heavier than normal, reminding him that all that energy from the day before had been more than he was used to exerting.

Standing on the other side were his boys and Grace, her eyebrow arched in a quizzical glance as she skimmed over his appearance. Looking down, his shorts were wet and probably gave the impression that he had urinated on himself. Colin rushed him with such vigor he staggered back, but even though he was weary and cold from the ice pack, the warmth of Colin's embrace filled his whole soul. Calvin followed suit, giving his dad a big hug and pat on his back, hitting a nerve Hank hadn't realized was slightly pinched from sleeping in the chair.

"Uh, do we need to get you diapers now?" Grace quipped glancing back down at his shorts with Hank returning her gaze with an annoyed arched brow.

"I fell asleep with an ice pack on thanks to your bestie smashing my nuts. I haven't even had time to go to the bathroom, thank you very much." Hank griped as he walked back over to the recliner to clean up the ice pack. Making his way to the small kitchen to dispose of the pack, he found Colin already rummaging through the kitchen cabinets and finding a bag of chips.

Following Hank into the kitchen, Grace went over to the almost completely empty refrigerator and started to unpack the items in the cooler bag she had brought with her.

"So, you did get hurt? You played it off pretty well. Now why don't you be a *good boy* and go potty." Hank turned on the good boy comment to see Grace with a half-cocked smile meaning that she knew about the comment.

"You know what the difference is between me and the shrew? I don't give a crap about a comment like that. I will go to the bathroom, but she would hold it just out of spite." Hank said as he marched down the hall to the bathroom. He had needed to relieve himself, and he wasn't about to let himself burst. As he stood there emptying his bladder he heard Grace's footsteps walking just outside the bathroom door.

"What is it with you two? Like, do you guys get some kinda high when you are going after one another? I just don't get it." Grace's voice muffled through the door, as he flushed and washed his hands. He looked at himself and was struck with how awful he looked, the bags under his eyes were puffy and the fine lines on his brow seemed to be deeper than usual. Grace cleared her throat, "I mean you are an ass so I get why she hates you."

That stopped Hank in his tracks of self-absorbed gazing of himself. Flying the door open, she stood on the other side grinning, knowing that would get his attention.

"Why shouldn't I hate her? She's been against me from the very beginning and I don't even know what the Hell I did." His shoulders were practically up in his ears as he shrugged. Blinking back at him completely unbothered by his heated tone, Grace just shook her head.

"Seriously?" Surprise etched across her brow and Hank was sure that her eyebrows were going to reach her hairline with how high they were.

"Yes, seriously, I have no idea." Frustration echoing through his words, he just didn't understand what he could have done to make someone hate him so much. Watching Grace look around the living room to the boys, and then back to Hank made him pause, this might have been a bigger deal than he realized. Stepping closer to him, Grace leaned in to whisper.

"I can't repeat what you said because the boys are around, but all I can say is that you went out of your way to completely embarrass her just moments after you had met. Like imagine the worst thing you can say to a single mom and then blow it up a trillion times over! Her hatred for you is well deserved, pal. Hell, people asked ME for years if I was okay, and if I needed a divorce attorney because you were that awful."

His chest felt tight, what was wrong with him? He still couldn't seem to remember what he had said. But if it was about being a single mom it must not have been good, and if Grace was holding back for the boys, it meant it must have been terrible. Unforgivable. Something that spurned years of loathing.

He knew he could be a jerk and considering that he had been raised by a single mother who was not maternal in any way, he knew it must have been bad. However, now as a single parent with shared custody he was learning just how hard it was and boy, was his tune changing. Although he had been a hands-off parent for years, he actually enjoyed spending time with them and they had a great routine which made him feel like he was actively doing something right for the first time in his life. He was learning about them and despite several hiccups in the beginning that challenged him, it was still progress. Grace, he could never truly expect a full reconciliation, but they at least talked and found a mutual understanding which had made co-parenting with her a bit easier.

Grabbing her bag for her, Hank handed Grace the bag and reached in for a hug.

"You are gonna leave me on a cliffhanger? Not gonna let me know exactly what I said."

"Nope, that is not my circus, not my monkey. But you can do the proactive thing and maybe have a conversation with Denise to discuss this. You know like human adults would." She turned with a smile heading out the door. Hank scoffed at that idea; Denise was impossible to talk to. All she would wind up doing is talking right over him, never allowing him to get to the real reason.

"Hard to have a conversation with Medusa over there, she takes one look at you with those hypnotically mesmerizing eyes of hers and you are stone. You can't even talk back." There was something about those eyes of Denise's that would stop him for just a brief second before he could counter. Those enchanting green eyes that changed to an amber yellow towards the iris, *why did he notice that*, he thought. Stopping dead in her tracks, Grace whirled around at that comment as she stood in the cold hallway.

"Huh, hypnotically mesmerizing eyes?" she questioned.

His mind raced, *why was he thinking about her eyes?* He tried to find any reason in his brain that made sense, she was aggravating and condescending, rude and far too blunt. If he loathed her, why was he thinking about her eyes, but the more thoughts of her that seemed to swivel through his brain the angrier he seemed to get. He could feel Grace's judging gaze over him, and he needed to toss these thoughts of Denise out of his mind.

"Yeah, Medusa was a gorgon, her stare would cause you to turn to stone. Come on you know the story, Medusa was beautiful once and all because Athena cursed her for breaking her oath as her High Priestess, and seducing Poseidon in her temple she wound up becoming a hideous creature." Having spent a million years listening about his Greek heritage and having to endure hours of mythology lessons, he was hoping it would change the subject, but he knew Grace was much smarter than that. The scrutinizing regard in her eyes had her arching her brow again, clearly trying to analyze the whole conversation.

"Right." Grace paused. "Well thanks for the mythology lesson I already knew. Now why don't you take your *perfect ass* and get in the shower. You stink, also Colin will want something to eat in a few minutes so good luck!" Turning on her heels she walked away, he wasn't quite sure why she had said that comment about his ass. Although, she wasn't wrong, his ass was great even if he said so himself, but it just felt weird and out of place for her to say.

Calvin sat on the couch playing on his phone as Colin sat with a bag of chips chomping away getting crumbs everywhere, Hank really didn't care he was just happy they were here.

"So, what do you guys say to pizza and a movie or we could do Uno? We haven't played that in a few weeks." Hank said as he lowered his sore body back onto the recliner. Colin responded in an inaudible noise that sounded like pizza and Uno as his mouth was stuffed with potato chips. Looking up from his phone, Calvin just shook his head at the ridiculousness of Colin's ability to always be able to think about food.

"Yeah, pizza and Uno is good. But we were hoping that we could watch a movie? There is a new one we've been wanting to see, Jim said we could get it at home, but we wanted to watch it with you, if that's okay." Calvin probably didn't know that the fact that they wanted to do something as simple as watching a movie with just him, had his heart soaring and his breath catching in his throat. The stinging in his eyes had him rubbing them as he had just woken up, acting like that didn't just make his whole month, Hank just grinned from ear to ear.

"Sounds amazing buddy. Let's do it." This was going to be an amazing week he could feel it.

CHAPTER THREE

Grace

Something was going on, and she knew it was not gonna be good. A gnawing in her gut had started just after she had talked to Denise the night before and right now talking with Hank; she just knew something was not right.

After all these years, these two would have never described the other person as having a perfect ass or mesmerizing eyes. Grace just couldn't put her finger on what exactly was both of their deals.

But she couldn't focus on it now. She and Jim were on their way to look at a bigger home for their brood to move into. They had spent the summer at the shore house which had plenty of room for all of them. But now with the girls and Jim having moved in, they were all practically on top of each other. The girls had moved into her office and were sharing the space, and if Grace was going to be honest she really didn't want to be in that house anymore, too many terrible memories and she had wanted something that was theirs.

Jim had been so great about not pushing her to sell the house once they were married, but with four kids and two adults they needed to be more realistic with this. They needed a bigger home. The girls needed their own spaces and the boys needed theirs, especially since the boys were eight years apart, and she desperately needed her office back. She could not write her book sitting in the living room with everyone buzzing around her, flitting in and out, asking her a ton of questions as she was working. It was great to have them all there, but she needed her own space.

Then she thought about her first home and what she was planning on doing with it. She could rent it out or –

"Hey, I was just thinking, what if I sold the house to Hank?" She said and Jim's head turned to her looking like she was speaking another language.

"You want to offer Hank the opportunity to buy the house? Really?" Jim questioned.

"Yeah, well that apartment is pitiful, and honestly, the boys wouldn't have to move their stuff out of the house. They've lived there their whole lives and I just thought that I would either sell the house or I can do what I have done with my other properties and turn it into a rental."

Always one to not do anything without thinking through every single aspect of a situation out and always ready to make a profit off of something, she had considered just using it as another investment property. She had four herself, one in Madeira Beach, Florida, two in Toselle Park, and one in Pocono Lake, Pennsylvania.

"Well, I'm not gonna tell you what to do with the house, it's yours. But I do think it might be good for the boys to have a bit of normalcy, I know the girls are struggling a bit. Between the move from our house, then to my parents, then in with you." Jim stopped and took her hand into his bringing it up to his lips placing a gentle kiss on the back of it before finishing. "not that I am regretting a single moment, but it's been a lot in a short time. Of course, if I hadn't been an ass in the first place this wouldn't have been a problem and we wouldn't be looking for a bigger house." Jim smirked, leaving another soft kiss on the back of her hand.

There was that word again. *Ass.* Grace was going to freak out if he mentioned her eyes being hypnotic or mesmerizing because those two conversations were driving her to the brink of insanity. Jim pulled up to the vast blue shingled colonial with black shutters and beautiful white window boxes overflowing with draping ivy and an overabundance of red blooms. Grace had always loved this home and swore she would buy it the second it went on the market. But this whole weird thing that was going on needed to get out of her brain. Unbuckling herself, she turned to Jim ready to tell him everything.

"Okay, totally off topic, something weird is happening and if I don't tell someone I am going to lose my mind. My gut is telling me something in the universe is off." Jim blinked at her as she stopped for two seconds. Even though they had been apart for twenty-seven years, Grace hadn't changed and she knew he understood that her brain needed a moment to digest everything. She just needed to find the right words because none of it was making sense.

"So, after the game, when we were at the Sun; and I took Denise outside to complain about Hank." Jim's indifferent expression was a clear sign to Grace that this was not a new thing since he had come back to Toselle Park. Grace continued, "Right, apparently after that play at home plate Hank told her to be a 'good girl' and to smile and wave." Jim's eyes popped out of his head on the *good girl* part, "I know, right, but that's not what is freaking me out. It was while she was complaining that she said he had a *'perfect ass'*," Jim spit out his coffee he had just taken a sip of; spraying it all over the dashboard causing Grace to tsk as she rummaged through the glove compartment in search of wipes while she continued. "And just now Hank said Denise has *'hypnotically mesmerizing eyes'* like Medusa turning him to stone." Jim had decided to take another sip of his coffee only this time he was choking on it.

"Good God woman, warn a guy! I'm dying, crash, death." Still trying to catch his breath and coughing to clear his lungs of the coffee he had just almost died drinking. As he looked over to the house to see if the agent had shown up yet, but sadly Grace's agent wasn't here yet.

"I did! I told you the gut, that should have been the indicator that this was fucked up. I feel like I've entered some kind of alternative universe, maybe a multi-verse. Because according to both of them, they both still hate each other, they just -" Grace wasn't sure she wanted to finish that statement.

"Want to fuck the other. Listen, I know I am new to this whole crew that you built here, but that is what I am hearing." Jim finished her statement as they exchanged skeptical glances and heard a car pull up behind them. Grace turned to see her agent Diane getting out of her car. Her stunning white hair shining in the last of the summer sun and warm smile on her face made Grace thankful that she was going to be too busy to finish this conversation.

Grace waved and with no further words or mentioning of Hank or Denise, she and Jim got out of the car. After a formal introduction, Diane hugged Grace tightly knowing the story about Jim from years ago. She had been Grace's agent from the beginning and Grace knew that if there was anyone who could make this dream of owning this house a reality, it was Diane.

It wasn't difficult to convince Jim to say yes to buying the house. This home was absolutely perfect for them and she would have her own she-shed in the back that would eventually be converted into her office. As Diane locked up the house, Jim stood behind Grace as he wrapped his arms around her waist and rested his chin on the top of her head.

"So, you think Hank will want to buy your house?" He said looking at the porch that had a bench swing on it and all the beautiful landscaping. Grace snickered at the comment, she knew he was worried about the price of this home, but he didn't have anything to worry about. Now that the divorce was finalized and everything had been transferred into her name from her parents, she didn't worry about the cost.

"I have a funny feeling he might actually. I really hate that apartment and I don't want the boys having to stay there with the three of them living on top of each other for very long." Grace sighed, worrying about the boys.

"I understand, but you can't just say buy the house because your apartment sucks, you also can't make things so easy for him. You already pack them food and stuff, you're gonna have to cut the cord and let him fall on his own, Gracie." Jim said, kissing the top of her head. She knew he was right, but she was getting tired of being a landlord of four other properties and adding another was going to be too much. Done with locking up the house, Diane walked over with a huge smile on her face.

"I'll get the paperwork over to you in about two hours, if you guys can go and electronically sign them, that would be great! Also, Grace, if you can get a copy of your financials I don't see them saying no to all cash and twenty thousand over asking. And since you aren't in a rush to close, that might help since it looks like they are gonna need some time packing up. Grace, I know you know this home, but do you have any questions for me?" The older woman said through a huge smile as she could tell just how happy Grace was. Diane had whispered to her as they had caught a second alone during the tour and told her how happy she was for her and also just how handsome Jim was.

"Yeah, how much is my house worth; I may have a buyer. Well maybe." Grace saw Diane's eyes widen in shock.

"Oh, really?" She said with a touch of sadness in her voice. "But you love that house. Why don't you keep it as a rental and just make a profit off of that one. That way I'll add it to my portfolio."

Grace just shook her head, "Give me a price, and let me see." She said as she hugged Diane goodbye.

As they stood there staring at the house in each other's arms, Grace pictured her getting old in this house with Jim right by her side like she had always dreamed; as a tear stung in her eye and her nose started running.

"Hey, don't go getting all emotional yet Miss, it's not ours yet." Jim spun her around, and with the pad of his thumb wiped away the tear that had finally escaped her eye and rolled down her cheek. Sliding his thumb down her soft cheek and then along her jawline to tilt her chin up to him, Grace couldn't help but smile and he lowered his head down to hers.

"All I heard was it's ours so shush and kiss me." She said as her lips dusted across his and he smiled while kissing her, because he had promised he would every day for the rest of their lives and she knew deep down inside it would be right here at this home.

Nikki handed Grace a glass of wine as they just sat there watching their husbands arguing over how the wood should be placed in the fire pit and the best way to start it.

"You guys want any help? You have two former girl scouts sitting right here who can start a fire with practically nothing." Nikki offered, shoving another two marshmallows in her face. It was couples date night and they had opted to keep it at Grace's house this week. Jim's girls were with his parents for the weekend and the McCarren kids were all home. As they sat there eating marshmallows, Mike reached for the lighter fluid and Nikki instantly made a noise that came from her throat. It was similar to a sound you would make to stop a child from doing something or an animal from chewing on an object it wasn't supposed to.

"Absolutely not! Step away from the lighter fluid or risk losing your chance at sex tonight pal! No blow jobs for a month, no hand jobs, nothing, you will lose, good day senor!" Mike looked like someone was telling him Santa Claus wasn't real for the first time and slowly walked away from the fluid. Stifling a laugh, Grace looked at Jim, giving him a knowing glance so as to not touch it as well. Shooting a coquettish wink, he must have known better than to tempt anything especially with no children in the house.

"Sex or kerosene, sounds like you picked wisely there bud." George said as he opened the gate to the backyard, as Denise and Nikki started screaming in excitement of their arrival. Getting up from her softly cushioned Adirondack chair, Grace walked over to the table, pouring a glass of wine for Denise and handed it to her as she joined them up on the deck. As Denise sat down and took off her shades, Grace stared deep into her eyes. Wanting to see if they truly were as hypnotic as Hank had made them out to be. Shifting in her chair, Denise looked back at Grace like she had gone mad.

"Are we having a staring contest, because I will win. Years of my father and I doing this has made me a master." Denise laughed, as she made funny faces while Grace stared on. Shaking her head Grace just sat back.

"Nope just admiring how hypnotic your eyes are." Grace said and she saw Jim's head pop up at the comment and she bit the inside of her lip to stop herself from smiling. Denise, however, gave her a flirty wink and took a sip of her wine.

"Look out Jim, your girl has a thing for me and she knows I swing both ways so I will attack her if she asks." Denise laughed calling down to Jim. Turning her head to Grace with her eyebrow raised, "Are you asking my *little minx*?" giving her a joking wink.

"No, my love, you are all Nikki's!" This was all too much fun as Denise started climbing out of her chair to molest Nikki. Only encouraging the madness, Nikki and Denise pretended to make out. Mike, having enough of someone touching his wife's breasts, lifted her up and over his shoulder pulling her away from Denise, leaving Grace to practically fall off her chair as tears of laughter streamed down her cheeks and she struggled to catch her breath from laughing so hard.

After several minutes of Denise chasing Mike with Nikki on his shoulder around the backyard, they went back to their usual spots and continued enjoying the rest of their night. Denise had already downed her glass of wine after the chase and was pouring another one but not before filling up Grace's glass and sat down.

"Okay, alright, so give. Why would you call my eyes hypnotic? You using me as a character in one of your books, I do have a really messy backstory you can use. It's called *my life*." Grace knew she was joking, but she also knew that telling her about Hank's comment was something that would send her off on a tangent.

"Maybe, I am always taking notice of different things or comments, and I guess I just never really noticed your eyes before. And I was trying to figure out if the word hypnotizing or mesmerizing would best describe them." Denise had been bugging her to use her likeness in one of her books since finding out she was writing one and knew that would be a good enough excuse. She definitely had very beautiful eyes, she just wouldn't use those words to describe them.

"I think your eyes are hypnotic, babe." George said from the fire pit as he took a puff of his cigar. Nikki pouted out her lower lip at the sweet sentiment.

"Of course, you would think that - you are obsessed with her. Like, don't get me wrong, your eyes are gorg, babydoll, but only someone who was entranced by you is gonna say that." Nikki looked over to Grace, "Tell me I'm wrong."

Grace shot a tiny glimpse over to Jim who was choking again, this time on his beer. The poor guy's lungs were going to be drowning in fluid between the coffee from this morning and now the beer. Noticing Jim's reaction, Grace watched as Nikki was starting to put two and two together to know something was up. Giving a slight shake of the head to Nikki not to ask, she gave a short nod back to let Grace know she would drop it.

"So where is Kevin and Jonathan? We haven't seen them in a while." Nikki had changed the subject, but just as she had, Kevin walked onto the deck from the backdoor by himself, no Jonathan in sight.

"It's because we broke up and I've been licking my wounds, crashing at Mom and Dad's." Kevin said, as he placed two more bottles of wine on the table and decided to grab the almost empty bottle as he sat down on Grace's lap to drink it. The saddened faces that looked back at him must have left him feeling even worse because he took a swig from the bottle and rested his head on Grace's shoulder.

She had known about the break-up and had promised not to say anything. The night it happened, he had come over and cried to Jim and Grace about it. He thought that he had found the person he could spend the rest of his life with, but when Jonathan had asked to make it an open relationship, he knew he needed to go.

"You are going to squish your sister, come sit on my lap." Denise said, patting her lap, but Kevin just shook his head and buried himself deeper into Grace.

"I'm afraid if I come over there you will hypnotize me into turning straight and then I'd have to fight George and he would completely obliterate me." Kevin quipped garnering a laugh from the crowd.

"Stop it! Babe, you don't mind sharing me with Kevin will you?" Denise asked looking over her shoulder to the fire pit. Grace noticed an odd look on George's face that she couldn't quite read, it was almost as if he was contemplating something. But that wasn't it, as far as she knew George was a monogamous person, so to share Denise for him didn't seem right.

"Uh-" George started but was quickly interrupted by Kevin.

"Oh babes, I love you, but you are just not my type, Dee. Sorry my dear, but George, you sexy thing over there better watch out!" Kevin jokingly teased as he blew her a kiss, but it was the blush on George's cheeks when Kevin called him 'sexy' that made Grace not know what was going on here.

Since the baseball game she had felt like she was watching the most insane show unfold around her. First Denise, then Hank and now some weirdness with George. She needed to walk away for a minute, excusing herself to the bathroom. Tucking herself into the first-floor half-bath, she sat on the toilet thinking about the past twenty-four hours. There was too much to process and everything in her reality just seemed like it wasn't real. Normally she could turn to her friends to work this all through, but with all the players involved, she didn't know what to do. As she finished and was washing her hands, Grace thought that perhaps she was just overreacting to all of this and that it was nothing.

Opening the bathroom door, she practically jumped out of her skin as Grace found Nikki standing there just on the other side.

"What is going on?" Nikki whispered as she stood there tapping her foot. Grace knew it would be a matter of time before Nikki started hounding her. Looking outside the backdoor to the crowd, Grace looked back at Nikki.

"Girl, I can't." Grace whispered back and Nikki started making a huffing noise to express her distress. Walking over to the pantry looking for more snacks to bring out, Grace was trying to avoid telling her. The truth was that Nikki was terrible at keeping secrets, she also didn't want to tell her what had been said between Hank and Denise, and now factoring into that weird reaction from George about Kevin, it was just too many people in her inner circle to divulge any information about. After all, Grace may be wrong about all of it.

"Fine! Let's just say, for shits and giggles, that someone is complaining about you but they say that your eyes are hypnotically mesmerizing like Medusa's and it causes them to feel like you are turning them to stone, what do you make of that?" Grace's question was met with a confused look on Nikki's face.

"Someone thinks you are Medusa?" There was that stereotypical blonde brain at work and Grace just shook her head no.

"Someone is complaining that your eyes are as hypnotic as Medusa's and the reaction they get from your eyes leaves them feeling like they have been stoned, frozen, unable to speak whenever they talk with you." Grace needed to elaborate in order for Nikki to understand. Nikki being a full-time work from home mom with three kids who were constantly involved in a bunch of different clubs and a husband who didn't just teach but also coached, may have fried her brain a bit. It wasn't that she was dumb, far from it, Nikki was brilliant, but she obviously needed help getting there right now.

"Well fuck, whoever that is has got it bad. Who has the hard dick for Denise?" Nikki asked but Grace just shook her head again. "Bitch, don't tell me no. Who the fuck wants to rail Denise?" Grace scrambled, she couldn't do it, she couldn't tell one of the biggest blabbermouths in town. Grace decided to lie, and couldn't believe she was covering for Hank, but it would be so much worse if Nikki found out.

"I don't know." She started trying to think on her feet. "Jim overheard someone at the game mentioning Denise's name and about her eyes and how they made them feel. I just found it interesting." That seemed convincing enough to her, but Nikki's unamused expression on her face told her she wasn't buying the lie.

"Thou speak-ith the bullshit!" barked Nikki. Fortunately for Grace, Jim walked in a second later looking between the two women and she could not have been more thankful to see him.

"He's right here, Babe, tell Nikki that I am not lying and that you overheard some *guy* at the baseball game say that Denise has them under her spell because of her eyes." Grace's tone must have given him the indication that he should absolutely agree with whatever she was saying. Luckily enough, he spoke fluent Grace, but sadly Nikki did too and convincing her was gonna take a miracle.

"Yup, I didn't recognize the guy though, so I couldn't even tell you who it was. It wasn't anyone I knew, but I'm still learning everyone's parents." Jim was nodding but Nikki was unmoved.

"I don't believe either one of you. But when you are ready to dish, I am the first to know." Nikki yanked the bag of chips that Grace had grabbed out of the pantry and left the room mumbling about how they were the worst liars and how they were pains in the asses. Jim walked over to Grace and hugged her as he kissed the top of her head.

"I love you, but don't ever make me lie to her again. She scares me." Jim said, tilting her face up to his and kissed her. She needed that kiss, because the rest of the night was going to be rough.

CHAPTER FOUR

George

Putting Denise to bed after five too many drinks was new for him, but their relationship was sort of new too. George had noticed that after the game she had been acting a little differently. He had been so wrapped up with keeping the peace and being the umpire for the game, that he hadn't noticed what had exactly transpired between Hank and Denise. There had been exchanged words that he knew for sure, and since these two had a history of fighting he figured it was a bunch of trash talking. But after they had shaken hands, something was off with her.

Dating Denise was fun, she was always ready to have a good time, but as he got older, dating women like that, who only wanted to have fun was starting to feel stale. He wanted more, he wanted a connection and despite the fact that he did care for her, George just wasn't sure if she was the one. The sex was amazing, she was always the one in control, a position he wasn't entirely positive he enjoyed, but he wasn't willing to risk asking if he could be the one in control sometimes due to her larger-than-life personality.

There was a lot about Denise he didn't know. Like - *who was Jodi's dad? Was he still in her life? Was he in jail or worse was he dead?* It seemed that when the topic was broached, it was always just shut down even before it started. He respected her space, but he thought that since they had been dating for a few months, that she would feel safe enough to tell him. He had asked about her parents and all she would talk about was her dad, who seemed like an amazing guy. But never anything about her mom, and when he asked she would again shut down or transition the discussion about all the things she and her dad had done while she was growing up.

Which had been the complete opposite for him. As the only boy with three older sisters, he wasn't shocked when his mom said that as lovely as Denise was, she wasn't the right person for him. Doreen Nicols was one of few words, but what words she had held true meaning even when she was being cryptic. Whenever he would introduce a new girlfriend, all his mother would say was:

"Georgie, baby, you know I love you but that is not your person. When the right person comes along, your heart will let you know."

He was sure it was because he was the only boy and the youngest that had her so protective, but she hadn't been wrong. All those women who had been in his life, had not been the right one. He liked them, found them attractive, funny, charming, but never that spark.

As he pulled off Denise's shoes and slid her long legs under the covers, he thought this was not fun. Having a glass or two was fine, but a bottle and a half of wine seemed like too much for him. His family were not drinkers, a beer, a glass of wine here or there was a lot, but the past two nights Denise had drunk more than he had seen her drink in the few months they had been dating. Something had happened and he needed to get to the bottom of it.

Turning off the light on her bedside table, he turned and left the room. Grace and Jim had been gracious and had offered to allow Denise to crash on their couch, but he could see in their faces that they really wanted to be with each other tonight and having Denise around was like having a house full of kids. He imagined that was not what they had anticipated for the night.

Her living room was filled with comfy blankets and pillows on the overly large eggplant colored couch that you could sink into. As a tall woman with an equally tall child, their furniture had to be large which he was grateful for as he would get a decent night's sleep. George could fall asleep standing up if need be, years of bad bunks when he was in the Marines or just long hours of sitting in a car for overnight shifts. His body was used to just instantly falling asleep the moment his head hit a pillow. But as he laid there on the couch, he just couldn't seem to find that peace that usually came to him so naturally.

Grace and Jim had been acting a bit odd the whole time and he had noticed. Something was up, Jim had mentioned that they were on edge about a new house they put an offer on, but deep down he knew that was not what was going on. It was the odd conversation about Denise's eyes. She did have stunning eyes, that he would guiltily get lost in, but it was the comment Nikki said about him being entranced by them that made Jim choke. Someone else must think that Denise is gorgeous or that there was something about her eyes that they were interested in. But then again, he wasn't surprised that someone else would find her stunning, because she was. Deep in the recesses of his mind and heart he thought he should feel concerned, *but he didn't*. It wasn't a self-confidence thing; it was more of a lack of something - he cared about Denise and she was fun to be around - but something had *shifted* in him.

George pulled the blanket up to his neck and turned on his side to face the empty fireplace. He thought perhaps, *if he made a fire the warmth would help him sleep*, but it was still warm outside so why bother. Closing his eyes, he tried to settle but it just didn't seem to be coming as easily as it normally did. For a comfortable couch, he was shocked he wasn't passed out already, but his brain just kept going. He knew Denise was too free of a spirit to be tied down and perhaps his mom was right, *Denise wasn't his person*, but maybe he could just keep it fun for now. Although he did want to be in a real relationship with someone, he knew this wasn't going to be the forever after and deep down that was what he truly wanted.

Then his thoughts turned to poor Kevin. He had been so sure that Kevin and Jonathan would be getting married soon because of how Kevin went on and on about him. But it seemed that those feelings were not exchanged equally, and after a lengthy discussion with the guys, Kevin had told them how Jonathan was just not emotionally in the same space as he was. *Poor Kevin*, he thought, he just needed to find his person, as his own mom had said.

Slowly but surely, sleep was starting to creep over him and the last thought before his mind settled was that one day he and Kevin would each find their person.

As the morning light cracked through the gauzy, lace curtains in the heather gray living room, George stretched and rubbed the sleep away from his eyes. Looking over to his phone he saw that it was nine a.m. and he wasn't surprised that he was the first one up. Denise was a night owl, so he knew it would be a while before she or Jodi would be awake. Checking his phone, he saw a text from Jim double checking that they had gotten home okay and wanting to know if he wanted to go for a run. Realizing that he needed to change in order to go, he grabbed a piece of paper from the printer next to Denise's desk and let her know that he would check in with her later.

Grabbing his stuff and locking up behind himself, he headed out to his car and let Jim know he would meet him at the track. It had been nice to have someone who enjoyed running and since he spent so much time behind the wheel of his patrol car most days, he needed to get out his energy some way. After heading home to change and brush his teeth, he hopped back into his car. As he pulled up to the parking lot at the high school he saw Jim and Kevin standing there.

"Hey, since when did you become a runner?" George said, as he looked at Kevin, who was wearing a pair of basketball shorts and his

Converse sneakers. Those were not running shoes and George did his best not to smile knowing that Kevin would be dying halfway through this run. Kevin pulled down his sunglasses and looked over to him with a face clearly indicating that he had no intention of running.

"Oh sweetie, do I look like I run? No. This body is for dancing only. I'm only here because my mother and sister are forcing me out of the house. Apparently, I have to blow the stink off of myself." Kevin said as he took a sip of his coffee he had in his thermal *'I'm a bitch without my coffee'* mug with a picture of a pug wearing sunglasses and a bow on its head. George smiled at the thought of Janie and Grace telling him to get out of the house. He really did feel bad for him as he deserved to be happy. He remembered a good amount of his old football buddies back in high school making fun of Kevin for being gay, but he let them all know that on no uncertain terms that if he heard anyone say anything about him again, he was going to walk off the team and then beat the crap out of them. George was not one to sit and allow someone to be made fun of, especially someone as great as Kevin.

He was always quick with a joke, had great taste in music, not to mention that he was super protective of Grace or just anyone who needed to be stood up for, yet he had had a hard time standing up for himself back in the day. He was braver than a lot of people realized, but the one thing that drove George crazy was the fact that he was the worst gossip in town. George wasn't one to enjoy gossip, probably because of his line of work, he liked concrete evidence, gossip to him was unsubstantiated information. But he did like hanging out with Kevin, he was a good guy.

As George and Jim stretched Kevin walked over to the bleachers and sat down scrolling through his phone drinking his coffee. Starting to walk onto the track, Jim turned to George.

"So, I'm assuming she's still passed out."

"Oh yeah, she won't be up before noon with the amount of wine she consumed." George confirmed; he really was a bit disappointed on how the night had gone. But running would help, he thought just wanting to forget the past couple of days. As they started a light jog for the first lap, he took his time to just get into a good rhythm, it was like music, he liked something that started off slow and then picked up. Despite having a good pair of running shoes he could feel the tread of the track under his feet, the maroon-colored turf and white lines keeping him going. If he just kept within the lines he was fine, he could keep pace with Jim who was starting to pick up his own.

His eyes trained on the track, staying within those lines, never straying, never looking up. The singular path only curving around the bend, but still a straight route. That's what his life was like, stay in his lane, never wanting to switch. It was easy, but if Denise had been here, she would have been changing lanes or weaving in and out, never wanting to stay on course. The longer he ran, he realized that perhaps he should try something different, maybe shift lanes, see if his pace would change if he went to the farther lane. As he came up along the bleachers he looked up and saw Kevin sitting, wiping his face as he looked down at his phone. His heart wrenched a moment as he knew Kevin was struggling, but he just needed to get this run done. Perhaps he should take him for a cup of coffee and let him vent out his frustrations.

But he just kept running, he had his own frustrations to deal with. One foot in front of the other, and the longer he ran the more he realized that maybe he was trying to outrun his own feelings. Maybe it was time to sit down and talk with Denise and see just where this was really going. Was she ever going to settle down with someone or was she just here for the fun? And if that was the case, was he willing to accept just that? His pace quickened and he passed Jim on his left, his heart racing as his feet hitting the pavement with such force he could hear them slamming down on each step. The burning stretch in his calves was not enough to make him slow down, he just felt like he was drifting, running away from what he really wanted, but it was just out of reach.

His lungs started to constrict and he realized that he needed to slow down or he was going to get out of breath. But just as he began to slow down he heard a second set of feet coming up on his right and when he thought he would be seeing Jim, it was Kevin. The shock of seeing him running caught him off guard and he swerved into the lane Kevin was running in and as his right foot came down on the track it bent the wrong way and then came the pain. His stride broken, he fell onto the track and rolled. As the foam tread of the track cut into his skin, he winced but it was his ankle that hurt the most.

"Oh my God, I didn't think seeing me run would stop you dead in your tracks. Are you alright?" Kevin came running over and not two seconds later Jim was slowing his pace and bending down to check on George. He didn't feel a pop or anything so it could just possibly be sprained, but his leg was definitely all cut up. The adrenaline running through his veins at the moment made him remember that he wouldn't know just how bad it was until it came down. As he sat there, he tried to focus on his breathing and getting his heart rate back to normal knowing that he wouldn't be able to figure out his pain level until he did.

"I'm sure it's just a sprain." The burning in his lungs had stopped, but the pain was definitely starting to kick in and as he looked down at his ankle which was beginning to swell.

"I don't think that is just a sprain, buddy. Let's get you to the hospital." Jim said, as he motioned to Kevin to help him lift George up. But he was not about to be some poor invalid who couldn't stand up.

"No, it's fine, I can get-" he started, until he went to get up but the sharp shooting pain from just trying to get his foot under him made him realize that hadn't been a good move. Crumpling back down to the ground, Jim shook his head as he placed his arm under George's.

"Yeah no, we are heading off to the hospital pal. Kevin, I'm gonna need you to drive George's car and follow me. Also text Denise to let her know." Jim said, as they carefully navigated their way back to the cars. Every step triggered a shocking pain through the length of his leg. He had never broken a bone before, sprain yes, but never broken anything and slowly it dawned on him that this pain that was coursing through his body might wind up being what he didn't need right now, a broken ankle.

CHAPTER FIVE

Denise

Denise opened the door to George's place and realized that this was the first time she was seeing it. The first-floor condo was all state of the art and immaculate. George had mentioned that he had recently remodeled the whole thing and it was gorgeous. The minimalistic aesthetic was truly George, it was all grays, white and black with tiny pops of color from the artwork on the walls. The black overly large sectional faced an expansive bookcase that housed the TV and a ton of books as well as a few framed pictures. Noticing that he had gotten a copy of the picture of all of them from Grace and Jim's wedding *and* that he had had it beautifully framed standing alongside ones of his family and caused her heart to flutter.

As Kevin helped George make his way into the condo, Denise turned to see him doing his best to maneuver through the doorframe with his crutches. She felt odd because she wasn't sure what to do. Unlike her place, there was nothing to move out of the way, and she hadn't a clue where things were. Although they had been dating for two months, she had never actually been here. They always hung out at her house because of Jodi or would meet up at the Sun for dinner, but with his schedule the past month it hadn't been easy to hang out. Their relationship was still new, so it was no wonder that she didn't know where anything was.

"Can I get you anything? Pillows, a blanket, water?" Denise had never needed to take care of someone with a broken bone before, and apparently he had done quite a number on his ankle and would be out of work for several weeks before he could just go back on light duty. George was going to need a pin put in within the next couple of days due to the way the ankle had broken and she would be there to help, but since it was her first time at his place she felt more like she was the helpless one.

"Uh, they said it needed to be elevated and I need to keep ice on it for now. There is an ice pack, if you go in the freezer on the top left-side drawer the gel pack should be there and the tea towels are in the top drawer to the right of the fridge. Kevin can grab one of these throw pillows but I definitely need that ice pack." George was trying to figure out where on the couch he was going to set himself up.

Wasting no time, she headed into the kitchen to find that he had carried the gray palette into the kitchen with stainless-steel appliances throughout, and the countertops were a gorgeous gray and white granite with tiny silver and black flecks throughout. It was something out of a magazine, and she couldn't help but be a bit jealous at how amazing his place was. Following his instructions, she found exactly everything that he needed right where he had said it would be. She even noted how it was all completely organized. *Who keeps their food organized this way*, she thought. It was like those crazy restocking videos you would see on social media, only it was in a *guy's* house.

Walking back into the living room, Kevin was helping George settle in with a pillow and a light blanket over his leg. It wasn't cold, but Kevin was going on and on about how his leg was gonna get cold once he had the ice pack on. It should have been her tending to George, not Kevin, but she understood why he was being overly helpful. The poor dear thought he was the reason that George had wrecked his ankle.

"Would you stop feeling awful about this, it wasn't your fault, I just took a wrong step." George said, reassuringly. Carefully placing the ice pack over his ankle, he gave a slight wince from the coolness and the weight of the pack, despite the medications they had given him he was obviously still experiencing some pain. Denise shot him a look and he just smiled.

"I'm fine, really. Why don't you go home, Kev's offered to stay. I'm sure Jodi needs you more than I do." She knew he was right, but as his girlfriend shouldn't she be the one to take care of him? Truthfully, if Jodi wasn't so flighty and could handle things around the house she would have argued with him, but he was correct. Denise couldn't understand why her emotions were all over the place, she wanted to be there to help but there was a deep sense of relief that he was releasing her from the obligation. Carefully avoiding his leg as she walked around the couch, bent down and gave him a kiss. It wasn't one of their usual supercharged romantic kisses and she chalked it up to him being in pain, but something felt off.

Pulling away and grinning down at him, Denise then turned to Kevin. "If you need anything, you call, got me, I'm not far." Giving him a quick squeeze, she walked out the door and headed to her car. As she sat there, she felt the inevitable adrenaline crash starting. Although she was hungover when she had gotten the call about George's accident she instantly sobered up, got dressed and flew to the hospital. It was like having a hero mode activated, no fear, no worry, just how can I help; but when she had gotten there, there really hadn't been anything to do. As much as she hated to say it, she had been bored. She should have been scared or hurrying people along, but there had been none of those feelings, just utter indifference.

As she started up her street, she realized something might possibly be wrong with her. All these people she had dated over the years, whether it was men or women, she felt absolutely no true connection with them. It was fun, they had good times, but nothing stuck. She had never felt any passion towards them, even when there would be an argument, there was absolutely no heat or fire behind it. It was just a difficult conversation that needed to be had.

The only person she had ever truly fought with wasn't even her own partner. If there was anyone, she loathed more than anything and actually loved riling up, it was Hank. But he was a complete and utter asshole. *Who was he to judge me, my life or my decisions*, she thought to herself. People with stupid ideologies needed to keep their mouths shut, but he just seemed to think he was God's gift to the world and could say whatever ridiculously awful thought in his mind. No, Jodi's dad wasn't in their lives, there was a reason for that! Who cares? Hank should have worried more about his own kids than her's. She would never forgive him for what he had said that first time they had met. She could still see his stupid ass sitting in those tiny kindergarten chairs.

"Denise, this is my husband, Hank. Hank, this is Denise Gagnon, Jodi's mom." *Grace had whispered as the other parents were still walking in and sitting in their kids seat. The unamused glare she received from Hank was her first indication that he hadn't wanted to be there and the slight hint of alcohol was the second. Holding out her hand with a smile, Denise waited for Hank to shake her hand, but he hadn't, all he did was look around.*

"Hey." *Hank muttered as he looked down at his phone checking text messages. Turning to Grace, "I could have stayed at the retirement party, Grace. I didn't need to be here. Denise's husband isn't here."*

"Oh, I'm not married, I'm a single mom and perhaps you should have stayed at the party. God forbid; you support your kid." Denise spat, she wasn't sure why she was even engaging with this guy. She looked at Grace and immediately felt terrible for her and Calvin. This guy was a total jerk. Hank lifted his head and then his eyes followed narrowing in on hers, it was apparent that he was not used to a strong defiant woman voicing her opinion, which shocked Denise because Grace was quite the force to be reckoned with at the PTA meetings.

"Divorced or baby daddy?" He smirked with an air of arrogance. Denise's eyes glowered at him, she didn't know this guy and she wasn't about to share personal information with him about her child's father.

"Neither; she was just a miraculous blessing." Utter disdain dripping in her voice, she still didn't know why she felt the need to talk to

him. Her heart rate was elevated and she felt herself slowly starting to get heated. He rolled his eyes at her, leaning in so only she could hear.

"You mean a one-night stand and a surgery you didn't have the guts for. Got it." His words slurring and the wafting of the vodka on his breath breezed past her nose, churned her stomach to the point that she almost threw up. Looking around to see if anyone else heard, it seemed that everyone around them was unphased and in their own little conversations, no one except her had heard what he had the audacity to say.

This person whom she had just met, who had never had a conversation with her until this very second had just suggested that Jodi should have been aborted. He doesn't know me, she thought, and then she thought, perhaps his mother should have swallowed him instead of having his father finish in her, if that was going to be how he thought.

Balling up her fist she thought it would be quick and painless if his face just happened to run into her fist, he was already drunk, no one would know. But not two seconds later the teacher walked into the classroom and started her speech on how exciting it was that their kids were starting school, however, all she could think was that she would have to interact with this asshole for as long as Jodi went to school here.

As she pulled into the driveway, Jodi was sitting at the window seat and holding up her phone waving it. Denise had programmed their phones so that they could track each other's whereabouts, which had come in handy whenever she couldn't make a game or tournament and the band was off playing somewhere for the football team. Smiling back at Jodi, Denise grabbed her bag and went into the house.

"Hey, how is George? Is his ankle broken or just sprained?" The concerned tone in Jodi's voice made her feel another pang of guilt for leaving George.

"He's okay, it's broken but Kevin stayed with him. I think he is gonna stay with him at least for now. I'm sure that one of his sisters or his mother might go over." Feeling inept was not something she normally dealt with. She was the problem solver, you gave her an issue and she would jump right into action, but with George, it was difficult. Being a single guy for this long, she knew he had his own routines, people and things in place so that should something like this happen, he would have it all sorted out, making her completely superfluous in this situation.

"Are we going to stay with him while he recuperates? I can make snacks and get him pillows or an icepack or" Jodi was spiraling, Denise knew this was all coming from the sweetest place in her heart as she walked over and started stroking Jodi's arms to try and calm her down. Denise made sure she made eye contact with Jodi and took a deep breath in, a silent reminder for her to just take a breath. She realized that Jodi must not have taken her medicine and vitamins yet, which helped with her ADHD, and even possibly had not eaten. George was right, Jodi needed her more than he did. As the teen started breathing normally Denise walked the two of them into the kitchen and started getting everything ready for the day.

While making a late breakfast Denise went over exactly what was going on with George and Jodi was rather insistent that they help in any way they could. Her heart warmed at the idea that Jodi was truly worried about George, but then that same worrisome tension in her neck she always got once her daughter started to care deeply for the person she was in a relationship with pulled at her muscles. It was going to be another conversation, wherein she would feel like she was letting her daughter down again. Denise needed to nip this in the bud.

"Sweetie, listen." Denise handed the plate that she had filled to the brim with all Jodi's breakfast staples, bacon, eggs and potatoes over to her as she started munching on some bacon herself. "George and I are just seeing each other, it isn't serious. I just don't want you getting your hopes up in anything too serious here."

Jodi shoveled a huge fork full of food in her mouth and nodded. "I know." She garbled swallowing hard on the mouthful of food. That simple two-word statement hung heavy on Denise's chest, *what kind of impression was she setting?* But the truth was, she didn't know what a normal relationship looked like.

Her own mother, Lavinia, would come and go as she pleased, always floating away like a feather on the wind. Her father, Phillipe, however, was the one who always was her rock, showing her love, security, something she could depend on and the bond between the two of them was something that she shared with Jodi. Perhaps that was it, not having that model of what a normal relationship between two partners was the issue.

There were parts of her mother in her, she couldn't get close to anyone, and to be honest the moment she did Denise ran in the opposite direction. Many times, she would see her mother come home from wherever she had wandered off to and her parents would reconnect. It was nice to see, but the moment that her mother had gotten too comfortable, or too close to either of them she would disappear in the night. She could remember waking up to the smell of warm buttermilk pancakes with warm cherry compote and she would know, which is probably why she hated pancakes. It was her father's way of softening the blow, but it never worked. As the years went by Denise detached more and more, hardening her heart to the idea that a relationship between two adults was entirely unnecessary.

Yet, as she sat there eating her crispy bacon, she looked across the table at the young person stuffing her face with food and realized that hard truth. That she herself had turned into the one person she hadn't wanted to, Lavinia Gagnon. Her father would claim it was her Bohemian blood, ever the gypsy, never wanting to stay in one place for too long. It would explain how Denise had only truly been happy when she was in the service and eagerly took on a new assignment anytime it would come up. But then she got pregnant with Jodi and things changed.

Denise finally had that one person in the whole world who would love her for all her dark parts and carefree behaviors. It hadn't been easy being a single parent, there wasn't someone she could turn to for help in the middle of the night or whenever Jodi was sick. Phillipe had come for the birth, which had been wonderful to have him there. Planning with his staff at the farm stand, he decided to stay for two months, and then headed back to Wisconsin, but not before trying to convince her to go back with him. If there was anyone who would know what it was like to raise a child alone it would be him.

But she didn't, she really enjoyed living in New Jersey, despite the taxes and some congestion, she loved being able to go from a farm in Califon to the boardwalk in Point Pleasant in just a little over an hour. Or that she could easily hop on a train and be in New York City in just 45 minutes, or if you were crazy, you could drive 80 miles an hour from Union and over the Pulaski Skyway at two a.m. on a Sunday and be in SoHo in 20 minutes, not something she would recommend or ever do again.

There were lots of things she didn't do any more since Jodi. She didn't take risks, she didn't party, she didn't fly by the seat of her pants anymore and she didn't decide to up and restart her life somewhere else just because she wanted to. Everything was a calculated, carefully chosen decision.

Except when she made bad ones. First bad decision post Jodi was Bryan, then Michelle, Rick, Kelly, and then Nash. And now within the deep recesses of her mind, she was starting to think George might be one too. She liked the guy, what wasn't there to like? He was tall, dark, handsome, smart, funny, had really great taste in absolutely everything and he was steady. He knew who he was and what he wanted, and she realized she was envious of him.

Denise wasn't sure what she wanted, she knew one thing with absolute certainty, she wanted Jodi to be happy, healthy and loved and that was all she cared about. But as Jodi looked up from her plate and smiled at her, something hit her. That deep down in the secret dark spaces of her heart, despite her constant flip flopping on the issue - she wanted someone to want that for her too - it's just that she hadn't found that individual yet.

Someone who would challenge her, make her think, make her feel powerful but was willing to take the reins from her when she didn't want to be the one driving the team. She wanted heat and fire, but most of all she wanted someone who would make her want to stay still, to never make her think of leaving or picking up and running away. Denise's plan was to leave New Jersey the moment Jodi graduated.

As great as her friends were, she knew they weren't enough to keep her in Toselle Park. It was cold, but truthful, would they be hurt if she was leaving, probably, but there was no one keeping her here. No one had met the challenge. All of the people she had dated had been gifted with wonderful childhoods, so they wouldn't get her or her trauma. They had lived sunshine, roses and cotton candy lives, never having to suffer to eat sad *"your mom left us again"* pancakes. She needed a spark, someone who got her, who stirred something in her and she was positive that there was no one on this Earth that could ignite that for her.

Later that evening, as she lazily laid there on her couch thumbing through her recent book with Jodi snuggled up on her side, when Denise realized that she hadn't talked to her dad in a few days. With him getting older and his back bothering him from years of running the farm stand she needed to check up on him from time to time.

Phillipe wasn't alone per se, he had the farm staff and they would always keep her abreast of any issues he was having with his health that he insisted on keeping from his daughter. Sally Jensen, whom she had gone to high school with, had worked at the farm stand since they were teens and had never left. Always sending Denise texts, she would let her know whenever Phillipe had hurt himself or just giving her an update so she knew what was going on. Her father may not have been a native to Wisconsin, but he was beloved in the county for always helping small farms get their products to all his customers.

Reaching for her phone she pulled up her dad and dialed. Twirling her silky long black hair around her finger she waited for him to answer.

"Ah, bonsoir mon amour. Que fais-tu debout si tard ? Is everything okay?" (*Ah, good evening my love. What are you doing up so late?*) Phillipe's thick French colonial accent was garbled as he was trying to catch his breath on the other side of the phone. She could hear him closing the large garage doors of the farm stand and she looked over not realizing that it was past closing time there.

"We're fine, I'm more concerned that you are still at work? Papa, why are you not letting Sally close like you promised?" Denise had originally called to chat about her problems but now she was suddenly more concerned about the aging man on the other side of the phone. Listening to the sounds of him struggling to get into his house she could tell by the creaking of the door in the background that he had at least made it into the kitchen from the side door.

As she grew up, Phillipe had been someone to never keep secrets from her. He would tell her stories about him and her mother, good and the bad. He believed that truth was much better for a stronger foundation of trust which was probably why she had no issues confiding anything in him.

When Denise was a teen she had so many questions about her parents relationship, something he had been a bit hesitant to reveal. And then on a cold winter morning while snow fell he told her their story. He recounted that when he had moved to Wisconsin after marrying her mother, he had never expected her to leave shortly after having Denise. It had been Denise that had bound him to his tiny cherry and apple orchard and the promise of a better life in the states.

Phillipe was an inspiration to her; his perseverance and dedication were unmeasurable. But it was his story telling that she loved. His romantic recounting of her parent's love story and how it had been a whirlwind of instant love. How without hesitation he had followed her back to the states leaving his entire family behind in the Seychelles.

They had gotten married in a beautiful intimate ceremony as the sun set on the horizon, casting an almost surreal effect on Lake Michigan making the water almost glitter at Cana Island Lighthouse in Bailey's Harbor. When he would recount the events, the word intimate was an understatement as it had been just him, Lavinia, two friends he had made after moving to the Door County area and a Justice of the Peace. Yet, despite Lavinia's constant leaving, there was never any disdain or hurt in his voice when he would tell the stories. To him it was a fairy tale, as if it was a dream he had created.

Phillipe would say that Lavinia was like a Crab-Plover, a bird indigenous to his homeland who were very social during their mating season but would suddenly leave and be impossible to find due to its desire to be alone. That is how Denise envisioned her, flying high and away not wanting to be bothered, it was a feeling that she herself sometimes felt when she got too close to someone. The desire to fly and be free, nothing like her father who was always a homebody.

As she listened to the scuffling of the chair being pushed on the kitchen's hardwood floors, Denise took a sigh knowing that it was probably the first time in hours that he had taken a break to sit. With the pop of a cork in the background of her father's favorite Cabernet Sauvignon and the familiar crinkle of the baguette being torn so that he could enjoy his nightly treat of cheddar and apples she knew that he was finally resting.

"Gary was running late. A storm blew in and we had to just wait it out. But he did give me a new wheel of his peppercorn cheddar, which is delicious, but before you yell at me some more Sally was with me." He mumbled as he chomped down on his apple and cheddar. Denise was truly thankful for Sally, but what she really wanted was for him to just sell his place and retire. She missed seeing him daily, being able to just be able to run up and give him a hug, which was why when Jodi graduated she was going to move back, there would be no one holding her here.

"Papa, I don't want to bring it up again, but-" she paused at his resistant huff, "Please consider selling. I know you don't want to but I would rather you retire and relax, you've been going non-stop." It was the same argument every time she called him, retire and relax.

"But if I leave what will happen to the farm, people will be looking for me. I have been here for so long and people know right where to find me." Phillipe said, with a tinge of sadness in his voice, there was something more, she could feel it in his words. "Now, tell me you didn't call me to yell at me?" he asked. He knew her too well, as she started twirling her hair again knowing she would need to rehash what was going on.

Denise didn't know why she felt the way she did, but it just felt like something was shifting in her. She hadn't wanted to say it out loud but she did want something more. The one thing she was absolutely sure of was that it wasn't with George. He was lovely, kind and outgoing but it just wasn't what she wanted. Perhaps it was because he was all those wonderful things that had her feeling so indifferent to him. Although she liked to be in control of things in the bedroom, she had been hoping that he would take charge, but he hadn't, maybe if she asked him to, then maybe she could be the submissive one for once, yet at the same time, why should she have to ask. George was a massive guy and the fact that he was so willing to be the one in the passenger seat had thrown her off, she wanted someone who wanted to take control. To have the passion, fire and desire that would incinerate her and crumble her to ashes. That was the heat she craved, someone to make deliciously bad decisions with, but she couldn't seem to find that person anywhere no matter how hard she tried.

CHAPTER SIX

Hank

Hank's office was framed with all glass which made him feel like he was working in a fishbowl, it also felt like every eye in the office was watching him ever since last summer. People had treated him like a leper and someone to avoid because of the scandal. Truthfully he had almost lost his job and it had been all Liz's doing, that and his stupid dick for falling for her.

Being in a marriage where you know that your wife doesn't love you had been soul crushing. So, was it any wonder when Liz showed up and got a tour of the office that he was immediately attracted to her? She was smoking hot and it seemed like after she had seen the pictures of his family she had taken a particular interest in him.

Of course, that had been because of Grace and a ridiculous one-sided feud with her, that she had started to come onto him. It couldn't be because he was funny or was good looking, no it was all to get Grace back because of some stupid contest. Man, he felt absolutely lame once he had found out.

He had gotten called into the partners office about the arrest and luckily with the number of clients he brought in over the years they had forgiven him. Their only contingency was that he and Liz needed to separate themselves. But when Dr. Mahoney had pointed out just how toxic Liz was being between hiring a private eye and then riling him up every second she could, he realized he needed to get away from her. He thought it was going to be a simple break-up. Calmly talking to her about breaking it off, at least until things settled down, blaming it on Grace possibly taking custody of the boys away from him. He warned her that Jim could do the same, but she was convinced that Jim was too kind to do something that hateful.

He had also started to doubt them as a couple after George had shown up with Grace's dad, Ken, and was asking all those questions to Liz. Something just seemed odd, that she would be involved with Grace's ex-boyfriend and then her husband, it was almost as if she was targeting Grace for some reason.

Liz kept trying to convince him that everything was going to be fine and that they should keep dating, but Hank had stayed firm. His boys needed to be the top priority from now on until he could work things out with Grace and that was when Liz lost it. She ranted and raved on how he was letting Grace get the best of him and how Grace needed to just go away. She had begged him if Grace went away, would he be with her again and his only answer he could come up with to get her to stop was a regrettable *maybe*. It was the glint of something in her eyes that scared him into saying maybe.

This was just to get her out of his office at the time, not realizing the level of hatred Liz had held towards Grace.

As he stared at the screen trying very hard to make sense of the numbers that his client had sent over for him to review for their tax return that he had extended months ago, he just rolled his eyes at the monotony of it all. He had asked them to send all this information to him back in April when he first filed their extension but they had finally sent it over to his assistant, Ginny, two days ago and now he was in a crunch with the October deadline looming just weeks away.

He tried not to think of the word crunch as his balls still ached from time to time because of Denise's giant head. She was a massive pain in his ass. Constantly taunting him like it was her job. She taught yoga and Pilates, wasn't she supposed to be all Zen and relaxed all the time. All she seemed to be, was wanting to constantly antagonize him, reminding him about what a loser he was, not getting laid and how awful of a father he had been to Calvin and Colin. He didn't need reminding of what a disaster his life had been.

Taking a few seconds to rub his eyes he looked up to see his messenger chat pop up.

Nick – *hey it's your turn to host drinks, where am I meeting you, are you heading into the city or am I crossing the Hudson and slumming it in Jersey?*

After Nick moved to the city, he would make it a point to make fun of New Jersey as often and as much as possible. Knowing that Hank had Dr.

M that afternoon, Nick would have to make the trek into Jersey because he was not about to do NJ Transit to get into the city.

Hank – *Jersey will have to graciously accept an asshole to come and visit it. I have a client I am meeting so just meet me at 6 at the Sun Porch here in town just let me know if you are running late.*

Nick must have been thinking about it a little longer and the three bubbles that were moving in the chat finally popped.

Nick – *So I should leave now cause you know how the trains suck ass?*

He had a point, the commute in and out of NYC was atrocious but if he left at five p.m. he should make it to Toselle Park in plenty of time. Letting him know not to rush, Hank looked up to see his mousey assistant standing in the doorway. Ginny was a sweet young woman, her brown hair swept up in a loose French twist, boring white button-down shirt and khaki colored skirt, he was still shocked that she had just gotten herself engaged.

There was a part of him who wanted to warn her of the dangers of being in a relationship, but based on the conversations they had had, this was true love. Something he was sure he would never receive, no one to accept him and love him for who he was - which sucked. Why was he so unlovable, except for his boys, they did love him and for right now it was going to have to be enough.

"Hank, you wanted me to remind you about your four o'clock and also Mr. Dupree messaged me to tell you -" she stopped, "I'm not sure what he means but he said you may need my help 'to ice them' I'm not sure what needs ice? Did you want me to get you a drink before you leave?" Ginny had no idea about his injury from the game, but because of their conversation after the event, Hank knew Nick was just being a dick, and poor Ginny had no idea.

Shaking his head, Hank got up from his chair and sent off a quick message telling Nick not to involve Ginny and that he would see him at six p.m. and he was buying dinner.

"No Ginny, ignore Nick, he is just being -" how was he supposed to explain that his friend told his assistant to help him ice his balls? It was best that he didn't explain, especially considering it was sexual harassment, "I wanted an iced coffee, but I can get one on my way to my appointment. Thank you, you can leave early if you want." Hank said, as he shut down his laptop and grabbed his suit jacket. As he walked out of the office he wondered why he was still friends with a jerk like Nick.

"So how was your weekend with the boys?" the short stocky older gentleman sitting in the large armchair asked as he looked over the rim of his glasses at Hank. Dr. Mahoney's office was small but inviting. A dark calming navy, silver and dark woods throughout gave it a safe space feel and the chocolate brown worn leather couch that had probably seen millions of tears shed on it was actually pretty comfortable.

Laying there, his back had hurt from that blow Denise had caused, but he wasn't here to talk about her. The boys had been great all weekend and when Grace came to pick them up she had shocked him by offering to sell the house to him.

"It went really well despite a small injury. We actually just kind of hung around my place and vegged out for the weekend." Hank really didn't have any issues this past week.

"Well, rest is important and considering that the three of you were just hanging out and you weren't being forced or were forcing them to do something. Sounds like things are definitely on the right track with the boys. You don't always have to occupy their time when you are together. You can engage in independent coexistence." Hank just bobbed his head in agreement and laid there just staring up at the ceiling which he noticed had a few cracks in it. "Do you have any other things you want to go over or news to share."

"Grace offered to sell the house to me and I'm actually considering it."

The impressed look on Dr. Mahoney's face made Hank snigger a bit, as he was also equally surprised. When Grace proposed it, he knew it was because she hated his apartment, which he was totally in agreement with. *It was awful.*

"Wow, well that is a lot of growth for both of you. Most ex-wives would have just sold the house and called it a day, but offering to sell you the house shows she cares about you and your well-being." Dr. M said, as he wrote in his notes.

"No, she just doesn't want to see the boys move out of the only home they have ever known, she also isn't a fan of my place. Besides, she isn't giving it to me, I have to pay fair market value." Hank grimaced, prices were through the roof with interest rates being so high and inventory being low, Grace could make a pretty penny if she sold it to someone else, but she had offered it to him before she put it on the market.

"That is what a good mom does. She puts aside her feelings and makes sure her children are happy. Think about it this way, if your mom had been in this same situation, would she have offered your dad the opportunity to buy the house when they got divorced?"

Hank just shook his head. "Nope, she would have burned down the house with me in it, just so that my dad's legacy was gone." Hank's matter of fact tone and statement must have caught Dr. M by surprise because he had begun choking on his tea.

"Well, that is the most disturbing thing I've heard in a while and that is saying something. Since we've talked about your mom in the past, I know she wasn't exactly maternal. Is it fair to say that Grace is probably the mom you would have loved to have had as a kid?" He knew what Dr. M was doing here; he was trying to get him to realize something.

"Perhaps. The truth is she is a billion times better than my mother was." Hank smiled, the truth was that during their marriage he watched as Grace wasn't just the boys' mom, she was their friend too. She knew all the things they liked, what their interests were, she took time to learn about their games so she could play with them, and he hadn't even bothered. Grace blew his mom out of the water hands down.

"So, let's revisit your mom." Dr. M hadn't realized the flood gates he was about to unleash. Taking a deep breath, Hank started slowly telling the jovial looking man who reminded him of Santa Claus all the awful things about his own mother. How when his father packed up his stuff, she screamed that he should take Hank along since she never wanted him to begin with. How if she had had it her way, she would have gotten an abortion because she never wanted to be a mother. The endless reminders that children were a burden and not a joy, just another thing to have to sacrifice her life to doing.

As Dr. Mahoney sat in complete silence making note after note, Hank just laid there. No tears, no anger or resentment. Just explaining it like he would explain to a client why you couldn't use a pet as a dependent whether they had a ton of medical bills or not. An occasional hm, or ah ha or an off um was all the doctor would utter. But as he went over all these awful things his mother had said or done, he was starting to realize why he acted the way he did. His father had left, never to return and a mother who hadn't wanted him was not the best environment for anyone to grow up in.

"Have you tried to reach out to find your dad?" the petite man asked as he took a sip of his tea.

"I wasn't sure I would find him, and honestly at this point I'm not sure I really want to. Having left and refusing to take me knowing how my mother felt was complete abandonment. So why would I want a reconnection now?"

"It's a great point, but is it something you have ever wanted?"

"Yeah the day he left, but when he walked out and didn't come back, I never wanted to see him again." Hank remembered secretly standing at his bedroom window every day for almost three months straight, looking out at every car that passed by waiting to see his dad's, but it never came.

"How old were you when this happened?"

"Six." Hank breathed out a long sigh, *six years old* and neither one of his parents wanted him. He was not the greatest parent in the world, but at least he wasn't like them. Never loving or caring or kind, he had been thankful that Grace had never met either one of them. His mom had passed two months before he had met Grace.

Nick had taken him out to karaoke to get him out of the house when he met her. Grace was sweet, kind, funny, but she was hesitant about engaging in a conversation or in a relationship. It had taken a few dates before she agreed, but there was always something keeping her from committing. Times when she would look over her shoulder searching for someone else.

Clearing his throat, Dr. Mahoney looked at Hank who must have gotten lost in his thoughts.

"Tell me where you went just now?" he smiled over to Hank to encourage him to open up. There was no point in coming to these sessions if he wasn't going to talk. So, he talked some more and just when he thought he was going to get to finish the chime went off. As the two men walked out of the room, Dr. Mahoney reminded Hank he could always email him or call if he needed to talk as they confirmed his next appointment. The tiny man held out his hand and Hank looked down at it and thought of Denise and their interaction.

"Actually, can we book something sooner? I did have something I wanted to talk about that's been bothering me." His brow creased with unease, he couldn't get that beastly woman out of his head and she needed to not live rent free in it. Making the arrangements, Hank thanked the doctor and left. He felt better as he walked out of the red-bricked office building, that was until he was practically ran over by a car pulling into the empty spot he was walking in to get to his own. As he looked up into the driver's seat he locked eyes with the one person he absolutely didn't want to see.

"Oh, for fuck sake, move the Hell out of the way, you are making it too easy for me to fulfill my dreams!" Denise yelled from the driver's side window as he backed away from her front fender and onto the sidewalk. He wanted to march back into the office and pray that Dr. Mahoney would kick his current client out so he could just vent it all out, but he just stood there staring at her as she shut the car door behind her. The pair of khaki shorts rode so high they accentuated her long curvy legs and he felt tingling up his spine as he watched her hips swish towards him. Frozen, his gaze moved up to the too tight purple tank top with the words *"Someone's FERAL Mom"* that hugged her waist and breasts perfectly. His mouth salivating as he noticed that her nipples were hard under the top from the breeze that should have been blowing but seemed to not be there.

What was happening, he thought. She was awful, but damn if she wasn't hot. Heat started to rise from his chest and up to his face as his pulse quickened as she closed the distance between them. He had to think quickly so she didn't notice him gawking at her.

"So, you are dreaming of me? Shouldn't you be dreaming of your flavor of the month or are you planning on ruining yet another relationship?" Hank smirked only to have a full handed slap smack him across his face. Denise had never struck him before. There had been plenty of times that he had deserved this sort of visceral reaction, but if it looks like a duck and quacks like a duck, you call it what it was.

"Fuck you!" The rage in her voice clear as a bell. "At least I am not a cheater, unlike you." He stared into those eyes and found nothing but rage and he matched it right back.

"I've apologized to Grace and the boys for your information. Not that it should matter to you. Now be a good girl and be on your way." He watched as her eyes narrowed when he said *good girl* and he couldn't help but enjoy the fact that he got to her. With his pulse rushing he could feel his breathing getting faster as his heart raced. Out of the corner of his eye he caught her pulling her hand back to hit him again and just as it was within inches of his face he caught her by the wrist. Smiling up at the fact that this slap was not going to land, he gave her a quick wink. *You only get one good shot,* he thought.

"I will never be a good girl for you. Now let go." Denise demanded, his thumb on her pulse point made him realize that her pulse was going a mile a minute and he felt the need to brush his thumb over her wrist. Her skin was the softest thing he had ever touched and he could smell a slight hint of honeysuckle, vanilla and some other kind of flower, it was sweet and addicting. He pulled her closer and surprisingly she hadn't hesitated like she had in the past.

"Say please." The words sounded more like a purr than a command.

"What? Fuck you!" Denise's enchanting eyes blinked back at him as she stared into his and it took him a second to respond. This time he lessened his grip ever so slightly, drawing her closer. He allowed his cheek to brush against hers so he could whisper as he took a deep inhale in of her scent. Her skin was soft, warm and enticing to touch. She was becoming addicting, this cat and mouse game they played with one another, the fire between them, the mutual hatred, *or* was it something else? Because God help him if it was.

"Sweetheart, I am a ride you will not survive." His words a languid whisper as he brushed his lips along the bottom of her ear and he felt her shiver ever so slightly. It had been months since he had been this close to another woman. And within the past few days their forced proximity to each other was making him start to question himself. Denise loved getting under his skin, but now that she was arms reach he couldn't help but want to touch or caress her.

"Now say please and I will let you go." Her breath quickened and he wasn't sure if the other hand was gonna hit him or if he had genuinely got to her. Could he have possibly thrown her off her game? Denise let out a ragged breath as his lips dusted her cheek. Looking directly into her eyes, he saw her pupils blown, barely able to make out any of the yellow center, all he saw was a thin green ring around her pupils.

It felt like months had gone by as they stared into each other's eyes before she breathlessly whispered, "Please." No snarky comment, no fight, nothing, just what he asked her to do. Realizing he had promised to let go of her, Hank slowly released his grip from her wrist, plastering on a lazy grin.

"See now you can be a *good girl*. Always a delight to see you." Hank said, as he carefully walked away. He hadn't realized that he had actually gotten hard at being so close to her. Adjusting himself as he sat in his car, he realized that these exchanges needed to end. Hank couldn't get involved with her, she was with someone else and was his ex-wife's best friend. This needed to end. And he had to try and do anything and everything to avoid her.

CHAPTER SEVEN

Denise

Denise had been running late for her appointment with her therapist. Dr. Mahoney was this sweet, plump adorable man who was used to her being a few minutes late to sessions. She had called him in the morning to see if he could fit her in because she needed to figure out what to do with her relationship with George. Being in a small town like Toselle Park, there were only two therapists, she could have gone to someone in another town but she liked supporting businesses in town but the best part was that he was in-network.

Flying down Maple Avenue, she pulled into the parking lot of his office building and saw a spot right in front, *perfect*, she thought. That was until she almost hit someone, Hank.

"Oh, for fuck sake, move the Hell out of the way you are making it too easy for me to fulfill my dreams!" Denise yelled from the driver's side window as he backed away from her front fender and onto the sidewalk. As she stared at him through the window, she noticed he was wearing a pair of jeans that were rather form fitting as it outlined the bulge in his pants. Her brain immediately went to the comment Grace had made about his dick and couldn't stop thinking about what it looked like.

Stepping out of the car, Denise took a deep breath and she caught the scent of his cologne in the air. It was rich and spicy, with hints of cinnamon, smokey tobacco and a pink peppercorn hint which was tantalizing her to actually want to get closer to him. Hating the fact that he not only was handsome but to smell that good was some sort of crime against nature when you have a personality like his.

"So, you are dreaming of me? Shouldn't you be dreaming of your flavor of the month or are you planning on ruining yet another relationship?" Hank's smirk and comment was the last straw as she landed a flat palmed smack right across his face. *God that felt great*, she thought. Honestly she had been wanting to do it for years, but now that they were actually alone and no witnesses she wasn't going to hold back now. *Dreaming of him*? Was he for real, maybe he lived in her nightmares like the monster that he was.

"Fuck you!" The rage in her voice clear as a bell. "At least I am not a cheater, unlike you." *That's right, I at least have some morals*, she would never cheat on any of her partners and to even think she would consider doing it, let alone with him was pissing her off. Hank stared into her rage filled eyes and he matched it right back.

"I've apologized to Grace and the boys for your information. Not that it should matter to you. Now be a *good girl* and be on your way." Once again there was that stupid *good girl* comment and her blood boiled. Pulling her hand back to hit him again, her hand flew through the air but he must have noticed because he caught her wrist just inches from striking him. Her eyes widened as his strong grip held her wrist, they had only ever shaken hands that one time on the ball field after all these years of knowing each other and it had caused an electric trigger through her body. This time his strong hand on her wrist was stirring her to practically melt right there on the spot and what made matters worse he had the nerve to smile up at her and wink.

"I will never be a good girl for you. Now let go." Denise demanded as she wrenched her wrist in his grip, if he didn't let go she might do something they would both regret. But then he brushed the pad of his thumb over her wrist. It was intimate and gentle, nothing like what he was like in real life. Pulling her closer, her breath stole at the back of her throat. What was it with him and wanting her so close lately? He hated her, so what was the incessant need to have her body pressed up against his. Feeling helpless, she needed to escape his clutches, she had an appointment to get to.

"Say please." He purred and her brain just exploded.

"What? Fuck you!" Denise hissed, her eyes drifting down to his lips with that tiny sneer on it and then up to those unbearable baby blue eyes, and then back to his lips as he drew her closer.

As the space between them got smaller, her head spun as his cologne sailed through the air, triggering a reaction. She was hoping this was nothing. That this was just the heat of the day causing her to feel so lightheaded. After all, this odd sensation that he was causing her was not something she wanted or needed in her life. She just wanted things to go back to the way it was, the mutual hatred, not this irrational desire she was suddenly feeling. Her heart raced as he leaned in to whisper in her ear.

"Oh Sweetheart, I am a ride you will not survive." He whispered as he brushed his lips along the bottom of her ear and her body betrayed her as she shivered from his closeness. *My God is he actually making me wet*, and to her agitation she realized her panties were now practically soaked. "Now say please and I will let you go."

Her pulse rushing at such an intimate gesture, she let out a ragged breath as his lips dusted her cheek. His scruffy five o'clock shadow felt like something she could get used to. That rough, heavenly gritty sensation drove her crazy. *A ride you will not survive?* Is he actually talking about sex with her? This needed to end, he needed to let her go, and if it meant she would need to say one stupid word she would.

Breathlessly, she whispered, "Please." No snarky comment, no fight, nothing, just what he asked her to do. Slowly releasing his grip from her wrist she felt like something was missing and she couldn't explain it.

"See now, you can be a good girl. Always a delight to see you." Hank said, as he walked away to his car, her eyes following him and never leaving his ass. She needed to get inside and away from this man, because he was dangerous and she had but one thought, *he was trouble and trouble only ends in bad decisions.*

Looking around the tiny room with Dr. Mahoney in front of her, she was avoiding his gaze. She knew he wasn't there to judge but something in her knew deep down he was.

"But if everything with your current partner is okay, why would you consider breaking things off?" She had told him that she wouldn't use anyone's names when she came to therapy out of a possible conflict of interest. In a tiny one and half mile wide town and only two therapists to choose from, she didn't want to share names. After she and Jodi had talked she realized that it might be best to separate herself from George. It wasn't the injury; it was just that she didn't feel like things were going to get serious with him, and he deserved to find the right individual to spend his time with.

"Because doesn't everyone deserve the right to be happy?"

"They do, but why do you think you cannot be happy with your current partner?" he asked, it was a valid question.

"Because, I have no idea what a normal happy relationship looks like for adults. I feel like I am stuck in this awful loop to be like my mother, who was never around and never showed me what a typical marital relationship is supposed to be like." Denise exclaimed in exasperation. She didn't want to be her mother, but the more and more she got into these relationships, the more she saw shades of Lavinia and her nature coming out.

"Denise, every person is different and not every relationship has to be two loving partners. What you need to remember is that not everyone will be paired off with someone. It doesn't make them a bad person, or that something is wrong with them." Dr. Mahoney looked over the rim of his wire framed glasses and continued. "Your mother was herself and she embraced it. You embraced being a single mother beautifully and you've done a great job with Jodi, but what you need to do is learn to love yourself, for all the light parts and the dark ones as well. You need to stop comparing yourself to your mother or to other people, but that is what we are here to do."

Not wanting to admit that he was right, Denise merely motioned in agreement. Because deep inside she did want a relationship with someone, but that suffocating fear of being like her mother had her all twisted. Being a mom had come so naturally, and it was something she prided herself on, and the truth was that that was the one thing that set her and Lavinia apart.

As she looked at herself in her rearview mirror, her puffy swollen eyes had become the telltale sign that the session with her therapist had been a hard one and had her rubbing her hands over her dampened tear-stained face. Lavinia, was not her present, she was in the past, and now was the perfect time to put in the hard work of regaining her life back.

Admitting that she had been jealous of the fact that her mom had been so carefree in her life and wanting it for herself had been difficult. But Dr. Mahoney had made her realize that perhaps her mom may not be as free as she was left to believe. He hypothesized that perhaps the reason Lavinia never stayed around was that she was afraid; it would be when she was getting too comfortable that she would leave, that it was the responsibility to stay and put in the work of being a wife and mother that scared her off.

There was a part of Denise that thought she should keep trying to have a real relationship with George. He was wonderful. There should be nothing standing in the way of possibly making it work, but she just couldn't get past these unsettling feelings she was having every single time she got close to Hank lately. What was it about him that had her feeling this way whenever he was around? No one should want to forgive him for the way he had treated Grace over the years, let alone for what he said the first time they had met.

But since Grace's accident something had changed; she still despised him, but he had been trying to get better. Except all she could think of was what he had said about her and that Jodi should have been an abortion, always staying in the forefront of her mind. How can someone think such an awful thing like that? No matter how much alcohol they consumed, no one should say that to someone else. He should have kept that to himself if he felt that way.

And then she thought about herself and how her mother had shaped this insane notion of what her life should be like and she wondered, perhaps Hank had suffered similar trauma that had caused him to have such a frame of mind. Grace had mentioned she had never met his parents and whenever she would ask he would change the subject. If there was anyone who understood those actions it was Denise. Always changing the subject to her dad whenever the topic of her mother came up. So perhaps that was it, his parents had scarred him as well. Of course, this was all her speculating but still there was just something off with herself every time she had been encountering him.

Be a good girl, she heard his voice echoing in her mind, and a slight stirring in her heart caused it to flutter. It was an order every time and no one outside of the Navy had ever put her in a position where she needed to do what they commanded her. Perhaps that was it, no one had had the gall to do that, to not be so intimidated by her. He didn't fear her or was it possible that everyone else was merely apprehensive in saying whatever they thought. Was that it? Was it the fact that she had finally met someone who wasn't afraid to say whatever they thought around her unlike so many other people before him. Denise knew there were times that she came off as aggressive and domineering, and that people didn't come right out and share what they were thinking, but Hank had no hair on his tongue with her.

Then her stomach flopped as her brain started thinking about his tongue and all the things she would have him doing with it. Reaching up and touching her cheek where his scruffy face had brushed against hers, her pulse quickening. Remembering how his lips grazed her ear and her breath was coming in shorter. *Shit!* she thought, this cannot be happening to her. She cannot be turned on by this man. As she pulled up to the red light, she closed her eyes and things just got worse as her mind went to his eyes, the piercing blue, the same color as the sky. She needed him out of her mind; she was going to move forward with George and that was it. Yet, as she opened her eyes her heart dropped, there he was walking across the street heading towards The Sun Porch. It would seem the universe was working against her.

That was it, she needed to end this whole thing. Denise needed to have it out with him and be done with whatever this insanity was because she would never be able to move on with her life if he was going to be doing whatever it was to her mind.

CHAPTER EIGHT

Hank

Hey Asshole, you and I need to talk!" Hank turned to find Denise getting out of her car in the parking lot running towards him just as he was about to meet up with Nick. His eyes following her voluptuous breasts bouncing as she ran, it sent a chill up his spine and a sudden tightening in his pants. *God Damn this woman and my dick, she needs to stay away from me*, he demanded his brain to keep it together. As she slowed down her pace, his eyes shifted down to watch her hips swishing as her long legs strode her towards him. She looked more like a caged lioness that had been released, stalking her prey like he was just a piece of raw meat waiting to be eaten alive.

"Trying to run me over wasn't enough today. You want to ruin my dinner plans too? Should I call you when I have a date so you destroy any chance of me getting laid as well?" Hank asked knowing full well there was no chance of him getting laid anytime soon. And then she was inches away from him and he could feel her heat. Standing there taking in deep breaths, she just stared at him, her eyes filled with some kind of pain or anguish. It looked like she had been crying and now his heart felt a pang of sadness for her which was completely unusual for him.

"I don't give a damn about whether you get laid or not, I just want to know what your deal is with this whole good girl business?" Denise demanded her breath was coming in short, which for someone who made a living off of teaching people how to breathe and meditate, it was obvious she needed to practice what she preached. He had gotten to her with two simple words and he thought for a second about that fact. He could continue this torture some more but he was truly trying to be a better person, yet.

"Oh, come on, you can't tell me no one has ever told you to be a good girl before. You of all people, with all these lovers you've had, someone has had to tell you to be a good girl." Hank asked as he moved out of the way of a family trying to get into the restaurant. Walking away from the front door, he thought it best to move this conversation away for any passerby and walked closer to the tall, bricked alcove bar area. If she wanted to have this conversation it was best to do this as privately as possible.

Despite his nonchalant appearance, the closer she moved towards him the faster his heart began racing. She still smelt like cotton candy, that is what he figured out she smelt like, like a floral delicious piece of cotton candy and he wondered if she tasted just as good, his dick hardening in his jeans again.

"No, and you need to stop. Whatever it is you think you are doing, I need you to stop." Denise was starting to get too close for comfort, if she got any closer she would practically be right on top of him and then she would know just how turned on he was by her. But Hank was not one to be told what to do.

"Why?" He felt this pull to her, as he moved away from the bar no longer caring if she felt his raging hard on. Denise's eyes fluttered back at him as he looked at her neck and then to her lips before his eyes landed on hers.

"Why?" whispering this time now mere inches from her face feeling the air between them mingling, and all the control in him holding him in check because what he really wanted to do was kiss her. As insane and as angry as she made him, there was just something about her that had been driving him nuts and he couldn't get her out of his head.

He followed her eyes as she looked down at his lips then back up to his eyes, he saw it then, *desperation*. But he wasn't sure what sort of desperation it was, so he took a chance and slid his hand around her waist pulling her close - right up against his body. Shockingly, she didn't tighten up. Denise didn't swing at him, if anything she pressed her body closer to him. *Holy Fuck, Denise wants me.*

"Because." Was all that she was able to choke out as she swallowed hard at his nearness.

"Because, isn't an answer Denise, now be a good girl and use your words." Hank was sure that was going to get him another slap, if not the comment, than the fact that he had wound his other hand around her and reached down to her toned ass. But instead, all she did was stare deeper into his eyes and brushed her nose against his as her hands moved up to the front of chest to grab a fistful of his shirt as he ground himself against her. He wanted nothing more than to pin her against the brick wall right this minute and have his way with her if they weren't just outside of the restaurant, but God help him this woman had him under a spell.

Their warm breaths mixed together as he felt her heart pounding under her breasts that she had crushed against him. Their weight and softness was making him dizzy at the thought of wanting to grasp them. But he would settle for the thrill of holding her ass in his hand for now.

"Please." Barely a whisper passed through Denise's lips and Hank grinned as he brushed his lips past hers causing his skin to prickle.

"'Because' and then 'Please'. Please what?" Hank whispered across her lips and then as he slid the hand he had around her waist down and grabbed her ass again grinding against her, her reaction to this caught him by complete surprise as she let out a shuddered moan.

"You want me to stop calling you a good girl?" his tongue skimmed the bottom of her lip.

"Would you rather me tell you to stop being a brat with all the naughty things you say to me? Do you want me to stop touching you like this." He purred as his hands trailed down to the hem of her shorts to lift them so he could get underneath. Gliding his long fingers along the soft skin just under her firm derriere, he managed to grab a full palm of bare cheeks as the tips of his fingers were perilously close to her ass seam. Wondering just how far he could take this with her, this slow painful process that they had been leading up to. He had finally caught his mouse and now he wanted to play with it before he devoured it.

The idea of what she tasted like had his balls tingling with anticipation and he could feel a bit of pre-cum escape. *Fuck, I need her*, was the only thing his brain could fathom at this point and by God, she wanted him because her hands were no longer grasping his shirt but playing with his hair.

"Denise," he growled, "tell me what you want." His fingers found their way to her thong which to his utter delight was soaked and he smiled to himself as he looked at her. Denise had closed her eyes at the sensations that he was eliciting from her, and his heart swelled at the idea that she was so turned on. He moved his fingers further down towards her core and she gasped as her eyes flew open to meet his.

"I need my brat to tell me what she wants. Do you want me to stop?" His pointer finger just centimeters away from her glistening entrance, he stopped. Staring deep into those mysteriously enchanting eyes he stood there frozen, Denise made no indication as to yes or no, moving in closer his lips grazed hers and he felt her shudder again.

"I will stop, and I will walk away this moment, never to do or say anything mean to you ever again or" he paused and her heavily lidded eyes flew open waiting for the foot to drop "you can say the thing you really came here to say and tell me to go fuck myself or" he paused again.

"Or?" Denise questioned as she licked her lips.

"Or you can tell me that you want me to fuck you against this wall like the brat you are." And then she did the thing he wasn't expecting and ground against him herself grabbing the back of his head crushing her lips onto his. Whatever beast inside his chest that had been lying in wait leapt into action as their lips connected. A snarling moan rumbled in his throat as he nipped at her lower lip begging for her to open to him, *and she did*. His tongue delved into her mouth to find her soft enticing tongue, and very much like her perfume, she tasted sweet almost like bubble gum. He refused to move his hands despite how desperate he was to grab her tits, but her pussy was practically screaming for him as he felt a slight tremor near his fingers.

Breaking their kiss, she looked at Hank with all the rage gone and nothing but passion. "Fuck me." She exclaimed but he truly wasn't sure that was what she wanted, but the moment she wrapped one leg around his waist and hoisted herself up he moved as quickly as he could to the patio alcove that had the highest wall for some privacy.

Now with some discretion and her lip caught between his teeth he kept one hand on her ass and managed to take his other hand and slid it down the front of her shorts driving one long finger into her dripping core. A tiny gasp escaped her lips despite her doing her best to stay quiet considering how out in the open they were. Her breathing was becoming ragged as he slid another finger into her. Denise apparently wanted more as she started to fumble with his pants and as much as he wanted to actually fuck her he was going to do something different in his life and focus on the other person.

Hank had always been greedy before, never taking care of his other partner until he had had his fill. But for some reason, he knew that with

Denise she would need to be served first. As he continued to slowly glide in and out of Denise and he could feel her walls constricting around his fingers. She herself had been very diligent in getting access to his rock-hard dick and once she had gotten her hand around it she looked up at him in shock.

"Holy Shit. Grace was right." She said, as she began to try and stroke him in the jeans, but his hand had stilled.

"Do I really want to know why you and my ex-wife were discussing my dick?" Hank asked as he curled his fingers inside her and slowly started re-stroking her core watching her head fall back, her mouth agape as she ground against his hand. Shaking her head she seemed to understand that he didn't want to hear about Grace while he finger fucked her best friend. Leaving her neck open for attack, he dove into her pulse point, sucking and licking it as he felt her growing closer and closer to climax. But then she yanked his head away from her neck.

"Stop going after my neck, I can't have a hickey." She said, as she struggled to play with him in the jeans, he was thoroughly enjoying the feel of her long fingers wrapped around his dick and it was taking everything in him not to let go. It had been a little over a year since someone else had their hands on him and it felt amazing. He knew she was close and he just needed to get her there. Taking his thumb, he went to work moving over her clit in a circular motion as he dropped his head down to her cleavage and started kissing the breasts he really wanted to be holding. But he would just enjoy this little dance they were doing, for now.

The only thing bringing him back to reality was his phone suddenly buzzing in his back pocket. He had forgotten all about the reason he came here, to see his buddy Nick. But first to get his brat to cum. Ignoring the phone, he picked up his punishment on her quim and as he crushed another kiss to her hungry lips she came. Wave after wave her core pulsated around his now soaked fingers. Collapsing down against the wall, he moved his one arm in time to catch her so she wouldn't hurt herself against the wall. They had been incredibly quiet, and for someone who had such a big mouth and always yelling at him, she was quiet the whole time.

As he looked up at her, Hank brushed her hair back away from her eyes as she caught her breath. She still had her hand down his pants and although he would want her to finish him off, he felt the buzz of his phone again and knew this wasn't the right time for him as he gently started to pull her hand out of his pants.

Denise just looked at him unsure of what was going on, but as much as he wanted this, *and he did*, he knew it was just a matter of time before someone found them and he really didn't want to be left with his pants down, both literally and figuratively.

"But" she started and he kissed her into silence. "What about" he kissed her again to stop her from talking. He enjoyed kissing her, there was fire and passion and something that hit him square in the chest every time their lips touched.

"I'm fine right now, another time. Besides, I came here because I'm meeting my buddy. Not to get into it with you." Hank fixed his shirt, what was supposed to happen now?

And then it hit him, George. He had just ravaged someone who was in a relationship, once again falling into bad habits again, he thought to himself. But was she still with George, unless that was why she had looked like she was crying when she arrived? Maybe they had broken up just now and if so that would make him what - a rebound?

"Hold on, you are okay with what you just did for me, but I can't reciprocate?" Denise's tone changed back to the one she had when she arrived. Wonderful, now she was pissed, but if he was the one that just got used, why wasn't he more mad?

"This isn't a tit for tat kind of thing, all I'm saying is that I had plans, you showed up all broken-hearted and picked a fight with me. How did I know things were going to go the way they did? I don't normally screw another dude's ex-girlfriend." Hank vented, raking his fingers through his hair smoothing it back down from where she had messed it up.

Denise stood there looking all dejected and he wasn't sure why, he just got her off, most women would love to not have to do any work. *What was her problem,* he thought to himself.

"I didn't come here all broken-hearted, okay. I came here because I don't get why you kept telling me to be a good girl and get you out of my mind, not to have your knuckles deep in my pussy!" Denise fumed and all that just happened was now becoming yet another fight where he is being left like the bad guy and what did she mean she wasn't *broken hearted.*

"You came here all puffy eyed picking yet another fight with me and let me have my way with you. You mean to tell me that you weren't just crying before you came here and that you just came here to start shit. You're right, you aren't a good girl, you're a bitch." Hank barked and all Denise could do was stand there. "And if you didn't come here all broken hearted then you are still with George, yes?" Hank asked his heart pounding in anger, how could she do this?

"Yes, I'm still with George that isn't why I was upset. I had been," Denise started, but Hank had had enough and he threw up his hand for her to stop talking.

"No, you know what, I don't care. But let me re-cap here so I have everything straight, you are still with your boyfriend, you were upset about something else, you hunted me down to pick a fight and then used me to cheat on your boyfriend and tell me to stop calling you a good girl? Am I right? This cheater just wants to make sure I got my facts straight." Hank needed clarification, he stood there waiting on her response, her eyes searching for something around them, *perhaps for the giant chip she kept on her shoulder*. She looked up at him with tears in her eyes now realizing the gravity of what they had just done.

"Got it." Was all he had the effort to get out, his heart dropped into his stomach and he felt incredibly sick. He had been played. Taking in a deep breath, he walked past her and all he wanted to do was reach back and shake her. Why did she do this, why did she like getting him all twisted and messed up? With his hand on the handle to the front door Denise called out.

"Hank, please."

"Got it, this won't happen again. Tell George I said hi and hope he gets better quickly." He said, as he walked into the restaurant and he meant it. He did hope George got better quickly, the faster he did the faster he could run farther away from Denise the better.

CHAPTER NINE

George

George hadn't been expecting company, his mom had stopped by earlier and had been thrilled to see Kevin helping out. He didn't know it in the beginning but with Kevin being there, he was actually thinking the healing process might go a bit faster. Driving him around to the orthopedist and helping him schedule the surgery had been a tremendous help. With Denise being occupied with Jodi, he didn't expect her to be able to assist him in any way so seeing her walking through the door was a shock especially since it was dinnertime.

"Hey, what are you doing here? I figured you would call me after dinner." George said, as he was adjusting the pillows next to him in case she was planning on sitting, but something was off and he could sense it. Denise just stood there looking around, not making eye contact. Her flushed skin, the pink mark on her neck and lack of eye contact. He knew and she didn't have to say a thing, she had just hooked up with someone the question was, *who?* Denise had made a bad decision again. Truthfully he was neither surprised nor upset that she had cheated, it had been clear that things had changed with her recently and with his injury he was honestly more focused on getting better than on their relationship.

Looking over to Kevin, George motioned his head in the direction of the kitchen and Kevin picked up on it.

"I'm gonna make a snack, Denise, do you want anything?" he asked looking over at her and she silently shook her head as he exited the room.

"You want to come sit? I don't think my leg will hurt any more than it already does if you actually sit and take a load off." George joked trying to lighten the already heavy mood. She was there to break up with him, he could tell.

Walking across the room, Denise sat next to him and for someone who was always so strong she looked as if she was four years old and someone had just yelled at her.

"Listen, I'm actually glad you came over because I wanted to talk with you but getting around has its challenges, do you mind if I say something first?" George asked, he knew that this was the part of her relationships that she hated, so he thought perhaps it was best to soften this blow. She just nodded in agreement, still not saying anything. Now that she was closer he could smell the mixture of her perfume and the spicy cologne that he recognized.

"Listen, I'm worried about Jodi." He started and Denise's head popped up. "She's been texting me to make sure I'm okay, and I'm afraid she is gonna get too attached to me. I mean don't get me wrong she is a great kid, but, and I hope I'm not offending you but I don't think this is gonna work out." George's comforting tone trying to make this easier seemed to be a relief because Denise released a sigh that she was holding in. Reaching over he took her hand in his, "You are amazing and so is Jodi, but I don't know, I feel like we are just amazing friends and I absolutely don't want to ruin that. If we got too involved and then broke up I would lose out on a great friendship, and I could never forgive myself for messing that up. So maybe we just go back to being friends and dance partners, if that is okay with you?" And that was all true. She was a great friend and dance partner, but she wasn't his person and he knew it. Squeezing his hand, she looked up at him with tears in her eyes and then moved close enough to rest her head on his shoulder.

"That was the sweetest break-up I've ever heard." Denise sighed and wiped a tear away from her cheek. "Couldn't you just be like, you suck, I hate you or something?" That made them both giggle and he kissed the top of her head.

"Nah, friends don't think each other suck. Does Hank think you suck?" George asked with a smile. He should have been pissed, but honestly he wasn't sure if it was spending time with Kevin that had him feeling lighter or not, but he truly didn't care. If anything, it was only a matter of time before those two finally hooked up.

Denise flew off of his shoulder and stared at him in disbelief causing him to break out in laughter as her cheeks started to blush.

"I can't even deny it even if I tried, could I?" she asked with tears forming again in her eyes.

"No, so tell me what happened from the beginning, not all the details though just the relevant parts." George said, as she settled back down and was about to start when they heard a throat clearing from the kitchen doorway.

"Can I come and sit at least, I'm gonna hear it from the other room anyway." Kevin said, as he moved from the kitchen doorway "You really need to get some carpets in this place because everything echoes." Patting the spot to her left Denise got comfy and let Kevin listen in as she recapped the whole story of what exactly had been going on.

A call to Jodi, a bowl of popcorn and two bathroom breaks later, Kevin and George were all caught up. George felt bad for her, but at the same time it seemed like these two lived to annoy the Hell out of each other. Although what started this was completely and unjustifiably cruel, with the work that Hank had been doing in therapy, it seemed to George that this was not the guy he met just last year. Kevin had known about this already but it seemed he was able to clarify that when Hank gets too drunk he would not be able to remember what he had said or done the very next day, not that it excused the behavior just that it probably would be the reason why he had never apologized.

"Have you forgiven him for the comment if you hooked up with him?" George didn't want to ask but it was a valid question. Denise shrugged her shoulders.

"No, until he comes right out and apologizes -" she paused, "I can't, that's my baby, how can someone be so cruel, alcohol or not?" Denise questioned and she was right. There had to be a reason why he would say such cruel things.

Kevin looked up from his phone, "Grace says he doesn't remember saying those things." Denise reached across to him trying to grab his phone.

"Oh my God, please tell me you didn't tell her what I just confessed to you or so help me God." She said, as she successfully grabbed his phone away from him and started searching his texts.

"What kind of person do you take me for? She's your best friend; I am not about to share what you just told me; she will lose her damn mind." Kevin said, stuffing another handful of popcorn in his face.

"I take you for the town gossip queen who will tell everyone everything, that's what I take you for!" The exasperation in Denise's voice ringing through the condo. George just laughed at the whole exchange, he hadn't realized it but he was actually enjoying himself at the insanity of everything going on in Denise's life, and a small part of him was glad that he wasn't her boyfriend anymore.

There clearly was an attraction between her and Hank, despite the past that Hank couldn't seem to recall. But as people get older and go through therapy like both were doing, George was sure that things would perhaps one day work out. But for now, he was happy to just enjoy this shit show from the peanut gallery.

Somewhere around seven p.m. Denise had decided to head home and make sure Jodi had everything ready for school and to get her winding down for the night. Realizing that popcorn was not a meal and with Kevin's stomach grumbling he went into the kitchen.

"Your mom left you a ton of dinners. Do you want me to warm one up or do you want a Kevin's special?" he yelled and George was now very intrigued at whatever that was.

"Oh, I am going to need to try a Kevin's special, I've eaten all my mom's stuff before, but do I at least get to know what is in it?" George asked, he loved to cook so he knew that the pantry was stocked with things he liked but he didn't have a lot of Italian ingredients and he was sure that Janie probably had more of that in their house.

"Nope, it will be a surprise." Kevin called out from the kitchen and he had been right about the echoing because it was almost as if he was standing right next to him. After several banging of pots and cooking sounds coming from the kitchen along with some slight cursing, George started to smell an amazing aroma of oil, garlic and something he didn't recognize coming from the kitchen. It smelt heavenly and considering that the only Italian sauce he used was jarred he wasn't sure what it was because he didn't smell any tomatoes.

Walking out of the kitchen, Kevin brought over a plate and on it was a stunning dish of linguine with tiny shrimp, sun dried tomatoes and garlic in a creamy pesto sauce.

"I had this stuff in my kitchen?" George asked as he brought the plate up to his nose and smelt it. Kevin smiled sitting down next to him with one of the lap trays twirling the pasta onto his fork.

"Oh God no, I picked some stuff up the other day with your meds. I figured I owed you something for making you almost kill yourself watching me run." Kevin said, as he brought the fork up to his mouth. George watched as Kevin opened his mouth and found himself gawking at how Kevin's tongue poked out ever so slightly to welcome in the pasta on his fork and then closed his eyes to enjoy the dish. Kevin moaned as he chewed, and George suddenly felt heated at the sound and sight he had just witnessed.

Unsure of what was happening to him, George just sat there with his mouth wide open and then shook his head. *What the Hell is going on?* He didn't understand why something as simple as Kevin enjoying his food, and the way he was eating it was suddenly so erotic, or why he wanted to watch him do it again.

Trying to get these odd thoughts out of his mind, he decided to eat. Maybe it was just that the taste of the dish was so good, maybe it was the fact that he had been hanging out with Kevin for the past several days that had him all confused. Twirling the pasta on his own fork, he took his first bite.

"Holy Shit this is fantastic." He said, with a mouth full of the delicate pasta.

"Thank you." Kevin blushed, flashing him a coy smile, "I told you it's my specialty. Mom makes it for Christmas Eve, but sometimes I like to make it when I'm down because Christmas Eve is my favorite night and it makes me feel better to think of happy times."

George realized that maybe Kevin was still having a hard time with the break-up. He and Jonathan had been texting about making sure the other person had gotten their stuff back and a few times Kevin had snuck off to the bathroom to have a good cry. His heart felt for him, as they sat there eating, George found himself amused with how Kevin ate. It was a mix of excitement, then at times slightly erotic, and George found himself putting the volume on the T.V. up higher because it was making him feel off. Not in a bad way, *just off* and he chalked it up to the pain meds still making him feel a bit loopy.

After Kevin cleaned up dinner the two of them sat there in a comfortable silence flipping through shows and he realized that it actually was nice having a roommate.

"Hey, I was just thinking, since you have been here helping out and I have an extra room, if you - want to move in I actually wouldn't mind a roommate. Since I own the place, you could just pay rent if you want." George said, with an odd sense of trepidation. He wasn't sure why he was actually nervous all of a sudden, he was just asking a friend to be his roommate, it wasn't like he was asking him to go out.

Kevin turned and looked at him over his glasses that had fallen down to the end of his nose which always made him look like a cute old man trying to read a paper with readers on. Making an odd pout on his lips, George felt a different pang in his gut like a feeling of butterflied nerves waiting for an answer.

"Yeah that works for me. That way I don't have to hear my mother drone on about me moving on and finding someone, I'll just get to come home here and hang with my person." Kevin smiled as he went back to reading his phone and doom scrolling. But something in that statement made George stop for a moment, *why did he use that term?* He knew it was a common statement, my people, my peeps, my buddies, but *my person*, was just a unique thing to say. But he was gonna let it go, it was probably his mother being over earlier and then the trouble with Denise that had him a bit off. As he sat there listening to Kevin laugh at the show he realized that having someone who just wanted to enjoy life but not want the fuss was what he wanted right now, a great friend, just someone who he could be himself with, whenever that may be.

CHAPTER TEN

Hank

The young waitress sat down Hank's fourth vodka and soda with lime in front of him, and he caught the amused look on Nick's face. Nick had been running a few minutes late, otherwise he would have interrupted what had happened with Denise. Leaving Hank to sit there stewing in his thoughts, now ticked that he hadn't stopped what had happened. He needed to stay as far away from that woman as possible; she was just a big, gigantic walking trap.

As he took another long sip, the sharp coolness of the vodka slid down his throat and he embraced the bitterness of the lime. Feeling Nick's eyes on him, he put down the glass and then reached for his water and gave him a salute of cheers.

"What?" Hank asked, almost allowing fear of what he would ask to take hold of him, but he steeled his nerves.

"Who is she?" Nick asked with a smirk, after years of friendship, he instantly knew. Taking in a deep breath and another sip of his drink, he got ready to finally concede.

"One of Grace's best friends, she is an utter prick tease of a beast that hates my guts." Hank snarked out, "Fucking Denise." He spat, and the worst part was that he was going to have to deal with her for anything relating to Calvin because if Calvin was in something, then most likely Jodi was too. It was the curse of living in a two-mile wide town.

"Why is it every Denise that I have met or dated is an absolutely awful person? You remember Denise Auer, awful woman with the sour look on her face like she had eaten a lemon? God, I used to see her coming and practically run the other way. She complained about the way I talked to some of the women in the office. Stupid bitch." Nick smirked and Hank had to laugh at that one. Denise Auer did look like she ate an entire bag of lemons and smelt like mothballs. She was the poster child for 'terrible human' with her super short old lady haircut, and patchwork matching outfits that she probably bought off of some kind of shopping network.

His Denise, however, was gorgeous, warm, full of life and unbearably hot, she was just messy as shit! Yet, he was no better, attracted to his ex-wife's best friend that hated his guts and had just finger fucked right outside of this restaurant. *What was he thinking?* He was supposed to be working on getting his life back on track, not sending it spiraling out of control. He had done that already and it didn't work out well for anyone. This craving he had for her had come on quickly and became insatiable, almost intoxicating, the scent of her still lingering in his nose. Feeling his dick getting hard again, he shifted in his seat to discretely adjust and Nick just laughed.

"You haven't fucked her yet have you? Please tell me you haven't been that stupid?" Hank's eyes flashed up to Nick's questioning gaze and his friend just laughed harder. "Christ, you are so screwed dude!" Hank knew it too, closing his eyes he let the back of his head hit the wall behind the booth as he tried to close out the image of Denise's eyes and cleavage. The taste of her lips and skin, or the scent of her perfume or the feel of how wet she had gotten from him. The only problem was that it was sinking him deeper into the quicksand that he seemed to be stuck in with her.

"Fine, then what was your Denise like, how do I get away from this one?" Hank asked, he needed to know how to escape. Nick looked at him skeptically and took another sip of his own drink.

"Shit, this was years ago, I guess back in 2008. The Guard Dog booted me, claiming I was gaslighting her, that I was too narcissistic and she caught me cheating. Honestly, I was glad to be rid of the bitch. She wanted me to go to some concert to just see some band she was into, who likes a band named the Dirty Mucks?" Nick grabbed a smothered steak fry and ate it. "I just wasn't into the things she was; I mean the sex was phenomenal but, honestly all she talked about was being in the Navy and how great it was and trying to get me to try yoga because she was an instructor, but seriously who gives a shit about some woo-woo bullshit. I was six months and done and that was fine. I bet she is married to some poor sap that just does whatever she wants, because it's the *Gagnon* way or the highway." Nick grabbed another fry and Hank looked up when he said Gagnon, instantly sobering up.

Was Denise the Gagnon he was talking about, was the person that Nick had just described be the very same Denise he was into? Former Navy, six months relationships, into herself unless it was Jodi, yoga instructor - Denise Gagnon. Pulling out his phone he scrambled through pictures of the recent game and found one that had included Denise. There had been one of the whole group and he looked at Denise and Jodi and then back up to Nick. Denise had pin straight black hair, but Jodi had the same tawny brown wavy hair as his friend sitting across from him with the same upturned nose. *No! It couldn't be?* Hank thought to himself.

Hank wasn't sure what to do, if Nick didn't know about Jodi, he couldn't be the one to show him or tell him but he wanted to know if this was indeed the same Denise. Cropping Jodi out of the picture he showed Nick the picture of just Denise.

"Denise's last name was Gagnon? This Denise Gagnon?" Nick took out a pair of readers to look at the picture because getting old sucked and his face said it all. The woman that was plaguing his mind and hormones was the same as the one Nick had been in a relationship with.

"You can't be fucking serious? You have a hard-on for the Guard Dog? Oh brother, don't walk, run as far and as fast as you can away from that one! Unless she has completely changed, I wouldn't date her for all the money in the world and I already have a ton of money." Nick said, eating the last of the smothered disco fries and took another sip of his drink as he glanced up at the T.V.

"When did you two date?" Hank's mind was racing, if they had dated back in 2008, it was possible that Nick could be Jodi's dad, but it would depend on the timing that much he knew.

"Oh man, that was years and other women ago. But that concert was back in September 2008, I think." Nick said, as he turned to check out the T.V. that was showing the Mets game, but Hank was doing the math in his brain. Jodi was born in June 2009, so if they had broken up in September 2008 and had had sex right before they broke up then, Nick could very well be Jodi's dad. "Why you asking? I'm telling you; you don't want to be in a relationship with this chick, she is highly toxic and a man-eater. Save yourself, I'm glad I have nothing to do with her."

With his brain running a mile a minute, he looked at his friend again, taking in all his features. He was a few inches taller than himself, had the same wavy brown hair as Jodi, the upturned nose and rich brown eyes. He knew Jodi didn't have the same eyes as Denise, but he couldn't remember if they were brown or not. It wasn't that he hadn't noticed, it was just that he knew for sure they weren't the same as Denise's. Jodi did have the same caramel colored skin as Denise, which was why he hadn't thought much about her dad before, but now that his friend had unknowingly confessed to being in a relationship with Denise right around the same time that she had gotten pregnant, he had to talk to someone else about this.

After their interaction he didn't want to talk to her, and since he had been trying to change his life for the better he wasn't about to throw her under the bus without actual proof. His stomach lurched from the mixture of alcohol, and nervous energy running through his system. He needed to talk to someone; he needed to tell someone else this information. He knew he couldn't tell Kevin or Nikki the two of them were major blabbermouths, and he was avoiding Denise. The only safe person out of the people who knew Denise was going to be Grace. Scrolling through his texts he pulled her up sending her a text that he needed to chat as soon as possible. This would weigh too heavily on him if he kept this to himself for too long.

Buzz – Grace

Is everything okay? You realize it is late.

Looking down at his phone he hadn't realized that it was already past nine p.m. and it was a school night but he needed to talk to her right this second. Texting back that he needed to see her right away, he let Nick know that he had to go, lying about something relating to the boys before leaving some cash and making plans to meet up again.

Living in a small town made it easy to get around without a car. The cool air blew against his face as he started walking over to Grace's house, which fortunately for him was only a few blocks away. Everything was still green as they were in that off phase of transition between the summer and autumn. But the brisk breeze let him know that the changing of leaves would start soon enough. Turning down his old road, he walked past the McCarren's house and could hear Nikki yelling to the kids to get ready for bed through the open windows and he laughed to himself. There was someone he was thankful he had never been in a relationship with.

As he drew closer to the house, he watched as Grace and Jim sat on the front porch in the rocking chairs. His nose tingled at the sight of a happy

Grace rocking away with the one who she would finally happily grow old with. Tears fogged his vision as he knew that he would never have that person, and that a happily ever after was not in the cards for him. It wasn't that he was wanting to get married this minute, in truth that was so far from what he wanted, but he was so twisted up with what he had endured as a kid that he was not sure that would ever happen for him.

CHAPTER ELEVEN

Grace

Grace watched as Hank slowly made his way up the walkway and noticed his eyes getting misty which was not his usual behavior. However, when he reached the top steps she noticed a slight hint of vodka and knew he was drunk.

"So how deep into the vodka bottle are we?" Grace asked knowing that either she or Jim would be driving him home. She watched as he wiped his eyes of the tears that had started and plopped down on the top step just feet away from her.

"Half the bottle." Hank confessed. Jim made an oof sound and Grace shot him a look that said not to make any sort of comments. Hank wasn't just drunk he was an absolute mess and considering years of being married to him, this was the worst she had seen him.

"You said it was important, so I'm gonna take a shot in the dark on this one." She started and he turned heavy-lidded towards her, and it took everything in her not to laugh at his face. "You hooked up with Denise." Grace bit her lip at the sight of Hank's jaw dropping. Jim turned his head, clearly trying his best not to laugh out loud at his reaction.

"How the Hell did you find out?" Hank, now completely sober, looked at both Grace and Jim looking to find some clarity.

"Well Kevin has been staying at George's since the ankle break, and I guess right after whatever the Hell you two did, she went over there." Grace said, watching Hank run his fingers through his hair, which had become disheveled. She could easily let him think that Denise and George were still together and that George was gonna beat him up, because she was positive that that was where his brain was going judging by his rather fidgety behavior *or* she could be nice. She opted to be nice. "They broke up."

Watching him snap his head up, she felt a tiny flutter for him and did her best to stifle her own laughter to his reaction. Could it be that after all this time, he and Denise had buried the hatchet, were they truly into each other? The look of hope in his eyes crushed her heart because based on her conversation with Kevin, Denise had been feeling torn when she had left.

"Why didn't you tell me you had feelings for her? I wasn't gonna get mad, slightly weirded out, but not mad. I mean I've talked about you in particular ways, you could have at least warned a girl." Grace was trying not to look at Jim, but she had caught him shooting her a look out of the corner of her eye, and Hank just smiled.

"I heard you had discussed a part of my body and she was surprised you were right." Hank sneered at Jim and Grace just rolled her eyes.

"Well considering that her best-selling book was her recounting of *our* sex life, I'm pretty sure you could have the biggest dick in the world, but-" Jim butted in on the conversation to defend his own virtue but Grace was not having it.

"Okay stop it, both of you! You are both gifted men, and I hate to break it to you but you are both the same size, no measuring tape necessary. Now can we get to the part where you tell me exactly why you came here?" Grace was getting impatient with the whole situation, but apparently she wasn't the only one as a voice echoed through her doorbell.

"Yeah speak up so I can hear too." Grace had forgotten all about giving Nikki access for whenever she isn't home and apparently she must have gotten a notification of Hank showing up on the camera. "Fuck it I'll be there in two minutes."

Poor Hank was going to be on show for the second biggest mouth in Toselle Park who was now scurrying across the street. Grace watched as Nikki held her boobs as she ran, it always made Grace giggle at just how ridiculous she looked. Hank, however, looked like he was going to puke. And not two seconds later, he did, right in her boxwoods, prompting Jim to get up and head into the house.

Breathless, Nikki walked up the rest of the walkway and made a disgusted face as she just watched Hank continue to wretch. Moments later Jim came back out of the house with a bottle of water in hand, and Grace took it, setting it down next to Hank - who had gotten the message, and once he was done throwing up made use of it.

"And now that you probably killed the bush, you will definitely be buying this house. Now tell us what is going on." Grace said, taking a sip of her tea.

"I think I know who Jodi's dad is." Hank's matter of fact tone had them all no longer breathing. It was like they were all frozen, Grace's mind was reeling from this statement and all she was able to do was rapidly blink at Hank. Hank just scrolled through his phone and brought up a picture and there was that old idiot friend of his, *Nick Dupree.*

She had met Nick a few times, he had been at their wedding but never came around once the boys were born. He was not someone who liked kids, in fact, when they had gotten pregnant with Calvin; he had told Hank that his life was officially over and life would suck from now on. He was an awful man and Grace made sure to exclude him from any events they had had, but Hank would meet up with him in NYC to have drinks or for work functions. It was one of the few things she'd been grateful for – the company's unspoken rule about having spouses and partners off the guest list.

"Please tell me you don't think it is Nick? He is awful! What makes you think it's him?" Grace was gonna need some clarification because as far as she knew, Denise doesn't know Nick, nor would she ever think she would want to.

Hank sat there and told them all about his dinner with Nick and his version of their relationship. Something in Grace's brain went to how Denise was now, she didn't know her before Jodi, so to think of such a dominant person like Denise actively being in a relationship with Nick made absolute sense. He was a pigheaded, arrogant, very rich asshole who Grace could never see dating someone as caring and kind as Denise. But if Denise knew that Nick was the father, then it might be possible that she didn't want to include him based on his point of view of children and herself. The most important thing in this whole story was that it showed a lot of growth on Hank's part not to give in and burn Denise's world down by telling Nick all about Jodi.

"Alright, I'm gonna say it. You may be an asshole, but the fact that you didn't throw Denise under the bus and then back it up over her by telling this douche canoe. I don't know how Grace feels, but I'm proud of you." Nikki said, looking over at Hank who still looked a little green around the gills.

"Nikki's right. Hank, you could have destroyed their whole happy existence by showing him the picture of Jodi. I mean now that I look at these two photos." Grace was looking at Hank's and her phone side-by-side and it was clear that she definitely had a number of his characteristics. "Like wow." She showed the pictures to Nikki who just shook her head at the resemblance. "You're a good kid Hank Nereid; I don't care what the neighbors say about ya." Grace quipped, getting him to laugh as he bobbed his head in acceptance of her compliment.

"Are you gonna tell Denise about Nick? I mean I get that this is just speculation and it's probably a huge violation of her confidence - but someone has to say something to her, right?" Jim asked. Grace had been thinking the exact same thing and as she exchanged glances with Nikki, Grace was sure she had the same question.

"I'm probably not the right person to say anything right now." Hank said, his eyes showing just how torn he was over the whole situation. Grace knew what his next sentence was going to be though. "Can't one of you talk to her, she will hit me again."

Grace's head snapped over to Nikki, it had always been a dream of Denise's, to beat the Hell out of Hank, and the fact that she had finally gotten her shot was shocking. Biting her lip she felt Hank's judging glare, knowing that there was a part of her that was just a little jealous, but very proud of her friend for finally standing up to him, not that Grace condoned hitting people, but if there was someone who deserved it after all these years, it was Hank.

The whole turn of events between the two of them had her feeling a range of emotions, but the one that stuck out the most was concern. Hank and Denise had been going to therapy, separately and for different reasons. So, if the two of them hooked up, it would eventually send one - if not both spiraling. That was not something she wanted to see for them, especially after all the progress that Hank had made.

Maybe it was best not to say anything at all, this was in fact Denise's personal life and as much as they were friends, this was the one subject that she never talked about. Was it possible that she already knew who Jodi's father was and had kept it a secret because of the fact that Nick was a narcissist who clearly would not want kids? Or perhaps there had been someone else? As much as the intrigue of the truth piqued her interest, there was a part of Grace that thought that it might be best to leave well enough alone.

"What if we don't? If Denise and Nick did date, and we all know how much he is not a fan of kids, perhaps she didn't say anything because of that specific point of view. Bringing up someone from her past and asking her out of left field - hey is this your baby-daddy - may not be the right thing to do." Grace couldn't possibly disrupt her best friend's life just to find out if this was true. Nikki's annoyed tsking and groan was echoed by Hank, but Jim's sigh let her know that at least one person agreed with her.

"I'll ask, I don't give a shit and she knows it." Nikki was never one to deal with secrets.

"Absolutely not, how're you gonna explain that Hank came here to talk to Grace about Nick and the possibility that he is Jodi's dad? If you went up to her and told her about tonight she will think we are talking about her behind her back - and with all that's gone on, I honestly think we should just let it go." Jim was trying to reason with the unreasonable but it worked as Nikki's tensed shoulders were now slightly relaxing. "If anyone should say anything it should be Hank. *I know* you don't want to, and maybe now isn't the time, but you are the only one who has a relative connection with both."

Grace watched as the weight of this knowledge started to settle on Hank's shoulders. This was a lot of information to process in a matter of a few hours, and with the alcohol paired with the late hour, it was probably best to see what a fresh perspective might bring after a good night's sleep.

The cool morning breeze brushed against Grace's cheek as it rustled the leaves in the tree and a few that were starting to change colors fell onto the porch. Rocking in her old wooden chair it creaked as she took another sip of her second cup of coffee, and out of the corner of her eye she saw the one person she wasn't sure she would see so soon – Denise. She was wearing purple leggings and a light gray jogging jacket as she made her way up the pathway to Grace's steps. Slightly out of breath, she stopped short of the old wooden stairs to catch her breath before climbing up onto the porch to sit in the other wooden rocker on her porch.

"Hey" was all that Denise could get out as she struggled to catch her breath.

"Hey, you haven't ran in a while. Everything okay?" Grace knew she only ever ran to clear her head; she would rather be doing a yoga routine than doing this.

"Oh, come on, don't tell me that Kevin hasn't texted you? I know you know already." Denise was at least cutting to the chase; it was one of the many things Grace appreciated about her. Cut, dry and to the point. Grace knew lots of things after last night, but if she was talking about Kevin, it meant that she was only talking about her hooking up with Hank.

"Yes, he told me. I'm sorry about George, but Kevin said that things are okay with you guys so that is good because he is one Hell of a dance partner and it would be a shame to lose that." Grace said, with a light laugh. Fortunately, Denise seemed to be okay with it as she smiled and gave a tiny chuckle.

"Yeah, well at least I get to keep that, what sucks is, the sex was good." Denise added, taking in a breath like she was going to keep talking, but then stopped before she said anything else. It was clear to Grace that she wanted to talk but wasn't sure whether or not she should.

"Speaking of sex, you and Hank." Grace started and Denise's neck cracked at how fast she turned to shoot a look at Grace. "You want to talk about it or are you too weirded out? Because I'm okay to talk about it, I mean I have in the past talked about how he barely reciprocates, so if you are expecting-"

"I almost don't want to tell you." Denise started and sighed, "I feel bad because that is not what happened." Denise finished biting her lip as her unease painted across her face.

"What do you mean? I've had sex with Hank for years, I know how he has sex. Did he try something weird because he was as vanilla as they can get." Grace asked recalling years of extremely boring sex with just a hint of passion. She watched as Denise actually started to blush, *Denise never blushes*, had Hank been holding back this whole time? Could sex have actually been interesting?

"Well, to get the record straight we didn't have sex, or at least one of us didn't finish." Denise said, biting her lip again, and Grace had a feeling she understood as she nodded her head.

"He is a greedy son of a bitch. You poor thing, I just got used to it, but if you guys are gonna start something you are gonna need to change that otherwise, you might as well walk away now." She said, taking another sip of her coffee, feeling terrible for her friend. Hank hadn't discussed details. All he said was that they hooked up, and that could mean any range of things.

She found it odd how when men say they hooked up but they don't specify, it wasn't until just recently that Jim had told her that all Liz and he had done back in college was make-out, and she played with him but that he never finished because of him thinking about her. Which was sweet at first but then slightly made it creepy as he had been thinking about her while he made out with Liz. But she understood, *served him right for wanting to keep things open.*

"That's not," Denise started and Grace could see the hesitation in Denise's eyes as she creased her brow. "He took care of me and then pushed me away." Now it was time for Grace's neck to crack as she whipped her head, eyes wide in astonishment towards Denise. *That motherfucker!* Grace looked down at her cup and noticed that all her coffee was gone, and knew she was gonna need a bucket in order to deal with this information. Gathering herself up from the old creaking rocking chair, she pointed to Denise and wiggled her finger for her to follow her into the house.

Still in disbelief, Grace and Denise made their way into the kitchen as Grace started making herself a much larger cup of coffee.

"He took care of you and wanted nothing in return? Are you sure you hooked up with Hank?" Perhaps Denise had hooked up with a different Hank, and maybe Hank hooked up with a different Denise, because none of this was making any sense. As Denise unzipped her jacket to get comfortable, Grace noticed the purplish mark on her long neck and stared at it. She hadn't meant to stare, but there was a part of her that was slightly pissed now. Not at Denise, but at Hank – where was this man the entire time they were married? Leaving hickeys, taking care of someone else and not expecting anything in return. She could feel the heat blooming across her face and based on the look Denise gave her – it showed more than she'd hoped.

"Stop, alright, this is why I was hesitant to come here and talk to you!" Denise said, as she drew a circle on the counter, and Grace took a second to collect herself. This was her best friend, she had listened to her, Denise had dried her tears and had been a shoulder to cry on - now she was looking for the same in return. It was just that the person she had complained about was the same one that Denise had been so angry and defensive towards for years.

"I'm sorry, it's just," Grace struggled to find the right words, but they kept slipping through her fingers. "It's Hank! The same Hank you have hated and listened to me complain about for years. So, you have to understand that it's just really," odd, weird, ridiculous "fucked up. You got the fixed version of him. I mean I'm happy for you, but it's just-"

"Fucked up. I get it. Listen, we don't have to talk about this if you can't handle it. I just wanted to come over and be honest with you before he came over here and said something." Denise sighed as she got up, walked over to the cupboard to grab a mug, and began making herself a cup of coffee. Grace's hand froze halfway to her mouth, mug suspended midair as she bit her lip and drew in a slow, shaky breath. Denise heard it and spun around, catching sight of Grace – who suddenly looked like a child caught with her hand in the cookie jar.

"God no! Please tell me he didn't." Swatting at Grace's upper arm jostling her cup in her hand, all Grace could do was flash her an uncomfortable smile and she watched as Denise hung her head. "Why would he do that?" Grace watched as Denise's shoulders fell her face smeared in remorse at what was now another bad decision in her life.

"Because he has no one else to talk to, apparently he was trying to confide in his friend Nick" she stopped short of saying his full name, Grace didn't even know why she was going to say his full name but she knew if she had this conversation would go in a completely different direction. "But he was just being unhelpful, but that is something that he is very good at. Anyway, he wanted someone to talk to. You went right to George, why didn't you come here?"

"Because weird Grace; I couldn't not go to George and let that relationship go on after what I did. I cheated on him, the least I could do was go to him right away and apologize. I wasn't expecting him to break up with me, I mean maybe I did, I wouldn't date me after that, but" throwing her hands up in the air she let out a gravely groan. "Once again I'm making another bad decision in my life." Slowly, her eyes misted and the tip of her caramel nose turned a shade of pink as she sniffled. Getting up from her chair, Grace walked over to her giant friend and embraced her. This was what she had come here for, *comfort*, she came here to be told that everything was okay, or at least that it would be.

"Hey, we all make 'em, none of us are perfect. That's why therapists make the big bucks kiddo. I'm sorry I reacted the way I did, it's just fuck why do you get the fixed version of Hank?" Smiling up to her friend it got Denise to laugh.

"Because therapy." Denise dryly said giving a half-hearted snicker.

"Son of a bitch! That is some bull shit!" Grace said, just shaking her head and it got the exact laugh she was hoping for.

CHAPTER TWELVE

Kevin

November, 2024

Kevin wasn't sure that this was a very good idea. He was not someone who liked gyms, not because he wasn't a physical person, he did enjoy Denise's yoga classes, it was more about people making fun of him for not knowing how any of the equipment worked. George was almost done with all his therapies, but he'd been cleared to go back to the gym – surprising them both – and practically begged him to tag along. George's begging was not something he imagined him doing often, but he had actually been sweet, with those big brown eyes of his and that pearly white smile that just turned his insides to mush.

George was not Kevin's type, he was just a really great, handsome friend who was now his roommate and he absolutely did not want to move back in with Janie and Ken any time soon. It wasn't that he couldn't get his own place, because he could. He made good money doing website designs during the day and then being a DJ by night, but it was lonely. It's probably why he had stayed with his parents for so long. But lately, George had been asking him about joining the gym he went to so that someone could drive him if his ankle got too weak after a session, and pulling the broken ankle card was a sure-fire way to get him to say yes.

Kevin watched on as other people in the gym noticed George and was asking him where he had been. Kevin hadn't realized that the gym wasn't just a place with machines that took a genius IQ to operate, it was a community. Which he thought was super sweet that they all seemed to know each other and was worried about someone they only knew at the gym. As George got engrossed in a conversation, Kevin felt a tap on his left shoulder and turned to find Hank standing there with a puzzled look on his face.

"Am I in an alternate universe? Because I'm sure that you are Kevin Cartino and I know for a fact that you don't go to gyms." He said, flashing a brilliant smile and Kevin stood there shocked at the fact that Hank was talking to him nicely and even smiling at him. Narrowing his eyes on Hank he cocked his head to the side and leaned in.

"Alternate universe, because I do not belong here and yet you are graced with my glorious presence." Kevin batted his eyes at Hank who just shook his head snickering. "I'm being forced to be here by my very large roommate who is making me feel guilty because of his ankle injury." He pouted. Kevin immediately observed Hank's demeanor change as he glanced over at George, who had noticed that Kevin wasn't alone anymore. Feeling this odd shift in the air as George walked over and Hank took a tiny step back. It was odd for Hank to suddenly look as if he was shrinking as George approached. Kevin remembered him as such a broody annoying man who got his jollies out of verbally berating Grace for years. However, this new Hank who stood in front of him seemed like an entirely different person and Kevin had to admit that actually getting mental help really was working for him.

"Hank." George said, as his gaze swept over Hank - who looked like he just got in trouble by his parents, yet he softened as George held out his hand to shake his. Kevin just stood there in complete bewilderment as this whole macho exchange as Hank hesitantly took George's hand.

"Glad to see the ankle is healing well. Grace mentioned that Kevin here has been helping in the recovery." Hank said, making Kevin feel like a fly on the wall that had just been spotted and he wasn't sure if he should leave the two men to chat or if he actually wanted to see if George landed a punch to Hank's pretty jaw. Never one to miss out on the drama unfolding in front of them, he stayed because making a fool of himself to figure out all these machines sounded like an awful idea.

George turned and flashed that amazing smile at Kevin and his stomach seemed to flutter, *why did he have to be so incredibly hot*, Kevin questioned. "Yeah, he's been super helpful, but Denise has stopped by and helped out as well." George smiled as Hank's head snapped up and Kevin bit his lip at just how quick his response to Denise's name had been. Although they had broken up, Denise and Jodi would stop by and hang out for movie nights, which the four of them seemed to really love. Last week had been *'Down with Love'*, one of Kevin's favorites, because who doesn't love *Ewan McGregor* as a romantic lead. With them no longer dating, everything between Denise and George seemed so much more relaxed. The funniest part was that from time to time she would bring up Hank, which would lead her down a rant about how getting involved with him was just another one of her bad decisions and how he is a jerk, but all George and Kevin heard was that she was into him and was trying to convince herself that she wasn't.

"Well, she's," Hank stopped and Kevin couldn't wait to hear what he had to say, *oh please say you like her, just say it you fool*, Kevin was wiggling his toes in his shoes waiting for the love confession. He loved a great romance, and these two were practically set up to be the shocker he had been waiting for knowing something like that would never happen for himself. "Denise is a good friend, just don't get on her bad side. Take it from me." There was a sadness in his voice and Kevin's heart just broke, *oh my god he is actually sorry about being an ass all these years*? Kevin shot a look at George trying to let him know it was best to change the subject.

"Good advice, luckily since we decided to just be friends I don't think that will be an issue." George quipped, and Hank's expression went from looking down in the dumps to hopeful, prompting a tiny giggle from Kevin. Who was this man in front of him, and where had he been his entire relationship with Grace?

"So, Hank, Kevin here has never stepped foot into a gym, I was going to do a circuit and see how the ankle feels, would you like to join us, maybe we can turn this kid into a gym rat." George said, and for some reason Kevin's heart felt a tiny pang of hurt at the word 'kid', he knew he was two years younger, but did he act like a kid? He stuffed the idea that someone would think of him as a child away, Kevin knew he loved to live a life free from massive responsibility, but it didn't mean that people could call him a kid.

"Um, I'm not a kid, just because I choose to do pilates and yoga, doesn't mean I am not physically fit, thank you very much!" Kevin barked, and the two men took a tiny step back from him. He hadn't meant for it to come out so defensive, but he didn't need grown men making fun of him.

"Listen, if you can help me up with no issues, I know you can do this. I just thought it would be something different for you to try." George said, in a very calming tone, he was placating him and Kevin knew it, but he was using that sweet tone that just hit him square in the chest. Kevin rolled his eyes knowing that if he kept giving him that look, his knees would buckle and they'd have to pick *him* up off the floor.

"Fine, but I won't like it." Kevin begrudgingly noted and it only spurned Hank and George to laugh.

Driving back from the gym, he was shocked at just how great he felt. The whole time it seemed like Hank and George were in competition with each other, which had made Kevin laugh to himself every time they would increase the weights on the machines. Wearing his brace, George did set the weights low on all the leg workouts unless he was doing individual leg work and Kevin was impressed by just how much he could sustain on the machine. However, he was equally thrilled at what he could do himself.

But what he wasn't expecting was actually getting to know Hank. They had been at what felt like thousands of family events or had been in each other's company all the time, but as far as he was concerned - this was a new person all together. He was still an ass, but there were times that he would say something rude or too sarcastic that he stepped over a line, but then immediately caught it- which was shocking. What was even more crazy was the fact that he was openly acknowledging that he was a jerk. Taking ownership of one's behaviors was not something that Hank would have done in the past, so it was rather refreshing to talk to this person who looked like Hank and sounded like him but was just not the same human he had known for twenty plus years.

What Kevin found hysterical though was how quickly Hank would lose his grip on the weights causing them to slam together whenever Denise's name was mentioned. It had become a game between Kevin and George, trying to see if they could trigger Hank just by saying her name, or something like it. It had become increasingly difficult to come up with word that rhymed with 'Denise'. Something Kevin found sweet on George's part was that it seemed like there was this unspoken forgiveness for Hank and Denise hooking up. Most men would have lost their minds and would have tried to murder the other one, but George seemed incredibly cool about the whole thing, and he wondered why he was just so lackadaisical towards the whole situation.

"Okay, I wasn't gonna say anything but, that was actually not horrible." Kevin confessed as he drove the car into the garage deck and heard a gasp from George, he knew what was coming next.

"See I told you! I was sure that when we saw Hank you were going to say let's leave." George said pointing to an open space and Kevin followed his direction and parked the car.

"Oh no, I was not about to leave. I wanted to see what you were going to do. It was too good to pass up." Kevin laughed as George gave him a disapproving glance. "I'm sorry but after years of how he treated Grace and then him hooking up with Denise, I was wondering if that big teddy bear that lives inside you was gonna go grizzly and tear him apart." Kevin still remembered how he had come to his defense back in high school and he wondered if he was still like that. But when it came to what happened with Denise, it was almost as if the whole thing didn't affect him at all.

"Well, I think after recent events of Hank's life, I was not about to pound the crap out of him, I think he has suffered enough." George said, grabbing his bag and closing the door behind him as they made their way through the garage.

"If he had done this to be spiteful or mean, sure, his nose would have been broken all over again. But this wasn't like what happened with Grace, no one was egging him on to be a jerk and he wasn't doing it to punish anyone." Walking into the smoothie shop he turned and lowered his voice and moved closer to Kevin, which stirred a very peculiar stirring in Kevin that took him by surprise.

"Besides, based on what Denise said, he thought she and I had broken up. Which meant if I was him, it would have made me feel like I was a rebound." George's face was just a little too close to Kevin's and he could feel the tingle of his words near his cheek as Kevin's heart rate seemed to speed up, *what is going on*? A sudden rush of heat flushed across his cheeks and he needed to take a step back but couldn't. This was George, and Kevin needed to focus only on the conversation. Hank and Denise, that was what they were discussing, not these off-putting feelings he was suddenly having.

Summoning the strength, Kevin stepped away collecting himself and thought only of Hank and Denise. If the two of them would take the time to talk to one another instead of avoiding the other one then they would finally be able to resolve this feud. But they were both so incredibly stubborn. Denise wanted not to be controlled and Hank found delight in trying to tame the shrew. But the truth was that as strong of a presence as Denise had, there was such an incredible softness in her. Hank was just as bad, wanting to be the dominant one in all situations; it was no wonder why the two were always at odds. Their constant struggle to be in control was astounding.

"Do you think they will ever talk to one another again? It seems silly that they are both interested in each other but not willing to be the first to break." Kevin asked as George handed him the protein smoothie he had ordered him. Taking his first sip, Kevin was shocked that it wasn't half bad and looked at George giving him a thumbs up as he kept drinking the green smoothie.

"My gut is telling me that one or both will finally break and give in to their feelings, but who knows with these two."

CHAPTER THIRTEEN

Denise

December, 2024

With amazing wins at all the local and state competitions the Toselle Park's Marching Farmers were heading to the National Conference in Williamsburg, Virginia. It had been endless hours of practice in all types of weather be it rain, humid heat and even an early snow in November. If they weren't practicing, then they were playing and supporting the TP Farmers football team.

With the costs that would be incurred by the parents for all the hotels and travel accommodations, Denise sprang into action. She figured if she could just keep herself focused – on anything other than those strange new feelings for Hank and the constant, gnawing fear of becoming her mother – she might be okay. So, she threw herself head-first into organizing the Casino Night Fundraiser.

"Considering that this is the first year we made it into the larger conference, I say we push for the football parents to help out for once. I nearly froze my ass off at the Thanksgiving game and they never come to competitions for us!" Denise was clearly annoyed at the one-sided support the school showed.

"You froze your ass off because you wouldn't sit still. All you kept doing was getting up trying to avoid talking or interacting with Hank." Grace glanced over the rim of her glasses as she made notes and Nikki just nodded in agreement.

"You two should just have sex and end this crap already. It's what we are all waiting for so we can move on with this." Nikki added, while Denise sat there feeling like she was being inspected under a microscope.

"I don't have time to argue about this with the two of you, but if you could both stay out of my bedroom activities and who they are with I would appreciate it." Denise snipped back at them.

She understood that this was a small town, but the fact that she was sexually attracted to her best friend's ex-husband was weird enough as it is. She caught the side-eyes that Grace and Nikki were exchanging and knew they were having that weird silent conversation that they liked to do at times.

Her top priority was not Hank and his perfect ass or his large dick, it was the Casino Night for the marching band. They had organized a casino night before, so this wasn't going to be an issue. The real challenge was going to be getting the other parents interested and involved. But right now, the most important thing was steering the conversation back to why they were all here for: the fundraiser.

"We can pull some of the extra big prizes from the tricky tray and use them to entice a silent auction. Also, I know we talked about having a DJ or a band, but I don't think that would make sense because if we have poker, people are going to be focused on playing their hand not listening to music." Back to getting work done, Denise tried to steer the conversation to the real topic at hand.

January was coming sooner than she had realized, and normally she would have this all squared away. But lately she's been pouring more time into therapy and focusing on work, leaving the event on the back burner. It wasn't that she didn't want to do the event, she actually loved it, it was just the idea of having to see Hank again that was bothering her.

Every time she spotted him at the games or competitions; the same dull ache stirred in her chest – unwelcome, but persistent. She couldn't quite decide if it was anger, or hurt, or something else. Perhaps it was all of it, Dr. Mahoney had been helping her work it out. Hank had called her a cheater and he had been completely unreasonable about wanting to listen to her side of things that day. But considering how she had ambushed him into having the argument - and with the weird turn of events that had transpired after - it was no wonder that he hadn't wanted to be finished off. It had all felt rushed and despite her orgasm she had left there feeling emptier.

She had just wanted him to stop calling her a good girl, and she just was getting tired of the fighting. No longer a spring chicken, Denise struggled to find any sort of inner peace with all their exchanges, it had become exhausting. It was an odd thrill to get him all hot and bothered and to poke fun at him, but as Dr. Mahoney had said it was all a bit childish. He had her working on trying to forgive the sins of the past - especially if Hank had been under the influence of alcohol when he had said that about Jodi, but it was difficult. To imagine her life without her daughter, broke her heart.

Looking down at her watch, she realized that she was going to be late for another therapy session. Packing up her stuff, she excused herself and said a rushed goodbye to Grace and Nikki, leaving them to figure out the number of poker tables and finalize the layout.

Heading to Dr. Mahoney's, Denise drove past the high school field and because of their conversation, Denise found her mind wandering to the memory of the Thanksgiving game.

The metal benches of the stadium were so cold and Denise cursed herself for not bringing the rechargeable heated cushion she had left at home. But Jodi had been so tired and Denise's mission was just to keep Jodi focused on getting to the field on time. It had been another sleepless night for the teen, her mind over-stimulated and excited about winning the division that she hadn't been able to settle at night. As the band marched onto the field, Denise worriedly nibbled her already short nails because she knew that there was a particularly difficult flag toss in the middle of the performance that Jodi struggled with and this particular performance was going to be aired on Toselle Park TV channel.

"What kind of music is called Medusa? I've never heard of it." A large man wearing the colors of the opposing team smirked from the row in front of Denise. Taking a deep breath, Denise tried her best to ignore the

loud comment and found herself with her right leg shaking. Not from the cold but from the nervous energy she was bottling up. A small hand reached across and steadied her knee.

"She is gonna be fine." Grace said, with a comforting smile. Leave it to Grace to always know when Denise was worried about Jodi.

"I know, it's just her sleep has been off and I honestly don't think she even went to bed last night." Denise said, before biting another stubby nail while Grace rested her head on Denise's shoulder.

"Listen, the competitions are done for now. This is just a performance; no one is going to judge her." Grace said, as she pulled some of the blanket she was keeping on her lap over onto Denise's. Denise gave a quick peck on Grace's cheek and then looked at Jim.

"You are very lucky that she has loved you as long as she has, because I would have turned her and this little sexy beast would have been mine." Denise joked and the group around them laughed, all except the strangers from the visiting team, who all clearly didn't have a sense of humor.

As the band started playing, Denise's attention was drawn to the person who had gotten up at the beginning of the performance and was making their way down to the field gate. Hank stood there silently watching the band. A tiny ache lurched in Denise's heart, he was close and yet so far. Perhaps she would finally gather up the courage to talk with him, but her focus right this second needed to be on Jodi. Watching the team, she could see they were all tired, not just Jodi. It had been a long and arduous season, but they would at least get a couple of months off before they would get back to practicing again. The program wasn't long and it was coming up to the difficult toss, as the flags flew through the air, just as she feared Jodi had missed hers and it landed on the ground. Denise's heart stopped and watched the crestfallen look on Jodi's face and heard the sneering laughter from the opposing teams fans. But then a shout came from farther down below them.

"It's okay Jodi, keep going. Woo, go Farmers!" Hank cheered from the gate and Denise's heart fluttered in her chest as she caught Jodi looking over to Hank nodding and getting right back into the routine as if she hadn't missed a beat. Denise's breath caught in her throat and looked down to Hank who continued cheering, encouraging the rest of the crowd to join in with him.

He didn't have to do that, Jodi wasn't his child, but there he was reassuring her to keep going and Denise felt the sting of tears in her eyes, that someone other than herself was caring about her daughter. Who was this person? This was not the Hank she knew, but there he stood cheering on the entire team as if he had spent endless hours with them. Wiping away a tear that had escaped Denise turned to Grace who was looking at her with compassion in her eyes.

"I told you. He's really trying." Grace whispered and she didn't need to elaborate any further. His actions were clear; he was actively making an effort to be a better person. The old Hank wouldn't even have been at this game let alone cheer the kids on. The crowd thunderously applauded as the band finished and exited the field. Denise knew Jodi was

going to be hard on herself and she wanted to be there for her as she exited the field. Making her way down to the gate to check on Jodi she was stopped dead in her tracks. As Jodi exited, Hank stood right there waiting for her and held out his arms to her. This wasn't her dad, but for some reason something on her face must have prompted Hank to show such a kind reaction to someone else's kid. Leaping into his arms, Jodi buried her head into his chest and hugged him for a brief moment.

Pulling into the parking lot of Dr. Mahoney's office all she could do was pray that she wouldn't run into Hank again. She hadn't known what to say or do after what had happened at the field. There was so much she had wanted to say, like *thank you* and at the same time she wanted to scream *you're not her dad*. Years had gone by with their lives being just her and Jodi. But to see someone else besides her friends actively making sure her daughter was okay was different.

She thought about Grace's comment about Hank trying and wondered what the likelihood of Hank actually going to Dr. Mahoney as well. *Did he talk about her?* She talked about him, or at least she had mentioned their interaction and how she handled it – or lack thereof. Did she actually care whether he did or not? During therapy, Dr. Mahoney had suggested that perhaps it would be best for Denise and the gentleman in question - because she never gave names - to actually sit down and discuss their issues. It was the mature and balanced thing to do. After all, he'd reminded her: how could she guide others to meditate and find peace as a yoga instructor, if she wasn't willing to face the hard things herself?

Finding a spot and seeing no one around, she took a deep breath and got out of her car. The Thanksgiving game had been the last time she'd seen Hank, and all that had been exchanged was a curt "Hello" and "Happy Thanksgiving". She had lost her nerve to say anything to him after his exchange with Jodi. Looking around the parking lot once more, she headed to the front door and then just as luck would have it - Hank walked out, stopping dead in his tracks.

Her heart stopped for a moment and it seemed like all the air had been sucked out of her, but somehow she managed a tiny, "Hi."

Managing only a tiny nod of his head in acknowledgment he opened the door for her. If he didn't care - if this was the old Hank - he would never have held the door open. Feeling the beginning winter breeze brush over her reddened cheeks she willed herself to say something else, anything. Because in truth she missed the heat, the passion, the fire she would feel when they would fight, but she couldn't. Nor could she move from her spot.

"Are you going in or not?" He asked his tone cold and unfeeling like the season that was just starting to set in, and yet in his reddened eyes she saw utter sadness. There was this urge in her to reach out and pull him close, to let him know that he would be okay, but she wasn't here to comfort him. She came to find clarity, or peace or whatever the Hell she needed. But what she wanted scared her more, because what she wanted seemed to be the man who stood in front of her. Broken, sad and not wanting her.

She steadied her breath as she walked toward him, watching as his eyes widened with every step. Even beneath the heavy peacoat, she could see the way his chest began to rise and fall – faster now, like he couldn't quite catch his own breath. What would happen if she just charged up to him and kissed him this second? Would he push her away again or would he take the advancement and run with it? Old Denise would have told him to piss off and she didn't need him, but the longer they stayed away from each other the more she felt herself falling for the asshole.

His eyes kept shifting – from her eyes to her mouth – lingering longer each time. When she caught on, she bit her bottom lip without thinking. His lips parted, just slightly, like a breath caught in his throat. And that was all it took. She rushed toward him, and he immediately let go of the door, his hands flying up in defense as if he expected her to strike him. But she stopped short just inches from him.

"What are you doing?" Denise was sure that she looked like she was trying to go and kiss him, not beat the living piss out of him. Moving his arms away from his face, he looked at her completely perplexed.

"I thought you were gonna hit me again, you weren't saying anything and I thought." He paused, "I don't know what I thought. I'm sorry, I have" he paused again. "I have to go. If I don't see you, have a Merry Christmas." With his head down he looked anywhere but in her eyes, something she was craving at this moment but instead he turned and ran off to his car. The sting of the chilling wind hit her eyes and they started to tear, but she wasn't sure if it was the wind that was causing the tears or the fact that once again she was blown off. Watching him drive off, she wiped the tears from her face and walked into the building and up to Dr. Mahoney's office.

When she finally got into the office his receptionist greeted her with a warm hello and must have noticed the tears as she handed her a tissue. *What the Hell was happening to her*, she questioned. This was not the strong independent woman she had prided herself in becoming. Perimenopause did mess with you emotionally and that was what she was chalking up all these feelings to lately, but was it possible that there was more? As Dr. Mahoney opened the door Denise got up and walked straight into the office without even saying hello and then went right to the couch and plopped down on it.

"Doc, you need to fix me and fix me now, because I'm not sure how much longer I can keep doing this thing with that guy I was telling you about." Exasperated Denise swatted at her cheeks, but the tears kept falling relentlessly. As Dr. Mahoney closed the door, he took his time to walk over to his large Queen Anne chair and gather up his note pad.

"Well, if we can narrow down what I am fixing, and what thing with the unnamed man you are talking about that would be helpful." Taking in a deep breath and sighing he went on. "Denise, you come here and you never mention anyone's names and I understand that you are trying to keep it confidential, but you do realize that is also part of my job as well and with a tiny town like this one, it is probably best to be a little bit more realistic in this approach of yours. My suggestion is, let's start at the beginning." Dr. Mahoney smiled down at her before taking a sip of his tea.

"Hank Nereid." Was all she could get out and he started taking his notes.

"And I'm assuming that one of these unnamed men that you have discussed is Mr. Nereid?"

"Yes, the one that I have been having issues with, about my feelings towards him." She was still being guarded.

"Denise, why do you come here? I mean it's your money if you want to waste it, that is up to you, but I thought you came here to get better? So how about you come right out with it." It would seem that the good doctor had finally had enough of her antics for the day, or perhaps the past several months.

"Fine, I have hated Hank since I met him. And then… something weird happened at a baseball event – the one the parents played to support the kids. He told me to be a *'good girl'* and ever since then things have been… I dunno, off? Then we ended up hooking up, and when I tried to reciprocate he brushed me off! Saying he had plans. I just, I don't get it. I only wanted to confront him about the *'good girl'* thing, but then he questioned me about George and when I told him we were still together he got angry and he called me a cheater – and to make matters worse, he just started ignoring me! And just a few minutes ago, I saw him leaving, so I went up to him… to I dunno, kiss him or something. And he threw his hands up like I was gonna hit him before running away again. And now I'm fucking miserable because I want to talk to him, but he won't stop avoiding me!" And right there on the couch that had caught millions of tears, Denise, 'the Guard Dog' added a few more as she broke down into tears for the first time in what was probably years.

Handing her over a box of tissues the doctor sat there letting her just cry it out and when she was close to being done he started audibly doing an out loud breathing method that she was used to doing in yoga, prompting her to follow suit until she calmed down.

"Thanks." She said, taking in a ragged breath. "I am just not *this* person. I've always been so independent and here I am feeling like an idiot because some guy I like won't talk to me. I'm never like this."

"What are you like? What have you done in the past?" The short man asked, adding more notes to his notebook.

"I've never had to get someone's attention or at least not have to fight for it. Most people just are stunned when I'm into them and are instantly ready to start something with me. I've never had an issue finding someone before." Denise wasn't being cocky; it was just a fact.

"It's just keeping you in the relationship that is the problem; and coupled with the fact that Hank is blowing you off, you are feeling off center." He stated, it wasn't a question. It was clear as day, he was making a statement. She wasn't liking where this may be going.

"Yes, but I don't want to be my mom, I actively want to have a relationship with someone. I think my biggest concern is that no matter how attracted I am to him, I don't think I could ever truly forgive him. Not after what he said about Jodi, and the one-night stand thing. Who even suggests something like that? He was drunk, sure, but still – it was cruel. And then there's the fact that he cheated on my best friend Grace. How do I trust someone like that? How do I even let myself try?" She had decided it wasn't worth her keeping anyone a secret anymore.

"Well, okay let's start with can you forgive him knowing he was under the influence?" *it was a fair question*, she thought. Was she willing to look past the fact that he had been drunk and not wanting to be there? That the Hank she had feelings for now was possibly not the same person?

"I think if I got an actual apology that would be a good start. I can forgive, but I'm not one to forget." She honestly thought that was a fair statement, forgiveness came overtime and considering how he has never actually apologized she knew that it would need to come first.

"Have you asked for an apology?" Dr. Mahoney asked.

"Why should I have to ask?" Denise asked, after all this time wouldn't he know he did something wrong?

"Well, if he was under the influence, do you think he remembers saying that?" That was a valid question, there were many things that she had done over the years while she was drunk that she didn't recall the next day and it wasn't until someone had told her what happened that she would at least try and correct her mistake.

"I don't know." Was it possible that he didn't remember?

"I think the first step for you to try and heal any distance is to have that conversation. If you ask him and he doesn't remember, then tell him. If he realizes that this is how this whole situation started and that he is remorseful of what he did, then perhaps, you can discuss a way forward for the two of you." He said, clasping his hands in his lap, looking at her with those warm soft eyes that always brought her comfort. "Communication with all relationships, whether romantic or not, is just that. Openness and honesty."

Closing her eyes, she wanted to shrink away from it all. There were just so many things that she had kept hidden, too many truths left unsaid. If she was going to embark on this journey of openness and honesty there was someone way more important than Hank that she needed to be truthful with, and that was the one person in the world who loved her the most - *Jodi*.

She continued laying there on the couch for a few minutes without saying anything and he wasn't pushing her to move or do anything, but then the buzzer rang and she knew her session was up.

"I think you have a good starting point on what to do. Start with being honest and then talk to Hank."

Dreading the idea of having to face facts and talk to Jodi was scary, but to have to talk to Hank and have that super hard conversation was going to be so much more difficult. What if he denies saying it or not even believing her? Nodding that she understood, she got up and started walking out the door to make her next appointment.

Denise had made all of Jodi's favorites for dinner, hot dogs, mac and cheese, and cut up raw veggies. If they were going to have a difficult conversation, the least she could do was make sure Jodi was enjoying her favorite foods. As she stood there making her plate, she now realized all these years later why her dad had made those pancakes, she only hoped that the same result wouldn't happen because it was bad enough that Jodi had food sensitivities and was a super picky eater.

As she served Jodi her plate of food, she nearly fell off her chair in excitement. Ever the typical teenager, she started shoveling food in her mouth like she hadn't eaten just two hours earlier.

"All my favorites! What happened, I don't remember getting an award? Did my grades come out? Are they bad? I thought I did good this semester." Jodi said, as she crunched down on some carrots. Taking a bite of her own hot dog, Denise chewed a little too slowly because she knew what she needed to do next.

"No, everything is fine, I don't think grades even came out yet, it's just that I need to talk to you about something." Denise took a big breath and braced herself for Jodi's reaction. "Okay, um, when I went to therapy today, Dr. Mahoney said that I needed to start with telling some truths and it's not that anything is a secret it's just that I don't talk about it."

Jodi's big brown eyes blinked back at her and just kept eating only now she was taking her time.

"About your dad. I want to talk to you about your dad." Denise said, as she watched her daughter stop eating, focusing only on her. Reaching across the table, she held Jodi's hand, not sure if she was doing this to comfort her or herself, gathering up the courage she went on.

"So, I was dating someone back in the summer before you were born. He was a complete asshole and I broke it off. However, a few days before we broke up we had sex, I was on birth control at the time, but apparently it didn't work." Pausing to collect herself, Jodi squeezed her hand letting her know that it was okay.

"I made some other mistakes after him and I had a one-night stand with someone else and when I found out I was pregnant I was in shock and I panicked." As tears collected in Denise's eyes, Jodi pulled her hand away and walked over to her mom wrapping her arms around her and the waterfall of tears streamed down Denise's face.

"I am so sorry I messed up. I've never told you this, but I was selfish. I wanted you, so badly, because I never thought I would get the chance to have a child. But I loved you from the very second I saw you up on that screen, you were a teeny tiny fluttering bean with that whooshing heart beating away without a care in the world and I fell in love with you the second I heard that sound. I thought, I would finally have someone who would just love me for me, not like Grampa does, I mean he does love me for me, but someone, I don't know. I just wanted someone to be mine." Jodi released her hug long enough to snuggle into Denise's lap as they cried together.

"Thank you for choosing me to be your kid." Jodi whispered, choking on the words, "You have been and always will be the best mom in the whole world, I don't need a dad when I have Stupend-o-mom as my mom." She said, kissing Denise's tear-stained cheek and all Denise could do was hug her as if the world was ending that very moment. That gigantic momma bear hug that always let her know that everything was going to be okay, because deep down in her heart she knew it was true.

"Well, I'm not sure I'm such a Stupend-o-mom because I do know who your dad is." Denise said, and Jodi pulled back. Sniffing and taking another deep breath Denise went on.

"After I kicked that boyfriend out he hadn't come by to pick up his stuff. He had left a brush behind that had his hair on it, so after you were born I had it tested and it was a match." Denise confessed and she felt a lightening in her chest starting.

"I'm sorry I have kept this from you but he is a bad man and I didn't want him involved in your life, but if you want-" Jodi shook her head stopping Denise from continuing.

"If you have kept him from me for this long then there is a good reason. You are a very good judge of character, so I don't need to meet him or talk to him. I have all I need right here." Jodi said, throwing her arms around Denise's neck and she felt that familiar tingle in her nose – the kind that always came right before her eyes filled with tears she wasn't ready for. She knew Jodi would eventually have more questions, but she didn't care, she felt like the weight of the world had just been lifted off her shoulders and she wondered why it had taken her so long to tell Jodi all this.

Allowing Jodi to get up and go back to her seat to finish eating they changed gears and chatted about the day and despite the cold weather and the light snow that had started to fall just outside their kitchen window, Denise's heart was the warmest it had felt in a very long time.

CHAPTER FOURTEEN

Hank

New York City was always pretty this time of year, the holiday decorations, the bustle of the crowds trying to make their way to Time Square and Rockefeller Center. But the thing he enjoyed most was that it was out of Jersey, and since he was trying to avoid running into Denise as much as possible – NYC was the better option for his night out.

Needing to go into the corporate headquarters that past week, left him commuting with the terrible train schedule and meeting after meeting. Figuring that he would need to grab dinner before he headed back to New Jersey, Hank begrudgingly agreed to have dinner with Nick and the only reason he accepted was because Keen's Steakhouse had been suggested and he never turned down a good steak.

It wasn't that Hank was avoiding Nick, it was just that Dr. Mahoney had mentioned that he had been making such amazing progress. That perhaps slowly pulling away from toxic people who encouraged terrible behavior would be best for him. But he didn't want to give up years of friendship and confidences that easily.

Nick had been there for him when his mom had died, getting him so drunk he ended up waking up next to some strange girl he never learned the name of, with no knowledge of the night before. He was right there after Kevin had dropped that bomb on him at the bachelor party about Grace not actually being in love with him. Hank had been devastated, and Nick's solution? Pouring more vodka down his throat, getting him a lap dance and paying the stripper extra to give Hank a blow job the night before the wedding. Nick's way of helping always seemed to be the same: drown it, numb it, bury it. But somehow, his version of making things better always ended up making things worse.

The restaurant was packed and as Hank sat across from him, Nick sipped his vodka on the rocks making fun of the fact that Hank was drinking a coffee with his T-bone steak.

"Dude, I still have to get home to the boys. Grace has been great and had them go over to her house so I can make the commute this week. I still have them for another day so I'm not about to get drunk before I pick them up." Hank said, enjoying the perfectly seasoned T-bone.

"Come on man, tell her to keep them and just crash on my couch. We can go and pick up some chicks, get them drunk, and take them back to my place and have a four way like we did when we were in college." Nick slurred as he stuffed a bite of his Filet Mignon in his mouth. The idea repulsed Hank, he wasn't a kid anymore, he was a grown man, with kids and a house. Kids which he had promised to take Christmas shopping the next morning, making staying over completely out of the question.

"No, it's my week and I promised to take them shopping for decorations." Hank said, with a smile thinking about the boys' excitement. "Colin wants -" he started and Nick just interrupted.

"Ugh, boring. Tell Grace she can keep them. She wanted those crotch goblins, anyway, let's just get plastered and laid. You haven't had your dick sucked in what, months? Unless you didn't listen and you fucked that bitch. Please tell me you didn't?" Nick pounded down the rest of his vodka and Hank put his fork and knife down, now so totally disgusted that he couldn't eat.

"Nick, I'm going to ask you to apologize this second about the comment about Grace and the boys." Hank's voice firm and even toned, trying not to make a scene right in the filled to capacity restaurant. He was finally seeing what Dr. Mahoney was talking about - and he wasn't going to take this, drunk or not.

"What the fuck for? Grace wanted the little brats, just let her have 'em." Hank could barely understand him - his words were mumbled and slurring together. He stared at Nick, not sure when things had gotten this bad with him, but it must have been noticeable even at work. It was no wonder why the partners had asked him and Ginny to come in to look over certain accounts that Nick had been handling. It appeared he'd been sliding down this slippery slope for a while now. Hank's boss had even gotten a call from Nick's senior partner, asking him to send Hank in. From the little he'd reviewed this week; something just didn't sit right with Nick's accounts. The worst part? He'd been sworn to secrecy – not allowed to say a word.

Glaring at the shell of the human who used to be fun to hang around with, Hank got up from his chair and pushed it in. Pulling a hundred dollar bill out of his wallet he threw it down on the table and looked down at the man who was supposed to be his friend and shook his head.

"You know what? I've thought for years what a great life you have, no kids, no wife, no hassle. But you know what I realized. I've got the better life. I have a family that loves me and needs me. And yeah I fuck it up from time to time, but *MY* boys are my entire world and I feel sorry for you that you don't have someone like that. That loves you for who you could be and I say *could be* because you are so fucked up you would need two therapists to get through your bullshit." Hank walked a few feet and came back to the still shocked Nick, who looked at him through glazed eyes. "And as for Denise, you keep her name out of your fucking mouth, you don't even deserve to even think about her let alone get to say her name. Hope you have a great fucking night."

The people around them applauded as Hank started to walk away, only Nick wasn't done with the conversation and followed him out of the restaurant.

"You're so fucked you know that, right? You don't see it, but you are falling for her. She is gonna break your heart and I won't be there to put that shit back together again. She's a fucking cunt that is gonna eat you alive." Nick screamed and Hank turned around staring at this pitiful excuse of a human.

Stone cold sober, he knew what Nick was like when he was drunk – and he knew his words meant nothing. But when he caught sight of Nick charging at him, Hank swerved just in time. Nick's fist sliced through the air, throwing him off balance when he failed to make contact. Before Nick could recover, Hank was already in motion – his own punch slammed into Nick's left eye and sent him crashing down onto the cement sidewalk. As he laid there on the ground, Hank checked to make sure Nick was still breathing and shook his head. He could be a great guy - if only he'd stopped acting like a child. As the hostess and Matre'd came out to check on things, Hank paid them for the whole bill and let them handle the rest. He was done with the spoiled child that laid there on the floor. *Let him be someone else's problem* – Hank no longer wanted to be a part of *that* circus.

Saturday morning came with a buzz of activity as Hank stood in the middle of the living room realizing he had no idea what he was doing. Although he had lived in this house for years, Grace had always been the one to decorate for every holiday. His only job had been to bring up or down tubs with decorations, and now that he officially owned and moved back into the house, he had no idea where to start.

"Boys, grab your coats! We're going shopping." Hank yelled, *a fresh start,* he thought. Even though it was the same house for the boys - he wanted to make new traditions that they could do together. Bundling up and getting into the car, he had previously checked out sales online, but Colin had made a specific request for a blow-up lawn decoration that was exclusively available at only one superstore. He knew it would be packed because of the weekend, but he would brave all types of shoppers if it brought joy to this kid's face.

Walking through the store he and the boys were trying to figure out which tree to get, Calvin wanted one with white lights and Colin wanted one with color. Fortunately, Hank had found one that did both with a bunch of different types of settings.

Grace had left behind a box of ornaments, but Hank wanted something that felt like his own. He just turned down the ornament aisle when a familiar voice had him stopping short.

"Jodi, it's one a year and we always get something new. What about this one?" he heard Denise saying. Waving his arms he tried getting the boys' attention as they had been walking ahead of him, but they turned down the next ornament aisle and he knew this was not going to be easy.

"What are you two doing here? Come here munchkin and give me a squeeze." Denise excitedly said, turning down the aisle Hank watched as she hugged Colin. Her black hair pulled up in a messy bun bouncing on top of her head as she whirled Colin around like a little ragdoll, his giggles echoing in the high ceiling store. Watching her slowly place Colin back down on the ground, Hank locked eyes with her and his heart immediately melted. *What was it about this woman?* No other person could make him distressed, annoyed and turned on all at the same time. His pulse began racing as she started approaching him, and he thought to himself *be cool, don't freak out.*

"Hhiii." Hank stuttered over a tiny word. "I wasn't expecting to see you." He said, as the boys and Jodi were looking at ornaments. Trying to appear nonchalant, he shifted his gaze to a display of ornaments – anything to avoid staring too long into her bewitching hazel eyes.

"Well, it's a small town with very limited stores to shop at. We're bound to run into one another. Unless of course you are trying to avoid me." She said, picking out an ornament and inspecting it causing his head to snap towards her. He was avoiding her. She always threw his whole world into chaos. Hell, just last night he had punched out his best friend because of her, and his knuckles still hurt.

"I thought it best after what happened. I never know if you are gonna slap me or pick a fight and it turn into-" he cleared his throat. Still unable to stop thinking of that day, he had taken himself in his own hand many times just thinking about her. Replaying over and over in his mind, the way she felt against him, the way she tasted, and that maddeningly sweet addicting scent. The same scent she was wearing this minute, making him get aroused just being near her. Moving closer to him, his heart rate escalated at her nearness and she leaned over to whisper to him.

"If it is at all possible, I would like to sit down and talk to you. No fighting, no funny business, just talk." Hank turned to her and her face was right next to his, he could just lean in ever so slightly and kiss her right there.

BANG, the sound echoing through the store as Colin had dropped a large box of ornaments and luckily nothing had shattered, well nothing but the moment. Watching as the teens helped him get the box back up on the shelf, Denise stepped a few inches away and he just nodded his head.

"Grace picks up the boys later today, so I will be home, if you want. Or we can meet up somewhere neutral." He prayed she would accept the neutral location he wasn't sure he could control himself at home.

"Having witnesses… yeah that's probably smart." She smirked, even she knew it was best not to be alone with each other. "I can meet you at Picasso's around 7 if that works." Picasso's wasn't in Toselle Park, so it was truly Switzerland, and he was completely fine with that. Bobbing his head in agreement he walked over to the boys to see which ornaments they were picking out. Hank reminded himself that his focus needed to be; *on the boys, not her.* But he could feel her gaze on him and a heated flush ran up his neck knowing just how close she was.

As they stood there going through ornaments, there was a normalcy he wasn't used to. He felt himself relaxing and after fifteen minutes Hank's cart was now filled with a brand-new tree, ornaments, garland and a star. It had all been so pleasant, there was no fighting, no tension, they had laughed and made jokes. *Was this how normal people acted with one another when they were interested in the other person,* he thought.

With all the work he had been doing with Dr. Mahoney, it had dawned on him that the way his mother had raised him had truly skewed his perception of how he was supposed to act. He wasn't a mistake. He had nothing to prove. He was merely a human, bound to make mistakes but also capable of facing those mistakes and making them right. Maybe, this hate feud between the two of them could be resolved, perhaps she would finally tell him what he had said that started it all.

Yet, she had things she had to answer for too. Like Nick, was Nick Jodi's dad or was it someone else? Then it dawned on him that perhaps it wasn't Nick's, and she had been sexually assaulted? That was a thing, some women still have their babies even after something as traumatic as that. He looked back at this woman and realized he truly knew nothing about her. She had kept so much of her personal life a guarded secret, to the point where even her best friends didn't know and he thought; *there had to be a reason for that.* To be what Nick had called her, a "Guard Dog" always on the defensive. That was the enigma, Denise Gagnon: so guarded and closed off, that her whole life before her living in Toselle Park was just as big a puzzle as the woman herself.

"Well, we have to get going. Enjoy setting up Christmas, and I will talk to you later." Denise said, with a wink causing Hank's heart to flutter. *Fuck, I can't with that woman,* he thought. If a wink and a smile could set his heart skipping; he was in real trouble.

Finally ushering the boys to check out, he somehow managed to purchase everything in his cart, and get the boys to agree not to buy any more goodies. He had sat down with Grace and they went over ideas on how to control the snack inventory in the house, and he had come up with a schedule and menu, which was really weird because he had never thought to do that. But it was like a spreadsheet with numbers and he did so enjoy a good spreadsheet.

"Can we stop and get some tacos?" Calvin said, as they were coming up on their favorite fast-food restaurant.

"Absolutely not, I have already gotten everything for homemade tacos and I was gonna make them the moment we got home. You guys can wait while I make them." Hank said, looking in the rearview to two very sad faces. "I get it, they aren't mom's but I'm trying, I swear she puts something extra in them because I use her recipe to a T and they still don't come out the same." Hank confessed, Grace really was the better cook, but he was trying. He had never really needed to cook but since the divorce he had been experimenting. There had been some successes, the boys did love his cheeseburger pie and spaghetti pie, but the chicken cutlets had been absolute disasters. Overcooked and some burnt to a crisp was an understatement. But he was great at grilling, ten out of ten would recommend his chicken souvlaki or his baked spanakopita, all those Greek genes finally coming into play for a good thing.

"Mommy told me she has a secret ingredient for her tacos." Colin chirped from the backseat and Hank snapped his head up, he knew she had been holding out. "Mommy said, her secret ingredient is love." *Of course it was*, Hank thought.

"Alright, then how about this, you two will help me make the tacos, that way you can put your love into it and it will be way better than Mommy's." Hank said, with a smile, Calvin rolled his eyes giving a quick half smile, but it was Colin's huge smile that touched him the most. He had never been a very touchy-feely kind of dad, but the more and more he spent time on his own with the boys, the deeper his love and appreciation for them grew. Calvin was practically a man, almost ready to take his driving test and starting to take an interest in girls; which was slightly nerve-racking. He had made it a point to talk to him about what he should and shouldn't do, but not before going over it with Grace and Dr. M first. He didn't want Calvin to make the same mistakes as he did, but at the same time he didn't want him getting hurt either.

Colin on the other hand was his little buddy. It wasn't that Colin was his favorite, because he loved his boys equally. It was just his innocence that he felt super protective of. The amount of love and support from one so young warmed his soul, years of trauma healed in just one of Colin's smiles. Hank had been spending time learning about all of Colin's games on his tablet, and they would spend hours playing, which made him feel like he was finally doing something right. It was tiny things, mini moments of giggles or bad jokes that warmed his heart.

After unloading the car, Hank went straight to work getting dinner ready. He needed to get it done quickly, *after all, Hank had a date to get ready for*, and the thought stopped him in his tracks. This *wasn't* a date; they were just going to a café. A dimly lit café with comfy couches and warm beverages on a cold night to have a deep conversation. Yet everything in his heart and pants were screaming that it was a date. *No, not a date, we are just resolving years of hate that is all.*

Calvin stared at him as he just stood there unable to move for a moment and his eyes were scanning the kitchen looking for something.

"Uh, you okay there?" Calvin asked, snapping Hank out of his train of thought. Nodding his head yes, he got back to looking for the spice mix for the tacos.

"Yup, just had a brain fart. Can you grab the tomatoes and lettuce out of the fridge?" Hank was trying to focus on just the tacos - and only the tacos - as he put the pan on the stove and turned it on to heat up the skillet. With a look of skepticism in his glare, Calvin just did as his dad told him and came back looking for a cutting board and knife to help.

"You sure you're okay. Something was up with you and Denise. Since when do you two not fight with one another?" The teen asked as he started cutting up the lettuce into shreds. Hank stilled his hands on the counter and started to panic; it was true he and Denise couldn't bear to be in a room with each other let alone say hello. Grace, Nikki and Jim all knew about the hook up, but now Calvin had noticed that something was up. Grabbing the packet of meat off the counter, he remembered honesty was the best policy.

"I am working through my anger issues and since Denise and I have had a feud for a long time, I thought perhaps it was best to work things through." *So, I can get back into her pants.* He couldn't believe he just thought that. Truthfully, he *was* working through things, one of them was this weird feeling he had about Denise, was it just lust or was it more. Dr. M had said, it was growth, it was some sort of growth, but it was more of something growing in his pants.

"So, you are going to bury the hatchet after all these years? What started it all?" Calvin asked the million-dollar question.

"Kid, I have no idea what the Hell I did or said to be honest. So hopefully I will find out tonight." Hank turned, opening the packet of meat and placing it in the searing hot pan. His stomach knotted as he thought about what Grace had said. About how Denise had acted like all these years and there was no doubt in his mind that the level of awful vitriol that had come out of his mouth could leave him apologizing to her for the rest of his life.

"Well, whatever it is Dad, I would just beg her for forgiveness, unless you want her to crush your nuts again." Right out of the mouth of his oldest babe. Colin walked in and sat down at the island with his tablet.

"Mommy says, if you did or said something wrong, it is best to apologize. But you have to mean it otherwise it isn't a real apology." For an eight-year-old who gave his parents a bit of grief some days he at least listened. Hank stood there looking at his sixteen and eight-year-olds, concluding that he clearly had no hand in raising them all these years, and it made him feel a twang of guilt in his heart. They were actually teaching him how to be a better person, and this is what happens when your parents either leave you or treat you like a mistake they couldn't get rid of.

"And this is why you are much better than me, kiddos. You are very fortunate to have a loving mom who has raised you right. I on the other hand did not, so that's probably why I'm so fucked up." He cursed as he pounded at the meat in the pan trying to break it up with the wooden spatula. Colin got up from his chair and hugged his waist from behind, prompting Hank to take in a deep breath. Putting down the spatula he turned around and hugged Colin tightly, then lifted him up and held him in his arms. Colin was starting to get too tall and heavy for this, but right now he needed this hug. Turning back to the stove, he let Colin use the spatula as he held him on his hip and they cooked the meat together, this was what he should have been doing with them their whole lives. But today was a new day, and new days meant new beginnings.

"Mommy, Daddy made the best tacos, they came out just like yours!" Colin yelled from the kitchen as he shoved the rest of his taco in his mouth as Grace walked in. The look of surprise on Grace's face was everything to Hank at that moment, because she prided herself on making the best tacos.

"Wow, so you added in a little extra cumin?" She asked and Hank's mouth dropped; she had been holding out on him with an extra seasoning as she took a taste and smiled.

"No, we just added love to it." Hank said, trying hard not to be a bit too happy that his were just as good as hers. Watching her bite her lower lip to keep from laughing, he had to chuckle to himself. It was funny, she had to add ingredients and he didn't.

"Alright, well then, my work here is done, maybe not yet though, you have to get better at making cutlets, that last batch was atrocious." Grace said, grimacing at the idea of those blackened cutlets that he had sent her a text message about. "If you guys are done, why don't you go grab your coats, boots and hats. The snow is really starting to stick out there."

Hank perked up at that, they had been having such a good time he hadn't looked outside. There was already about two and a half inches of snow out there which meant that driving later would be a bit difficult because the DPW never went out until there was at the very least three inches of snow. But at the rate that it was coming down it looked like they would be out within the hour.

"I didn't know it was supposed to snow; I had plans tonight." He said, from the window and he heard a slight "oh" from Grace.

"I guess you are gonna have to reschedule that date. I didn't know you were going to start dating after the events of September." She smirked glaring at him over the rim of her glasses. Calvin, however, never one to miss the chance to make things a bit worse spoke up.

"It's not a date." He said, through a mouthful of tacos. "Dad is supposed to meet up with Denise, but he's been acting like a goofy teen since we saw them this afternoon."

Hank closed his eyes as he heard the sharp crack of Grace's neck as she whipped her head quickly to look at him. Waving his hands in front of him, trying very hard to diffuse the whole thing he walked over to Grace who now had a shocked smile on her face.

"I have not! I'm just worried about what she is going to say, that is it. We are going to try and bury the hatchet." Hank defended himself.

"Dad wants to bury something in her and it isn't a hatchet." Calvin quipped, garnering him a quick slap on the arm from Grace and Hank as they both called his name.

"Calvin James Nereid, that was disgusting, apologize right now." Grace said, with a hint of disgust at his comment.

"What? I'm a teenager. Dad, if you think I'm blind to the fact that you were staring at Denise like she was a Sunday roast in the store, you are sorely mistaken. Even Jodi said her mom has been acting weird whenever Nikki goes over for coffee and your name comes up in conversations." The teen said as he put on his boots and hat. *Was it possible that this wasn't just a one-sided thing then? Was this just as difficult for her to comprehend as he struggled with?*

"Calvin James, apologize to Daddy now. They are both adults and they are just trying to work through stuff, I think it is very adult of the two of you, trying to talk things out. And don't you dare say one more snarky comment, mister." Grace defended Hank and Calvin just smiled.

"Sorry Dad. But you are a bit obvious. But sorry for the comment." Calvin apologized as he walked up to Hank looking for a hug. Smiling at his son who was almost his height he gave him a huge hug.

"It's alright, all fair really. But thanks for the apology kid. Don't give your mom a hard time this week, Jim you can bust all you want." He laughed.

"Henry Nikolaos Nereid." Grace this time hit Hank on the arm, and he just laughed as he shrugged away from her trying to hit him again. He just couldn't help himself. After helping Colin put on his gear, Hank walked them out onto the porch and watched as Grace slowly drove away being the cautious driver that she was.

Walking back into the house he checked his phone, shocked to find a text from Denise.

Looks like we are gonna have to reschedule.

He didn't want to reschedule; this was years of not knowing why she hated him so much, and then there was the whole big question about Nick that he wanted to ask her. With the two of them avoiding each other for months he just wasn't willing to chance it. Throwing on his boots, coat and hat, he locked up the house and started the four-block walk to her house, but not before waving to Mike who had started to shovel his sidewalks.

CHAPTER FIFTEEN

Denise

The banging at her front door was so loud it actually startled her as she threw the long, wooden match into the fire she had just started in the fireplace. Wrapping herself in her small, crocheted gray blanket, she slid her feet into her old ratty slippers and walked to the front door as the echoed knock persisted. Shivering as she got closer to the front door, she realized that a short summer nightgown had not been the best idea, but her perimenopause had kicked in again and the night sweats had been unbearable. Since cancelling with Hank due to the weather, she had decided to just light a fire and fall asleep on the couch. But whoever was at her front door was not letting up.

"Who the Hell -" Denise started as she was shocked to find Hank covered in snow standing on the other side of her door. Scanning her eyes over his appearance, there he stood, snow caked around his boots up to his ankles and clinging to the front of his pants and coat. His cheeks windblown pink and his lips were practically purple. He was an absolute mess.

"Oh my God, come in. Did you walk here? I sent you a text that we should cancel tonight and -" was all she got out before he crushed his cold lips onto hers. She hadn't even had time to close her eyes and all she saw was this insanity and fire in his eyes. Hank pulled back from her probably because she was blinking at him as he had kissed her.

"I'm sorry, I know I shouldn't have come over, I should have -" was all he got out before Denise needed him to shut up. She didn't care about the snow dripping off of him onto her lavender colored nightgown, that cut off at her mid-thigh. Or on her slippers as she helped him out of his coat and tore off his soaked snow-covered hat. All she cared about was the fact that he was so determined for the two of them to talk, that he walked in this snowstorm just to be here in her home. Sliding his tongue along the seam of her lips, the mix of the coldness of his lips and the heat of his tongue caused an overwhelming stir as she opened her mouth to sigh, and he dove right in. Helping him remove his gloves and tossing them onto the floor, she felt the cool dampness in his fingers along her back as he finally embraced her fully pressing her up against him.

Enveloping her arms around his neck, she grabbed at his hair and pulled hard, eliciting a moan out of him that she hadn't heard before and it was utter music to her ears. She couldn't believe she was feeling a thrill at hearing such a sound coming from him, and she couldn't help but want to hear it again. As she ran her hands through his hair again, he broke the kiss to trail his mouth down her chin to the curve of her neck. Just before he could suck too hard on her pulse point she gave his hair another firm tug – and the low rumbling moan that escaped him made her smile. It would seem her little Hank likes having his hair pulled, and she decided to store that little nugget of information at the back of her mind.

She opened her eyes to see Hank's baby blues had barely a ring of blue around his black blow out pupils. As they stood there just looking into each other's eyes, she couldn't help but smile a little - if someone had asked her to put money down on a bet of whether tonight was going to ever happen - she wouldn't have even wasted a dollar bet on it.

"What's my favorite little brat smiling about?" His voice low and throaty as he gently brushed back a stray hair away from her face, causing her to narrow her eyes back at him.

"I'm your favorite little brat again, am I?" Denise breathlessly uttered as she rubbed her nose against his and he walked her back against the wall; it was cold and compared to his body she felt like she was trapped between fire and ice, causing her to shiver with an anticipation she hadn't expected.

"Yes, you are mine. My addictive," he kissed her nose and she closed her eyes to his gentle lips, "hypnotic" he kissed her right eye lid and her brain stopped, "mesmerizing" he kissed her left eye lid and she remembered, "favorite little brat." Her eyes were hypnotic and mesmerizing. She had heard those words before. Grace had said those words. Had Hank said this to Grace about her before?

The memory tugged at her – after the game, when she'd vented to Grace about him, She'd gone on about his ass being perfect, and Grace made that offhanded comment about his dick -which to be fair, she hadn't been wrong about. She couldn't wait to get her hands on it again. But now she was distracted by the thought that they had said these words to Grace. Wanting to test a theory, she reached down and grabbed Hank's ass wanting to see if Grace had shared her words to him.

"So, if I'm your favorite brat, then this is my perfect ass." Denise said, keeping her eyes open this time as she kissed him only to see his eyes come instantly into focus.

"You're the one who thinks my ass is perfect, not Grace?" He asked and she smiled, biting her lip.

"Yes, and you are the one who thinks my eyes are hypnotic!" She said, screwing up her face to show him that she knew all about that comment. They both huffed at the idea that because of their proximity to Grace this may in fact be more difficult than they had imagined. As he pulled away from her, the coolness of the vestibule made her nipples harden and she noticed he caught sight of it as he bent down to finally unlace his boots and walk out of them. Not wanting to have her neighbors enjoying their show much further she welcomed him inside.

"Did you actually put the fireplace on just for you?" He asked as he stood in front of it with his damp pants facing it trying very hard to dry them and failing miserably. Walking down the hall she ignored the question and went into her laundry room to grab a pair of her spare pair of shorts which happened to be a pair of extra-large boxers. Walking back, she saw him looking at her as if she was carrying a lit firecracker.

"It's my lounge shorts, the least I could do was get you a dry pair of something to put on, unless you want to attempt to put on a pair of my yoga pants, I might have a pair of Jodi's booty shorts if you really want to wear those?" Denise said, holding out the boxers.

Shaking his head, he held out his hand and she pointed him over to the half bath around the corner from her living room. A few minutes later Hank came out wearing the boxers over his slightly dampened boxers and laid his jeans in front of the fire to dry.

"I was also missing home. Whenever there was a snowstorm my dad always made sure we had a really strong fire going in our hearth, he grew up in the Seychelles so he wasn't sure how to handle Wisconsin winters but he has learned over the years." Denise smiled as she recalled the memories of cold nights and her dad playing games with her.

"Then you at least had a better childhood than me. Mom would keep the heat super low in the winter, leaving me to freeze and never putting the air conditioning on in the summer so I would sweat to death. She had a unit in her room that she kept on just for her and would crack her bedroom just enough to barely get any in the rest of the house. On the hot nights I would sleep outside her room on the floor near the crack just so I wouldn't overheat." Hank said, as he warmed his hands against the heat of the fire and she sat there shocked. She had no idea that someone could be that cruel to a child. Watching as Hank enjoyed the dance of the flames she saw a wonderment in his eyes and yet a great sadness.

"My mom was never around. It was only me and my dad. He has a farmer's market and orchard where all the local farmers come to sell their crops, or meats or goodies. And my dad sells his honey, cherries and apples. He has a massive collection of hives and he has family who still live in the Seychelles, so they send us the caviar they harvest and we sell it at the stand. But mom is somewhere gallivanting across the globe probably or dead, we don't know." Denise said, as she got up from her couch and made her way to the kitchen. Hank followed her in, it was actually kind of nice to have someone she could talk about this to, that seemed to have a horrible mom. The rest of their group all seemed to have these amazing families and running gags with them, but she didn't have that and it seemed neither did Hank. And then it hit her, she had never shared any information about her mom with anyone before.

"What's your dad like?" Hank asked and she smiled.

"The best, just the best." She reached up to the side of the fridge and pulled down a picture of herself, Jodi and her Dad from their last trip to Wisconsin. It was the three of them taking a selfie all holding their fishing poles and Jodi having a large rainbow trout on the hook. Her father's dark complexion compared to herself and Jodi must have been a bit of a shock as Hank had never seen or heard about her dad before, but all he did was smile a wistful smile.

"It looks like you guys are all best friends, that must be amazing." The tiniest hint of envy in his words made her realize that it must not have been just his mom that was also so cruel but also his dad. "My dad, I haven't seen since he left when I was six. Probably off with your mom somewhere right?" She knew it was a joke but all she heard was the pain. The pain of a man who never had love given to him until he met Grace and by the stories, he had never truly been welcomed into the family. It wasn't that they were awful people, not even by a long shot, it was just that Grace was so in love with Jim and the whole family knew it. Of course they would be rooting for someone who they all loved, not this stranger with a damaged past.

She turned and pointed to the coffee machine to see if he wanted coffee and he just nodded. Since the night on Grace's deck, she had been avoiding alcohol and having a night cap was either a cup of tea, cocoa or coffee depending on the day. After brewing his, she went to work on making one for herself and she handed him his mug, holding hers up for a toast.

"To the messed-up kids, who became very messy adults." She said, as they clinked their mugs together and laughed. This was different, it was odd, but it wasn't bad - it was actually rather nice. Walking back into the living room they sat back on the couch in a comfortable silence for a few minutes. She wasn't sure just what to say or do so they just sat near each other and watched the fire.

"This may sound crazy, but I honestly don't remember how this feud all started." Hank explained, and she sucked in her breath knowing that eventually they would need to talk about it. "Please, Grace told me I said something awful and that I should ask you because she wasn't going to get involved. I know this is too many years late, but please, what did I say that made you hate me?" The agony in his voice twisted her gut and she knew he was being genuine. Taking a sip of her coffee and a deep breath, she turned and faced him.

"You were drunk." She started slowly, and he just sat there without interrupting. "You had come from some party and I could smell the vodka on your breath. Grace introduced us and you asked about me having a husband, I said no, you said baby daddy, I said no and that Jodi was a happy blessing." He gave a slow nod because at that point it must have sounded like him, but she continued. "Then you said, 'so you had a one-night stand and couldn't go through with the surgery', implying that I was a whore and should have had an abortion."

Hank's calm understanding face, suddenly changed to one of complete and utter disgust and her eyes began to sting. "You have no idea how hard it was for me. I have PCOS and the fact that I even got pregnant while on birth control was like a one in a million chance. My doctors had told me that it was very possible with the severity of my condition that I may never have children so the moment I found out, I knew I could never give up something as precious as my blessing. No matter who the father is." And then the tears came, the strong woman, the façade of the unbreakable broke right in front of him, and all he could do was rush immediately to her side to comfort her.

"Denise, I am - I am not even going to try and defend myself. It is a relief to finally know what I did and said and all I can say is that I am so unbelievably sorry. My mindset back then was so jaded and fucked up. I had been hanging out with someone I should have separated myself from for years and it wasn't until very recently that it dawned on me that I outgrew this person. Maybe it's the therapy I go to, or maybe it is just finally dawning on me that I need to grow up in order to help my own kids be better humans. But that doesn't excuse what I said. I truly am sorry." Hank said, as he looked at her and with the pad of his thumb, wiped away the tears on her rosy cheeks. It was the apology she had always wanted but never expected and then she heard Dr. Mahoney's voice in her head about telling the truth.

"Thank you, it's been a long time coming." Denise said, with a tearful smile as he bent in and kissed her reverently and almost hesitant. "But the truth is, you weren't far off from it. I had been dating this guy Nick and we broke up a day before a concert that I had gotten us tickets to. I was so excited because it was a band I loved and I had been dying to see, anyway, I decided I wasn't gonna miss the concert simply because I broke up with him and when I was there I met this couple and we had a thing that night." The insight of the situation was hitting him and slowly his pained expression turned to one of comprehension, he had called out the one-night stand.

"But then a month and a half later, I found out that I was pregnant, the problem was that I didn't know if it was Nick's or this other guy's. Jodi knows all this, I told her not too long ago actually, but since we were being open I thought you should know that you were sort of right, but very, very wrong for saying it."

There it was, all out in the open and the same feeling she felt when telling Jodi started up again. It was like she had been Atlas, holding the world on her shoulders and she had been carrying all of this while on her knees barely getting by, but now she felt incredibly lighter as if she could float away. Hank, however, looked a bit off, his brow was furrowed and he sat there contemplating something.

"So, this Nick guy, have you ever spoken to him after you broke up? Did you ever find out if he is Jodi's dad?"

"Nick, oh God no, he probably would have forced me into an abortion. He abhors children, he told me that almost a month into the relationship. And I did find out and Jodi's his, I just don't want her anywhere near that man, he is a narcissistic gaslighting asshole, the amount of trauma he would cause either Jodi or myself would warrant me needing bail money." Denise quipped as she took another sip of her coffee and something struck her. There was a knowing glint in Hank's eyes and a smirk spread across his lips as he reached over and held her hand.

"Huh, it's funny that you list all these wonderful attributes about your Nick. It just so happens an old college buddy of mine fits that same description to a tee. Well, former friend, his name's Nick Dupree." Denise's heart stopped, she hadn't heard that name since September 2008, what were the odds that there was another Nick Dupree?

"He sounds just like yours. And like I said with my therapy, I need to separate myself from people who will not support my desire to be a better person. So, I stopped hanging out with him." Hank said, bringing her hand up to his lips kissing it. It was an out of place reaction to his statement and she wondered what was going on.

"Oh?" She uttered; she wasn't sure why he was sharing all of this but she wasn't going to interrupt.

"Yeah, it's kind of funny because I had hung out with him right after our encounter back in September. That was who I was going to meet that night." He looked up at her sheepishly causing a blush to Denise's cheeks from the heated gaze he had in his eyes. A quiver in her belly reminding her of just how enjoyable those events had been before it all went sideways.

"He had mentioned dating some girl he called her 'The Guard Dog' because that was what her last name translated to." Trying her best to be unreactive was not working. Her face was not helping because she knew Gagnon was French for guard dog but she allowed him to continue.

"He mentioned he dated her back in 2008 and how she was awful and all these other things. But you know what? Even after all the awful things he said about her, I wondered if perhaps she was just too mature for him. He's always been a spoiled individual and has never truly grown up and I thought, I've worked too hard to become a better person to want to stick around people who are unwilling to change."

A stray strand of hair had fallen into her eyes and as Hank gazed into hers, he brushed it away so he could see her. It was a tiny movement, yet the gentleness of such a small thing melted just a little more of that ice around her heart.

"I've realized that my kids are the most precious thing to me. And if your Nick is like my Nick, then I don't blame you for wanting to keep Jodi safe and as far away from someone like that." He said, rubbing his thumb lazily over the hand, he was holding almost trying to sooth her to let her know that it was okay. Deep in her bones she knew, he was basically telling her that he had figured it out and for all these months *he* had kept her secret. So why would someone who *didn't* care, someone who *hated her,* why would they ever do that – unless...

Looking up into his eyes she saw no rage, no lust, not even heat or fire, but something more dear. Something sweet. It was reassurance, a silent promise that he would never say anything. It was unnerving, this really was not the person whom she had been so angry with for so long. As tears started to collect in her eyes, she just shook her head.

"I can't ever tell him. I won't do that to Jodi." Her words but a pleading whisper.

"I know." Acknowledged Hank as he moved closer to pull her into his embrace.

"I have spent my whole life protecting her from people like him, please I'm begging you." Tears fell from her face, scared that he would do the right thing and tell Nick all about Jodi and then her whole world would be turned into utter chaos. His hand went up to her face to wipe away her tears as he smiled.

"You don't have to beg me to protect Jodi. I may be a domineering asshole at times, but I wouldn't do that to a child. However," Hank's sweet tone changed throaty as he uttered 'However'.

Looking deep into her eyes with a longing she had seen only a few times, as he grazed his knuckles down her cheek trailing his light touch down to her chin, lifting it ever so slightly. "I will take you begging me to do whatever dirty things you want me to do to you, my brat." He finished as he brushed his lips against hers. The simple faint sensation sent ripples of desire course through her entire body, and she could feel a dampness starting to gather in her thin cotton panties.

Initially she hated being called a *good girl* and now here she was with a tangible thrill coursing through her veins as he called her *my brat*. Brats were bad, un-behaved children who needed to be taught a lesson on how to behave properly. As a gentle parent, her father had never once hit her or treated her unkind and she had carried that through with the way she had raised Jodi. But the idea that Hank saw her as misbehaving meant that he planned on some kind of treatment and he wanted her to beg for it. The idea of someone else taking control over her, to drive her to the point where she would plead both excited her and scared her at the same time. She was always the one controlling the action when it came to sex, but this man right here, it was very clear that he would be in control and the idea sent a course of electricity through her.

As he continued this slow torture of brushing his lips against hers, his hands slowly trailed over her body with deliberate care sending shudders through her with his exquisite touch. She could tell he was holding himself in check the entire time as he moved even closer placing one hand on her right leg, he moved it behind him so that he was sitting between her thighs. Never rushing, almost doing this to drive her to a brink she was so close to escaping to.

"Will you beg for me? All you have to do is say please. I know brats normally don't say please, only good girls do. And since you insist that you aren't a good girl you need to learn to say please Denise." His tongue skimmed along the seam of her lips as she parted them praying he would just give in and kiss her. But he didn't, his body now rigid and unrelenting, she felt him guiding her body to lay down onto the couch as he hovered over her. His hands planted on either side of her torso as if he was ready to start a push-up, his closeness was so far and yet she could feel the heat his body emanated.

"Please." She whispered as her hands ran up his taut arms pulling him closer, and he cocked a half smile staring down into her eyes.

"Please what, Denise? I've told you before, you need to use your words." Hank commanded as he moved his head down to her chin and nipped at it ever so slightly, triggering yet another current of electricity through her body, and she wrapped her long muscular legs up around him as she tried to get closer to him. But he was steadfast in keeping the distance between them until she told him what she wanted.

"I need you. Please Hank, I need you." She begged because she couldn't take this torment much longer. She had dreamed of him touching her again. The last time they'd been intimate, she's kept so quiet – holding back everything she wanted to feel. But now she could be as loud and unchecked as she wanted, since they were in the privacy of her own home. No sneaking off, no fear of being found and no one to stop anything.

Slowly lowering himself down onto her vibrating body, she finally felt the weight of him and he was much heavier than he looked. But then she could feel just how muscular he was under all those clothes that hid his form and just how hard he was for her. The way he moved reminded her of going from one yoga position to another, and as she ran her hand along his arms, she could feel just how toned his arms were under his sweater and she realized that it needed to go.

Sliding her hands up and over his back, she reached for the end of his sweater and grabbed a fist full of the wool sweater and shirt he was wearing underneath it, pulling it up and towards his head. With a half-cocked smile he looked down at her as he straightened himself up kneeling on the couch between her legs helping her remove his shirts. As she sat there looking up at him, she recalled she had seen him shirtless before while on the beach, but in the amber glow of the fire he looked like some kind of Greek God and it stole her breath. He had been working out, and she couldn't help herself as she ran her hands over his torso, starting from his shoulders and working her way down over his abs.

Locking eyes with him as she moved her hand, never once leaving his gaze. It was odd to be looking up at him, considering they were always eye to eye with each other because of her height. But to be in such a submissive position, it gave her a thrill. As her hands roamed lower, he finally let out a throaty moan when her fingers had finally found the waistband of the boxers he was wearing.

"I let you take my shirt off for free, these you will need to say please." He said, as he lifted her chin up and kissed her again, this time he wasn't holding back. His invasion was fierce and determined, it spurred longing and as good as his tongue felt in her mouth, she wanted it on her clit even more. Not willing to say *please*, she worked her hands into the boxers and grabbed his bare ass. He immediately pulled back with a firm shake of his head.

"I said, say *please*." His tone this time was stern and it took her breath away.

"I don't want to say please, I just want you." She mumbled, planting soft, deliberate kisses along his pecs before letting her tongue flick his right nipple – her eyes locked on his the entire time. She didn't miss the way his cock twitched beneath the thin fabric of his boxers. But then he grabbed her chin, holding it steady in his hand.

"I said, say please, or I will put all my clothes on and go home right now, even if that means I have to walk home in all that snow with a raging hard-on." He meant every word that he said, she could see it in his eyes, and that was the very last thing she wanted. She was already wet for him and so she would have to beg, but it didn't mean she couldn't be cute about it. Twisting her face into his palm she placed a tiny kiss in it.

"Please." She whispered. With the simple word he released her chin. Moving lower she placed another kiss on his left pectoral.

"Please." Denise uttered, kissing his abs slowly and languidly as she moved further down towards his boxers.

"Please." She said, once more as she slid the boxers down over his ass, allowing his dick to spring free right in her face. She looked up into those bright blue eyes and smiled.

"Please." This time, she demanded finally breaking his resolve. Letting her tongue slip out between her parted lips, she swirled it around the head of his shaft as she grabbed his tight well-trimmed balls with one hand and stroked his length with the other just before she took him into her drooling mouth causing him to shutter. The moan that rumbled from his chest seemed to reverberate against the walls of the living room, and she smiled again knowing she had this power.

His hands roamed over her shoulders, finally making his way up her neck as Hank laced his fingers up into her hair. Her tongue pulsed against his twitching cock, sucking in his veiny girth as she bobbed her head back and forth. Swallowing, she relaxed her jaw so that she could take more of him down her throat as she looked up at him through her lashes. She noticed his breathing was coming in shorter as he seemed to start thrusting his dick further into her mouth.

As much as she loved giving head she would rather him be in her pussy, which was pulsating at the idea of his dick thrusting in and out of her. She moaned at the idea. It had been with that moan that she felt his balls tighten even more in her hand, and it dawned on her this could bring him to cum right this second. With tears at the corner of her eyes, she looked up again and swallowed deep to get as much of him in her throat. Catching the way he was looking at her - this was something unreal - the fire in his eyes was only for her, and she moaned again. The vibration from the trapped sound had his eyes rolling to the back of his head, and the next thing she knew he was cuming right down her throat. As she sucked and licked him clean, he tried catching his breath.

"God damn it, why did I have you stop that other time?" He murmured, easing her to lay back against the couch cushions as he peppered her in sweet, tiny kisses. He kissed her forehead, cheeks, nose, lips and chin – leaving her wanting more as he worked his boxers off kicking them to the floor.

"Because you're an asshole, who didn't know just how good it could have been." Denise wasn't sure if calling him an asshole was going to get her in trouble or not, but it was true.

"Did you just call me an asshole? Are we back to being a brat again?" Hank asked, propping himself up on his elbow as he stroked her leg working his way up her thigh. Would he stop if she said yes, would she need to apologize?

"Yes, I called you an asshole, and I told you before I'm not a good girl, it's hard for a leopard to change their spots." His hand had made its way up to her panty line, and all she wanted was for him to pull them off. Hell, she would do it herself if he wasn't laying across one of her legs, pinning her down. Drawing his finger to the seam along her inner hip, he slipped his finger inside and dragged his nail along her crook of her hip causing her to suck in her breath.

"I know it's hard for you, baby. But I know you want this." He said, as he lowered his head to the top of her night gown nipping at it to pull it down allowing her breast to spill out exposing her to his face. Grinning down, he took his tongue running it around her taut nipple and sucked it into his mouth as his finger slid closer to her wet seam causing her to moan at the exhilarating feeling leading him to stop.

"Ah, so that is what you sound like when you moan? What do you sound like when you scream?" He asked as he continued his torture on her breast, licking, sucking and nipping at the surface of her skin – she couldn't help but to close her eyes, throwing her head back allowing herself to revel in the feeling. But then, he stopped and removed his hand from her panties, prompting her to produce the saddest whimper she had ever uttered as she looked at him furrowing her brow.

"Why did you stop?"

"Just one word." He said, brushing his lips against her now raw damp nipple. He had her right where he wanted her and she couldn't fight it.

"Please? How many more times are you gonna make me say, please?" she hoisted herself up on her elbows and now her bare breast was literally in his face. Grabbing the back of his hair and pulling him closer, she watched as his eyes rolled into the back of his head - enjoying the way she pulled at him.

"Please, I will moan, I will scream but for the love of God and all that is holy just fucking please." Her voice cracked from the sheer level of desperation in her, and he laughed as she crushed her lips to his. But it seemed that he was just as done as she was, as he pulled away and got up from the couch.

Holding out his hand to her, she took it as he pulled her up to stand in front of him as he scanned his eyes over her body. She was the only one still wearing clothes, yet she felt like she was already naked in front of him. Slowly he took the straps of her nightgown off her shoulders, exposing both her breasts to his gaze as he reverently ran his fingers over her body and pushed down the nightgown over her hips, allowing it to fall to the floor.

He said nothing, but his breathing and his body's response to what she looked like undressed gave her every indication that he was just as turned on as she was. Allowing both thumbs to slowly slide her panties down onto the floor, she was finally naked in front of him, and he couldn't pull his eyes off her body. For some reason, just his gaze had her breaths coming in short, erratic bursts. Something in her caught that he was memorizing every part of her body, he wasn't just taking her in, he was searing in every single detail of her and no one had ever made her feel this wonderful before. It was something more, he was stirring up something greater than just desire. Her heart leapt as he slowly ran his hands ever-so gently over her, almost as if a ghost was touching her, as if he was afraid of breaking her. The man in front of her was driving her to the edge of the world and he was barely even touching her; *no, he was worshipping her*.

"Hank" she whispered, and his head snapped up to her eyes. In them she could see only one thing and it scared her, but what scared her more was what she was going to say next. "Make love to me." She didn't want sex. She didn't want a good fuck - she wanted more. She had never had more, but no one had ever made her feel like she was the greatest thing in the world. And despite this whole teasing thing he enjoyed doing, there was more in his touch and his kisses. And God help her she was desperate for it.

"Please."

CHAPTER SIXTEEN

Hank

Hank couldn't believe what she had just said, she wanted him to make love to her. He had seen love in people's eyes before, but never someone who had looked at him the way Denise was right this second. He knew his boys loved him, but this was different and if he was going to be honest with himself he was nervous. What if this went wrong? What if he messed this up all over again? But there he was, standing in Denise's living room naked in front of her, and her in front of him as vulnerable as they both could be, and she was asking him to make love to her. Those bewitching hazel eyes filled with a love and passion, he never thought he would ever see from another living soul.

Clasping her face within his hands, he kissed her like tomorrow was not promised, and the fire that was returned in her kisses was just as intense. Could they have healed years of hate so quickly? Probably not, but what they had learned in just one night was that they were two lost souls floating around this world alone, fighting their own demons by themselves and perhaps they just didn't want to do that anymore. He knew he didn't, he was so tired of all the self-loathing and the trauma of the past. But here standing in front of him, begging him to do something he wasn't even sure he was capable of doing was someone who had seen him at his worst. Yet still, she asked for his love.

Releasing her face, he let his hands wrap around her waist, her soft skin was like satin as he pulled her so close - it was almost as if he was trying to fuse their bodies together - two souls trying to become one. He felt her nails on his back as she scratched at him and he couldn't hold back the moan that escaped his lips, or the tears that seemed to want to leak from his eyes. Someone wanted him, not to exact revenge or to be a stand-in for the one they really wanted, someone who was willing to accept him for all the morally gray things he has said and done. But for Denise, he would be better because _she_ wanted _him_.

Pulling away from their kiss he dropped to his knees, wanting to worship at her feet, to make her feel like no one has ever made her feel what he felt for her. He placed tiny reverent kisses on the underside of her breasts as she ran her fingers through his hair and then trailed kisses down her abdomen to the top of her waxed quim. Steadying himself, he grasped her hips and kissed ever so slowly around, her damp pussy not quite ready to dive in.

That sweet addictive scent she wore mingled with the heady scent of her arousal and he was afraid he would lose it right then. But he stayed strong as he allowed his tongue to slide down her seam and she let out a moan again – the sound like music to his ears. Widening her stance to open herself to him, he smiled against her soft pussy as he dove in. Her breath caught the second his tongue slid between her folds and swirled her clit. Raising her right leg over his shoulder opening herself up to him he continued his swirling ministrations on her clit with his tongue and proceeded to pulse suck on her bundle of nerves causing her knee to buckle a little. And Hank couldn't help but produce a pleased groan against her. Gripping her ass with his left hand he maneuvered his right hand up to her dripping core and slid one finger in – laughing against her mound when she let out a small screech.

"I'm sorry did I do something wrong? Does this help?" He asked as he slid another finger in and curled it up into her as she seemed to slump against him and ground herself against his hand.

"No, please don't stop." Denise was back to begging, and he was happy to oblige as he went back to licking and sucking on her clit. He slowly moved his fingers methodically in and out of her, making sure to curl his fingers so that he would hit her g-spot. As she tipped her head back to the languid ministrations he was performing, she dug her nails into his scalp, and although there was a tiny bit of pain - he didn't care as he felt her thighs starting to quiver, and her breathing coming in short pants. Then her core started to constrict tighter and tighter around his fingers and he sucked down hard one last time on her clit. Her climax hit, rolling over and over as her cum dripped down his hand, and he tightened his grip on her as she fell onto him in the final release of her orgasm.

Unhooking her leg from his shoulder, he scooped her up and placed her onto the deep aubergine colored couch continuing to kiss her body. He started with her ankles and worked his way up, placing kisses everywhere, not leaving a single spot un-kissed as he crawled up between her thighs. His hard cock pressed against her soaked pussy, but then he realized he needed to get up to grab the condom he had in his wallet.

It wasn't that he was expecting this all to happen, it was just an in-case sort of thing he had done for the past four years. He had had a vasectomy right after Colin, but one needed to be careful no matter what. Shifting to get up, Denise looked at him and seemed to hold him a little tighter.

"Where are you going?" She asked and then she followed his gaze to his jeans and bit her lip.

"Well, I need to get something if we are to continue." He explained, teasing her teeth away from her bottom lip to kiss her. He stared down into her eyes and he felt himself once again getting lost in them.

"I'm not normally this kind of person but-" she paused, "I'm clean, if you are."

He glared down at her and the idea of having unprotected sex meant that she was willing to take a risk, or perhaps there was something even more, it was that she trusted him which was an odd notion. The only person he had only ever had unprotected sex with had been Grace, he had been smart while having his affair with Liz and never even considered having unprotected sex - even though he was sure he didn't catch anything, he had still gotten tested and knew everything was fine.

"Denise, I need you to be sure. This is not something that I normally do. Hell, I didn't even think this was going to happen." He confessed, in truth he thought if anything he would come over, talk things out and maybe they would get slightly carried away, but not this far despite wanting it, and it still felt like it was an incredible dream. But here she was laying beneath him, wanting him to make love to her. To make love was not just sex, it meant something far greater, something *sacred* and *profound.*

"I asked you to make love to me once, don't make me ask again." Still gnawing her bottom lip as she moved her hips so that his hard cock swept her core, catching him off guard, he released a groan at the overwhelming sensation of her warmth.

"No Denise, I'm going to ask you one more-" was all he was able to say before she pulled him down for another kiss. Her lips tasted like coffee and a little salty from the sweat she had been kissing on his body, inhaling her in he couldn't get enough of this goddess he had laying beneath him. Hank wanted to stay there between her legs as long as he could, he wanted to bask in her fire, anger and love; and the notion stopped him in his tracks. Did he want her love? Was this divine creature - the one that he had been fighting with and then lusting over for the past ten years - someone he wanted to be loved by, and to love her in return? Her kisses told him she wanted him, and her plea to be made love to meant something so great that his heart raced at the idea.

A primal instinct started thundering in his heart as she scratched at him crushing him down on her and as her long legs wrapped around him, attempting to grind against his hard throbbing cock. The ecstasy of the sensation rippled goosebumps over his body as he let out a guttural moan. She had asked to be worshipped and he was just starting. Releasing her from their kiss he started placing tiny kisses down her chin and along her jaw line and then slowly working his way down her long, graceful neck.

"Do we want to stay here or would you like to continue this in your bed?" He asked while sucking at her neck and collar bone. She shook her head, unable to speak as her breathing increased and she threaded her fingers in his hair.

"Please don't make me move, you feel too good right now." Pleading sounded good out of her mouth, smiling to himself as he ran his hand over the outside of her breast, eliciting a shiver as a tiny giggle escaped her lips. She was ticklish, and he was not gonna let that go by without hearing her laugh again. He had heard her laugh a million times, usually with a sarcastic air to it. But this was different, it was innocent and sweet, yet breathy and sexy at the same time. Squirming beneath him she had managed to line his dick right up to her core, and he wanted nothing more than to glide right into her, but she wanted to be made love to - and he knew that was not something you could rush. Unhurriedly massaging himself against her wetness, he grazed his hand on the outside of her breast again. And as she began to giggle, he slowly let the tip of his now soaked shaft penetrate her opening, robbing her of her breath.

Her eyes flew open as she dug her nails into his back, and he was sure she had drawn blood this time as he could feel her walls constricting around his thickness - the sensation unbearable. Wanting to have this go as slow and as pleasurable as possible, he held himself in check, determined not to let this end too soon. The feeling of her beneath him and around him was something he had never truly fathomed, and as much as he was going to make love to her, so much of himself wanted this as he guided himself a little further into her drenched pussy.

"Oh Hank, yes, please. I need you in deeper." As she tilted her head back enjoying the stretch of him in her. Since she had asked so nicely, he was happy to oblige as he grabbed at her thigh lifting her ass off the couch and buried himself deep inside resulting in the two of them moaning at the same time. It was perfect, she was perfect as she dug her heels into his ass drawing him to get closer still. He felt her moving on her own and he was happy to start his slow strokes, gliding in and out of her slick channel. Bending his head down towards her, he went after the other side of her neck leaving tiny bites and licking them afterwards to soothe the marks he was leaving behind. *My little brat needs to know she is mine*, he thought, and he didn't give a shit who saw them or didn't. *Mine all mine*, and he picked up his pace.

Hank wanted her to be his, he knew the risks of even thinking something like this was only bound to get him hurt, but he didn't care. She had mesmerized him with her hypnotizing glances and ways that she moved, the smell of her lingering in his nose and the sounds coming from her was a song he wanted to hear ringing in his ears forever. There was no denying it now, Hank was falling in love with her, the hate had turned and changed into something different. It was passion. With this dawning he looked down into her eyes that had been closed for just a moment but as she opened them, there he found those fields of green and amber wheat that had him spellbound. He wanted to look into them every day and see the heat in them that he was seeing right this second. Crashing his lips down against hers he picked up his pace and felt her core start to pulsate and he knew she could actually be close.

"Tell me what you want." He said, against her lips and he buried himself as deep as he could and she threw her head back at the depth he was able to reach and gasped.

"I want -" she started and stopped. Unable to speak as he kept up his punishment on her pussy.

"I need -" and he slid his hand down between them and started to play with her overstimulated clit, dragging a scream from her soft lips as he felt her thighs starting to shake around him. "Oh God, Hank I want you. I need all of you."

And all of him was what she was going to get as he drew her closer and kept strumming her bundle of nerves, his thrusts becoming harder and faster, not willing to stop. And then that glorious moment, her climax came in hard and fast as she pulsated around his cock, and that was his end. Unable to take any more of this prolonged torment of holding himself back, he allowed the glorious feeling of her walls milking his shaft bring him closer to his own end. The tingling in his balls let him know he was just seconds away and as she had just seemed to be calming down, his own release came in hard and fast as he exploded inside her, letting out his own rapturous yell.

Doing his best not to collapse onto her, he moved her so that they could both lay on their sides, still attached to each other not wanting to release her. She was perfect and she wanted him. Gathering her up in his arms his heart skipped a beat as she kissed him again.

"Thank you." He said. Her brow furrowed clearly not understanding why he was thanking her.

"Thank you for forgiving me, for wanting me and for starting to understand me. I've -" he could feel the overwhelming sting of tears as they formed behind his eyes.

"I've never -" his words caught in his throat as he looked deep into her eyes seeing nothing but warmth and what he thought could be love.

"No one has ever just wanted me for me." A single tear escaped his eye and she wiped it away, her own eyes starting to glaze over with tears.

"Hank, I don't just want you; I meant what I said. I need you; I've never known someone who has made me feel as many emotions as you do." She said, and they both laughed knowing the rocky relationship they had had. "You challenge me, but what we just did, I've never had anyone or experienced anything like that before, so I'm really the one to thank you."

In one night, life for him had changed and he knew it was for the absolute better. The only thing that could make it perfect was if she would be his.

"You don't have to thank me, just -" he took a deep breath and closed his eyes praying she would say yes. "Be mine, be that one person that I get to say, this is mine and only mine." She pulled back her head and looked a bit shocked.

"Wait this isn't some proposal is it? You just want us to date, right?" Denise's tone slightly panicked, his eyes widening to the idea that she was thinking he wanted more.

"No, God no, I mean not like NO. I just meant, yes like us dating." He felt his cheeks start to flush as he watched a sly smile spread across her face. Brushing her nose against his placing a quick peck on his lips.

"Say please, good boys say please." She smirked, and he couldn't help but let out a relieved laugh as she was playing with him and he knew it.

"Fine, you little brat, please be mine." His grin wider and truer than any other he had smiled before as he watched her eyes sparkling in the dimming fire light.

"If I have to." The sarcasm dripping in her words, but her eyes showed just how bad she wanted him, and he laced his fingers through her hair, bringing her face back to his for another kiss. But this time, there was no questions or hesitation, because finally someone was his and his alone.

He woke up in Denise's bed the next morning to find all his clothes folded neatly and smelling freshly washed, but she was not in it with him. Listening to see if maybe she was just in the bathroom, he noticed the familiar scent of coffee creeping up the stairs and into her room. Putting on his boxers, he checked the time and it was still rather early. Making his way to the kitchen, he found Denise dancing to music on her earbuds, cooking eggs as she sipped a cup of coffee.

Leaning against the door frame he folded his arms across his chest, watching her body move as she sang off key to some song he had never heard before. She couldn't sing to save her life, but she could move, and he watched as she swished her hips and ass in that same tight little summer night gown she had on last night he smiled to himself. Hank wondered if this was what she was like every morning, but then he remembered she really wasn't a morning person - only when she was on vacation.

He remembered one time down the shore when Nikki was shocked that she was up so early, and she explained how she couldn't sleep when she was extra excited – especially when she was super happy to be on vacation. He smiled at the notion that she was happy and it was because of him. Considering his clean clothes and the fresh cooked bacon she had definitely been up for a while. Whirling around mid-song, she screeched when she saw him standing there and he couldn't help but smile.

"Oh my God, you scared the shit out of me." She said, walking over to him with spatula in hand placing a kiss on his lips like she had done it for years and started walking away, but he wasn't done with her. Catching her by the wrist, he whirled her around pulling her close to him lacing his fingers into the hair at the nape of her neck – he brought her in for a proper good morning kiss. Dropping the spatula to the floor, she wound her arms around his neck deepening their kiss and melting in his arms. *She was perfect,* he thought, *sweet and fire,* all the heat he had wanted and needed his whole life.

Opening her smiling eyes, she nipped at his bottom lip and the sting shot through his body, sending heat right to his groin.

"You can't do that and think I'm not gonna fuck you. Because right now it is taking everything out of me not to bend you over this island and have my way with you again." He said, and then she went and did the thing he hadn't been expecting - she nipped at his bottom lip again and slowly sucked on it. She had issued a challenge without saying a word, and all he could think was, *this is going to be fun*. Whirling her around he did exactly what he had said he would do only; he figured he would warm her up first.

Starting at the nape of her neck he started kissing her, first her slender neck and then down her shoulders as his hands made their way around to the front of her body. His left hand lazily worked its way to her soft full breast as his right made its way to the bottom seam of her nightgown. Pulling it up he found that she hadn't bothered to put underwear on, almost in anticipation of him.

"Now there is the good girl I love." He said, and they both froze. His heart raced as he openly out loud just said he loved her. Was it truly Denise that he loved, or was it the fact that she wasn't currently wearing underwear that he loved and then it dawned on him, why was he actually questioning this? He threw caution to the wind and kept going as he picked up on kissing her shoulders and playing with her breast as she seemed to relax again in his arms.

Slipping two fingers between her slick folds he smiled to himself when he found she was already for him. Massaging her bundle of nerves dragging more of those magnificent moans from her delicious lips he enjoyed listening to. Releasing her breast, he kept playing with her engorged clit and placed a hand on her back, guiding her to bend over the island and spread her legs. His hard cock was already weeping in his boxers as he unsheathed it and guided it up towards her quivering hole. Languidly, he slid in easily and he buried himself all the way in, not being as gentle as he was the night before and she let out a shuddered gasp at his speed.

"I'm sorry my love, I can't hold back you feel too exquisite." He said it again, only this time he didn't care, this time instead of freezing she pushed back against him wanting more. Straightening herself up she leaned against his chest and rolled her head back to look at him, and he saw wanting in her eyes.

"Say it again." She begged as he bent his head forward to kiss her parted lips.

"My love." He said, as he kept pumping in and out of her while playing with her bundle of nerves, and unlike last night she was already close as he felt her walls squeezing around him while he thrust over and over. His left hand released her breast and gently grabbed at her throat as he whispered in her ear, "You are *mine*." Hank uttered as a throaty growl tenderly squeezing to remind her who she belonged to.

"You will always be mine, my love." His words a promise and she broke, her moan loud enough for the neighbors to hear as her orgasm exploded around her with his following just a second later. Her legs must have been weak because she fell back against him, and they stood there with the mixture of the two of them leaking down her legs, kissing in the kitchen to the smell of coffee, bacon and now burnt eggs.

After helping Denise clear a path from her door to the garage, he trudged through the foot and a half of snow that had fallen and walked home. The cold crisp air felt amazing on his face and he smiled waving at people as they shoveled. He felt incredibly lighter and the best he had felt in his whole life - except for when the boys had been born.

That was until he saw Jim shoveling the sidewalk in front of his house. Why would Jim be shoveling his walkway? It wasn't his house, and then he remembered having waved at Mike the night before as he charged through the snow to get to Denise and the damned doorbell had a camera. He hadn't changed it yet, and that meant that Nikki might have seen him leave the night before.

Jim stopped his shoveling as Hank approached and tried catching his breath.

"So, you went for an early walk in the snow?" Jim asked, probably hoping to keep it light. Hank looked towards the house and prayed Grace wasn't inside.

"You could say that." He smirked and Jim just laughed, shaking his head. "She in there?" Thankfully Jim just shook his head no.

"I just thought I'd come over and do the neighborly thing and help you clear your walkway, wasn't sure how long you were gonna be out." Jim said, passing the shovel over to Hank so he could shovel the rest.

"You live two blocks over that is not being neighborly, that is your wife sent you. And don't deny it, I was married to her for twenty years, I know how she operates." Hank knew that Grace would have convinced Jim to come and find out what was going on, knowing that he might have talked to him rather than her. Looking down the road he watched as Mike trudged his way over to them and Hank didn't realize this was going to be some kind of meeting of the minds. Huffing as he walked through the snow, Mike waved and caught his breath before getting to them.

"You know they know right?" Mike said, as he whispered so that Nikki couldn't hear through the doorbell. Huddling closer together so that nothing could be heard from where they were standing.

"Of course they know, your wife still has access to my doorbell. I had a package delivered the other day and she texted me to let me know." Hank said shoveling.

"I actually came over to make sure you were okay, when I overheard Grace chatting with this one's wife she got concerned about it being a one-night stand. Especially after your first hook up. We just don't want to see you fall down some rabbit hole." Jim surprised him with the concern he had for him, he had shown up here after that time at The Sun drunk, but that had been an intense night with his brain overloading with so much information.

"This wasn't a one-night stand."

"Wait, you two are-" Jim started in a hushed voice "are you two actually dating now?" He said looking over his shoulder to the house making sure the light around the doorbell wasn't lit but it was and then they heard a muffled voice coming from the porch.

"What are you saying?" Nikki's voice garbled through the speaker. The three men turned to the porch and Hank threw his hands up in the air.

"I said it wasn't a one-night stand, okay!" he yelled at the porch so she could hear, "I'm in love with her and yes, we are dating alright, not that the whole damned block needed to know. Yes, I slept with Denise and it was the best damned sex I've had in my entire life because the other person actually wanted me for once! Now get off my ass and stop being a nosey busy-body Nicole!" He yelled at the top of his lungs in the middle of the snowy sidewalk as people were starting to come out of their houses to shovel. He turned around to see eighty-five-year-old Mrs. Locke coming out of her house to pay John who had been shoveling her driveway and stairs. "Hi Mrs. Locke, if you need anything let me know, I can run to the store for you." He said, with a new blush spreading across his face at the utter shame of being caught by so many announcing this all because Nikki was so damned nosey.

"Well, I'm pretty sure Denise heard that over on her block." Mike said, looking around at everyone who was looking at them. Jim just patted Hank on the shoulder and laughed as he shook his head.

"Honestly, I don't care. Let people talk, what are they gonna say, she's nuts and he's a jerk. News flash we know. We are both in separate therapies to figure shit out and to be honest, it's the best thing that has happened to me. Don't tell Grace I said that; she will murder me; she wanted me to go for years." Hank said turning to Jim, who just bobbed his head in agreement.

"So, you're actually in love with her? How the Hell does this happen; you guys have wanted to kill each other since you met. Hell, last year she almost punched you right before Jim did." Mike asked, reminding the two of them of the fight in the kitchen down the shore and the two men just stared at each other.

"I am well aware of how this doesn't make sense." Hank glared at Mike; he didn't need a reminder that his nasal passages were still a mess thanks to Jim's big fist. "Listen, I'm not perfect and neither is she; we are two messy people who just accept the mess. I don't have to be perfect for her; she's already seen me at my worst. Do you know what that is like, because before Denise, I didn't. I was a replacement for you!" Hank said, turning to Jim who looked taken aback. "I have lived in the shadow of someone else my whole adult life, I've been raised on the idea that I'm a waste or I'm second best or Hell, even used as bait. Do you have any idea what that does to someone?" The frustration rang in his own ears as his blood pressure skyrocketed, neither of these two men had ever had to feel this way - and the trauma of dealing with that takes a toll.

"So did you tell her you felt this way?" Jim asked not intentionally being nosey, just wanting to know.

"Yes, she knows."

"Does she feel the same, did she tell you she loves you too?" Jim asked, trying to get a handle on this story. Hank stopped shoveling and bent his head, closing his eyes. She hadn't, all she had done was ask him to make love to her, but she didn't say that she loved him. Denise had kept so many secrets for so long, so he wasn't surprised that a woman who had them would also keep her feelings close to the vest. *Or was it possible that she didn't feel this way*, and then the anxiety hit as his stomach churned at the idea that he could have just put himself in a one-sided relationship. Her eyes though, he had seen love in them and felt it in her embrace and kisses. But was it possible that because he had never received true love before he could have mistaken lust over love?

"I, I'm not sure, but she -" He stopped, his heart sunk, never feeling so defeated - which was saying a lot, considering how awful his whole life had already been. Jim looked behind him and Mike slapped his arm causing him to turn. Speaking of the devil herself, Denise was just a few feet away running through the snow. Had Nikki told her about what he had just announced to everyone on the block? Was she here to beat the shit out of him for proclaiming all this without her being there? He didn't know what to do as her eyes bore down on him; he stood there frozen in the snow not sure of what to expect. Her stride was long and closing the gap between them, he braced for a punch or a slap. Instead, she threw herself towards him, wrapping her arms around him, kissing as intensely as she had earlier. All the questioning, all the wondering gone as he got lost in her all over again.

Dropping the shovel into the snow he embraced her and held her as if she was going to float away. Their kiss was sloppy, but it was cold and he couldn't feel his own lips, but hers tasted of mint and the warmth of them soothed his soul. The broken child and man healed with just a second in this woman's embrace and his heart roared the tighter she held onto him. As she broke the kiss, he watched as she looked past him to Jim and Mike and just smiled.

"Morning fellas. Aw, were you two being good little boys and coming to help my boyfriend shovel snow?" Denise asked, her voice dripping with sarcasm, and he wanted to eat her alive right then for that *good little boys* comment.

Hank couldn't seem to wipe the smile that was extending from ear to ear off his face, even if he tried. Her boyfriend, it was such a silly word at their age, *boyfriend*, but what he loved more was that he was hers. Still with his arms around her, he turned to see the stunned looks on Jim and Mike's face and he choked down a laugh.

"They did, wasn't that neighborly of them?" Hank said, she had that intoxicating scent on and because he had zero fucks left to give, he nuzzled his cold nose towards her scarf clad neck to get the scent of her as she lazily titled her head back allowing him access. She giggled and he wasn't sure if he was tickling her or it was because the whole display was bizarre.

"What?" she asked, Mike who had actually taken his phone out to take a picture.

"I'm sorry but Nikki isn't going to believe me if I didn't have pictorial proof of this. How the Hell did this happen? I'm sorry it's just, well you guys are so you and this is like something out of '*The Twilight Zone*'." Mike blinked at them, and Jim just stared - stunned into a mystified silence.

"If you must know, and I know your wives must, you can tell them -" she paused and Hank was intrigued at how she was going to explain this. "I will tell them later when I come by to pick up Jojo. But right now, I came to have coffee." Hank wasn't sure why she was coming over to have coffee; they had just had a cup before he left, but there was a glint in her eyes and he felt himself hardening right there in the cold with her body pressed against him.

"Right, I did promise you coffee didn't I? Sorry guys, I have to go, I guess I'll finish this later. Coffee calls." Hank said with an enormous smile, and even Mike and Jim couldn't help themselves as they just grinned right back at him. They patted him on the shoulders as they watched Denise walk up the path to the front door, both tilting their heads to the side watching the way her hips swished and he laughed out loud.

"Mine, mine, mine." Hank said, sounding like the birds from 'Finding Nemo' practically tripping up the stairs to follow after her. Reaching into his pocket for his keys Denise stood by the door and he saw that the ring around the doorbell was still lit. He grimaced knowing Nikki was watching the feed. Yanking it off the plate he threw it down on the ground stomping on it until the light went off finally ending any sort of connection to Toselle Parks' second biggest gossip.

CHAPTER SEVENTEEN

George

As George stepped out of the bathroom, he turned to see Kevin drop his phone with his mouth wide open, and he could hear a female voice coming from it asking him if he was okay. Furrowing his brow, George walked over and picked it up trying to hand it back to Kevin who was still standing there motionless.

"Hello?" George asked not sure who was on the other end.

"Oh my God, hey George, I was just talking to Kevin, is he there?" Nikki said. On the other end sounding shocked and slightly winded. Glancing over to Kevin, he caught him blinking rapidly – clearly stunned into silence at whatever Nikki had just told him having blown Kevin's mind.

"He's here, but he is unresponsive. What's going on?" George questioned and Kevin immediately snapped out of it finally, trying to snatch his phone out of George's hand, which only made him smile.

"No, no give me my phone. You stop this, don't get sucked in, this is for the professional gossips only." Kevin said, as George held the phone high in the air, and Kevin tried jumping to get it. George was having far too much fun and Kevin was now trying to climb up his body to reach for his phone. With George being off duty due to his recovery, he had been working out and rehabbing as much as possible and Kevin had been coming with him and working out as well. His body had started to change and his untoned, slightly flabby arms were now lean and building muscle. Kevin's strength had definitely increased, making it a tad more difficult for George to keep his arms up as Kevin was practically pulling them down - something he wouldn't have been able to do just three months ago.

Finally giving in, he smiled down at Kevin and handed his phone back to him, leaving Kevin only rolled his eyes. "It's about time, now take your sexy chocolate ass over there, you are too distracting." Pointing towards the couch, George gave him a salute. He wasn't going to argue with him, Kevin had been a great roommate and George was allowing him to get away with calling him sexy, something just a few months ago would have weirded him out. Living with Kevin, he had learned that it was just Kevin's little way of making endearments and meant nothing. He had even told him how he called Jim, Grace's 'hot dick on a stick' and George understood that it was not meant as a come on, he just liked to make up fun terms for everyone.

"Is she over there now?" Kevin asked and whatever the answer was he gasped. "No, wait, how long has she been there?" George was trying hard not to pay attention; this had been a regular thing between him and Nikki and at this point he just ignored the conversations. "Shut up? And he was at her place all night?" Clearly someone was sleeping with someone as the muffled Nikki went on. "Wait Grace sent Jim over there and watched him do the walk of shame, so hilarious. Why didn't Grace just go? Why send Jim?" There was more muffled talking, prompting George to sit and shake his head to himself, but the clearing of Kevin's throat got his attention. "Nik, babe, shut up for a minute. Um what are you shaking your head about?" Kevin said, putting his hand on his hip and holding the phone away from his ear.

"You, you are like an old woman, I'm shocked you don't sit at the living room window everyday just to watch everyone going by so you can keep tabs on them." He said, reading the news on his tablet and propping up his ankle, since the injury when the weather got too humid or cold his ankle seemed to bother him.

"Oh, I do, I just do it when you aren't watching me." Kevin said, as he walked over to said window watching people. "Anyway, continue, uh huh. Right." George was trying very hard to read the article about the town wanting to add another dispensary, but that the residents in town had shown up en masse to try and have the council vote against it when Kevin gasped again. "So, wait, where was Jodi all night if he was over there? Oh, okay well that's good, could you've imagined her waking up to Hank in the house?"

It now dawned on George why Kevin and Nikki were so invested. Turning from his spot on the couch he looked over at Kevin who was biting his lip. Pointing at him, George curled his finger and gave the come-hither hand gesture watching Kevin to screw up his face as he handed him the phone.

"Nikki, it's George, I'm gonna need you to start from the beginning now that Gossip Gerty over here spilt a whole cup of tea with no context." The reluctant sigh on the other end let him know that Nikki wasn't sure that she wanted to dish to him.

"Fine, Kevin, why you are rooming with a detective is beyond me. Now I have to go over this all over again." Nikki whispered, clearly she wasn't wanting other people in her home to hear her but George was patient as she launched into the retelling of the story of what she knew. Everything from catching Hank leave the night before and watching him heading into the direction of Denise's just as the storm hit, then about talking to Grace who was concerned about both Denise and Hank. How this morning Grace convinced Jim to go over and shovel once Nikki had checked the device recordings that showed that Hank was still not home, and ultimately about the display in front of the house as Hank professed that he was in love with Denise. That she had texted Denise to let her know what was going on, and how Denise showed up and made out with him right in front of everyone, and called him her boyfriend, and the last thing she knew was that Hank had broken the doorbell so she didn't know what was going on anymore.

Then there was silence. Kevin looked at George who was still processing all this information. "Well, it's about damned time." George laughed. Truthfully, he was wondering when the two of them were going to pull their heads out of their asses and finally get together. When he had seen what happened at the Thanksgiving game with Jodi and Hank he was wondering if Denise would finally soften and talk to Hank, but she had instead avoided him. George had been hoping that the two of them would have figured it out by then, but it would seem it would take them a few more weeks for them to come to their senses.

"That's it? It's about damned time? You aren't shocked and or pissed?" Kevin asked, rather hesitant to even bring this whole dating thing up.

"Why would I be pissed? Yeah we dated but she wasn't into me, she was into the sex, we didn't have anything in common. Her and Hank however, these two whether you all realize it or not are made for each other. They've been at their absolute worst with one another and now they really only have one place to go from here and it's up. So good for them." George looked over at Kevin, who had the look of complete shock on his face and was doing the same rapid blinking from earlier.

"Nikki, I think we short-circuited Kevin because he is doing that weird blinky thing again."

"Oh, just hit him, that usually works." Nikki said, as George watched Kevin continue to blink rapidly. Not exactly sure he should hit him, George pulled back his hand.

"Don't you dare." Kevin said, looking over at George pulling himself out of his trance. "Have the kids figured it out?"

"Cal and Jodi caught the two of them being all practically hot for each other yesterday when they happened to meet up at the store. According to Grace, Cal was busting his chops until they left and the kids have been texting non-stop so I'm pretty sure they knew, they just don't know the details." Nikki just laughed. "It's funny because Jodi has actually been incredibly happy, but with her I don't know if she is just excited for the snow or that her mom got laid." She added.

"How is Grace holding up? That is the big question, her ex-husband and her best friend fucking and in a relationship. I mean she is a big girl so I'm sure she is okay with it."

"I don't think she is thinking about that aspect, I think she is more worried about their mental health. They have both come so far, especially Hank, he has almost become like this other person which is nuts. I mean, I think it is nuts, but honestly guys, when he came here after whatever they did back in September and him trying to figure out if his old friend is Jodi's dad -" she stopped and must have recognized that she had said too much. George and Kevin looked at each other like the biggest explosion just went off at their door.

"Say what now? Hank knows who Jodi's dad is? Is he Jodi's dad?" Kevin apparently had not heard this news, and considering all the conversations that Denise and George had had the fact that Hank might know was crazy to him.

"Okay so it's not concrete, but Hank thinks it is his old college buddy that he works with, he claimed to have dated Denise around the time she got pregnant with Jodi. I remember meeting him maybe twice, his name is Nick something." Nikki said, as Kevin screwed up his face only this time he fake dry heaved as well – giving George the impression that Kevin had met him before.

"Oh God, please no! Nick Dupree is the biggest douche on the planet. If you want to talk about someone who hasn't grown up past the ninety's that is your kid. Ugh, he tried to buy me a lap dance at the bachelor party, like dude, no thanks. I let him buy me one and the dancer and I just sat there for ten minutes talking about all the guys that were there and which ones we actually thought were hot and which moisturizers we use. She handed me back the money and I bought some drinks with it so it worked out." Kevin said. To George, this Nick person it seemed would not be the best person to be a parent.

"Okay so I have a couple of questions, one is, is Hank still friends with this guy and two has he asked her if he is the dad? Like is this confirmed or is it just speculation?" George clearly missed work because his brain went right to getting down to facts.

"I don't know, this was back in September, so who knows. I know that Grace had the boys go to her house for dinner Friday night because he went to dinner with Nick. She mentioned that his mood was a bit off and he was super lovey-dovey on the boys when he got home and even hugged her, so something was definitely up." Nikki mentioned and George just felt like he had more questions and not enough answers. He knew it wasn't his place to butt in; however, curiosity was killing this cat. Trying to piece this all together, Nick and Denise dated back when she got pregnant, Nick was a jerk, Denise loved being a single mom and never talked about Jodi's dad, so in his brain it sounded like she got pregnant with this guy and didn't want him in her life. As the youngest brother to all older sisters, one of which was a single mom herself, he understood the rationale behind that. Was it right? Probably not, but if this guy Nick was as bad as Kevin was saying - then if

George was Denise, he wouldn't want this guy knowing anything about Jodi either.

CHAPTER EIGHTEEN

Denise

Christmas morning came with another snowfall, and a warm cup of coffee on her nightstand. She could hear the snowblower going outside already - only Denise knew that Jodi was still fast asleep because she was laying next to her in the bed. Grabbing her phone to check the time, she saw it was only nine a.m. and she wracked her brain, trying to figure out who would have been in her place this early shoveling and bringing her coffee without waking her up. She had given a copy of the key to her house to several people, Grace, Nikki, and recently she had given it to Hank, but she figured that since he had the boys overnight he would be home. Then she smelt something familiar, it was soft and sweet, something she hadn't smelt in years.

Sliding her feet into her old ratty slippers she trudged over to the window and saw Hank and Calvin shoveling and snow blowing outside as she stood there in total disbelief. It was Christmas, what was he doing taking

Calvin over to her house just to shovel, and who was watching Colin? Furious at the idea that he had come over here when she was completely capable of cleaning up the snow, she ran down the stairs throwing on her robe ready to launch into a full yelling fit. But as she passed the kitchen doorway, she stopped dead in her tracks and turned around.

Walking over to the doorframe, her eyes widened and instantly filled with tears at the sight in front of her. There sat Colin, already eating a stack of pancakes and in front of her stove stood the second most important person in her whole life.

"Oh, ma douce crème au caramel, tu es censée dormir. Joyeux Noël ma fille." (*Oh, my sweet caramel cream, you are supposed to be sleeping. Merry Christmas my daughter.*) Phillipe said, as he walked over to her, placing a sweet kiss on her cheek and embracing her. Closing her eyes the tears that had collected in them leaked down her cheek as she found it increasingly hard to breathe. Her father was standing there in her kitchen on Christmas morning. She had just talked to him the day before and he hadn't said a single thing about coming. They had talked about tree sales and how Sally Jenson was starting to take over a bunch of new tasks at the market because his back was starting to get worse, and Denise told him he just needed to retire already, but all he said was that he wasn't done just yet.

"Pourquoi pleures-tu ? C'est Noël, j'aurais pensé que tu serais ravi de voir ton vieux?" (*Why are you crying? It's Christmas, I would have thought you would be happy to see your old man?*) He said, as he wiped away the tears that stained her freckled cheeks. Standing there ugly crying in her father's arm, all she could do was shake her head in disbelief.

"Of course I'm thrilled to see you, but how did you even get here? I just talked to you yesterday." Denise said, between sobs as she hugged him again to make sure he was real. Jodi had finally woken up and stood in the doorframe smiling.

"Papi Phillipe you made it! How was your flight? How did the tree sale go? I cleaned up the spare room so that you can stay in there, it's right next to mine." Jodi excitedly exclaimed and Denise turned her head; she hadn't even noticed that the spare room was set up to receive a guest or that Jodi had apparently known this whole time that her father was coming. Embracing Jodi, lifting her up off the floor Phillipe kissed his granddaughter.

"My sweet, you are always so inquisitive. Merry Christmas my dear. The flight was a little rocky, but nothing I haven't experienced before and the tree sale went better than last year, so I am pleased. Sally really did a great job; she is going to make a great owner." Phillipe said, with a sly smile, Denise's head spun on that comment.

"Wait, you are retiring? Why didn't you say something sooner?" Denise was beyond shocked, she had pleaded with him for years to finally sell due to his back issues. Running the stand and taking care of the orchard and hives had been his whole life's work but it came with a price. Loading and unloading all the items at the market had taken a toll on his body and with her living in New Jersey she hadn't been there to help. Always reaching out to the staff to make sure he wasn't overdoing it the past couple of years had been a weekly thing, but to know that he had finally decided to sell and retire made her feel so much better.

"Why would I want to ruin my Christmas present? Now you can stop worrying about ton père mon amour." Phillipe smiled as he went back to making more pancakes and Denise went over to hug Colin who was stuffing my pancakes in his face.

"I thought you being here was your Christmas present?" Denise questioned as she heard the front door and the stomping of feet in her vestibule. Hank and Calvin must have finished outside and she could hear Hank instructing Calvin to take off his boots. With her brain still reeling, she tried to piece this all together, Jodi knew Phillipe was here and so were Hank and the boys, which meant Hank had orchestrated this whole thing and kept it from her. Otherwise, how could her dad have gotten here? Kissing Colin on the head she headed to the hallway and stood there with her hands on her hips as Calvin and Hank just looked at her as they walked through the living room. Calvin smiled, knowing that his dad was about to get yelled at and walked up to Denise giving her a hug.

"Merry Christmas." He said, "Don't be mad at him, he's been planning this with Jodi since you guys started dating." He whispered and gave her an extra squeeze before walking into the kitchen. Looking at Hank, she didn't know whether to kiss him or slap him. She couldn't believe it, Hank and her own daughter behind her back. Hank slowly approached and reached down on to the couch to pull out a box from the bag they had brought with them and held it out.

"Merry Christmas?" Hank questioned because he knew how she could be, years of fighting must have traumatized him into thinking that she was always ready to throw a punch and not three months ago she had slapped him, so it was a fair response. "Listen, I'm sorry I didn't tell you, but I overheard you talking to your dad the other week and I know you are worried about him. So, I thought; 'why should he spend Christmas alone, and you here'."

Who was this man standing in front of her? Yes, things were obviously tremendously better, but who starts dating someone, and then flies their girlfriend's parent out on Christmas? No one! She knew no one who would do this.

"You flew him out here at this time of year? Hank, that costs a fortune!" Denise would never be able to repay him, but all he did was smile.

"My love, they are called airmiles. I don't rack them up for no reason, I just finally had a good reason to use them." She looked down at the box and rustled it around as she took it out of his hand, it sounded like shoes which was a really odd present to give a new partner. Narrowing her eyes on his sky blues she was really struggling with the desire to smack him or kiss him. He stood there very proud of what he had done and she could see that cocky air in his gaze, but she gave in as she wrapped her arms around his neck. His hands felt cold against her back as they stood there in each other's arms.

"What am I going to do with you?" Denise asked as he brushed his lips across hers setting a tingle in all the right places and raising the hairs on the back of her neck.

"Whatever you want, just as long as you can wait till tonight. Grace invited me for dinner this afternoon and your dad has already agreed to watch Jodi so we can have a night together at my place." Hank whispered, kissing her soundly on the lips. She was still in shock, but more shocked that her dad knew and agreed to all of this. Sure, he didn't know the details but the fact that he had just met Hank and agreed to watch his granddaughter so that his daughter could get plowed by this new stranger was just slightly off putting to her.

"Wait, my dad agreed to this?" She pulled back and he kept placing tiny kisses on her face setting little flames all over her and along her chin.

"Your father is a lot more open minded than you realize, he practically begged me to take you off his hands. He said you would hover over him the moment he got here, so just let it be and let me spend my night and tomorrow morning unwrapping my present." He added a nip to her chin as he nudged her chin up so he could continue setting her aflame, kissing down her neck and she melted right there. Her father was right, she would hover, he had done so much and been there for her through all the rough times, but the fact that Hank had convinced him so easily shocked her.

"Your pancakes are getting cold and I brought presents all the way from Wisconsin. So come and eat, you can finish whatever you two are doing later." Phillipe called from the kitchen and the kids made gagging sounds prompting Hank to start laughing. Denise wasn't sure when or how, but his gruffy laugh made her heart flutter just a little. This man was not the same one she had known for ten years; he was lighter and he had this sweetness she never knew he could possess. She needed to remember to give Dr. Mahoney a massive hug the next time she saw him, because whatever magic he was weaving with Hank was truly a miracle.

Making their way into the kitchen, she spotted the kids devouring their pancakes and for some reason the scent of them was not the same ones she recalled from her youth. These were different, there was a sweetness in their aroma, almost as if her dad had changed the recipe. Hesitant to take a bite for fear that they would be the same sad pancakes of her youth, she looked to her dad who just gave her one of his amazingly warm smiles and she closed her eyes, taking a hesitant bite. They did taste different, they were buttery with a tiny hint of vanilla and their texture was better, these were light and airy, by far the best ones she had ever eaten in her entire life. Taking a second bite, she still held skepticism in her mind that it wasn't possible that they could be this good, but they were.

"Okay, what did you do to the recipe? Is it more vanilla? Did you add the cane sugar?" Denise asked stuffing another large bite full into her mouth, but all Phillipe did was smile and look at Hank and the kids, then back to her.

"Mon cher, quand la vie est plus douce, tout ce que vous mangez l'est aussi." (*My dear, when life is sweeter, everything you eat is too.*) Phillipe said, looking around the room at the group that surrounded her. "La vie ne doit pas être amère. La nourriture peut être de l'amour, mais l'amour est la nourriture de l'âme." (*Life should not be bitter. Food can be love, but love is the nourishment of the soul.*)

Hank finished his bite of food and took a sip of his coffee. "Your dad is right. Life can be bitter, but like Phillipe said, when it is sweet, everything else can be too." Denise and Phillipe exchanged glances, neither one of them would have guessed that Hank understood French, and their shocked looks made Hank laugh.

"What? I took French in high school and a number of my client's work for a large French cosmetics company that have offices here in the states. It's good to be the only one in the office that can handle all those clients." Hank said, before taking a sip of his coffee.

"Daddy speaks Greek too, it sounds so silly when he does." Colin chimed in, now chomping on the thick cut bacon that Phillipe must have brought with him from Wisconsin. Denise honestly didn't know what to make of all of this, but what she did know was that this was the first Christmas that everything she ate was going to taste amazing.

The morning flew by as quickly as it had started, and there was a small part of her that was sad when Hank had to take the boys to Grace's for dinner. But Jim had extended an invite to Hank as well, so he was going to be able to celebrate with their families too - which he confessed to Denise he was a bit skeptical of. Positive that he was going to get grilled about their relationship by Kevin, Janie and Judi, he promised to tell her all about it later. But she was getting to spend her Christmas with her Dad and Jodi and she couldn't have expected a better time.

"I still cannot believe you are here." Denise laughed and Jodi smiled.

"It was my idea." Jodi confessed, "I just didn't know how to get Papi here, but when Mr. Hank was picking up me and Cal from game club he said he could help, so we called Papi and the rest is history."

Denise sat there in her brand new purple fuzzy slippers that Hank had gotten her for Christmas, still in disbelief that they had done this and watched as Phillipe and Jodi exchanged winks to each other like they were in some kind of cahoots about something. Then she thought to herself, *dear God I hope he isn't going to propose.*

He brought her father here, and her daughter was in on this whole thing – all she could think was that the two of them were acting a bit too squirrely. She needed to know because she couldn't marry Hank, it was just too soon.

"Alright out with it, please tell me he isn't proposing." Denise said, slamming her fork and knife down on the table, and the startled pair stopped eating.

"No, he has not asked me. Although at this point, and at your age, do men still ask permission from the father? I do not think he is going to propose." Phillipe said, wiping the bearnaise sauce off his lip, Denise turned and looked at Jodi who clearly just sat there in complete bewilderment.

"Then why are you two acting like a bunch of idiots with the side glances, it is driving me nuts." She exclaimed, taking a sip of her Cabernet Sauvignon and Phillipe just sighed. Denise watched as Jodi and her dad exchanged glances again to one another and she saw the resolve in his eyes that something was indeed up.

"It is because I am moving to New Jersey. I have decided that I am tired of living too far away from my fille et petite-fille and I want to be close to you. I am tired of waiting for something I lost years ago to come flitting back into my life, when my constant is right here." Phillipe's eyes glistened and it finally dawned on her that he had been staying in Wisconsin all those years because he was waiting on her mother to finally come home and stay for good. But they both knew that wasn't possible. Her heart sank, realizing that he had put his whole life on hold for one person that never felt the way he did, someone who didn't share the same feelings or dreams that he had. That he had stayed in place watching other people move on and grow, fall in love and find peace, when he should have been doing that for himself.

"Papa, you" getting up from her seat Denise walked over and embraced her father from behind. Bending over, she kissed his cheek as tears fell down the stoic man's face and onto her sleeve. Jodi got up from her chair as well and joined their hug, and in this moment Denise's emotions were all over the place. The sadness that her father had wasted years waiting for a woman who would never return. The joy that he was finally moving not just on with his life, but to New Jersey to be with her and Jodi, and a little angry that all of this had been kept from her. But she understood, some things took time, very much like some plants - not all of them bloom the first year you plant them, sometimes the blooms don't show until years later allowing the bulb in the harsh soil to mature. Time always has a funny way of making you learn patience.

As her father wiped away the tears of regret, she knew that although there was years of unspoken pain to them, he must have been relieved to know that he was loved and would finally be starting his life over. It had seemed that this whole year had been about new lives starting and yet not a single new baby between all of them had been born. Musing that sometimes a new birth doesn't happen when you are a child, perhaps bad decisions lead you down paths that send you so off course that you need to start anew, to reinvent yourself. New paths that help you find your true self.

Finally, sitting back down in their seats, they got to enjoy the rest of their dinner filled with laughter and plans of the future they would get to have together, and Denise thought to herself that today couldn't get any better than it already had.

"You need a new doorbell." Denise said, as Hank looked slightly winded answering the door. The mischievous smile that spread across his face let her know that he was still rather pleased with his own destruction of the original one, and although she didn't condone violence, she had been a bit happy that Nikki no longer could keep tabs on his coming and going. Closing the new app she just installed she slid her phone into her dress pocket - she had a surprise for him but it could wait until later. Hank turned to her with a light twinkle of something naughty behind those baby blues of his, and she knew he had a surprise of his own. It always amazed her at how his eyes looked all sweet and innocent, but the looks he would send her was on a level she had never experienced before.

"I don't need Nosey Nikki hacking into my doorbell, checking to see just how often I have you coming over here." He said, winding his arms around her waist as one of his hands slid up into her hair, pulling her head back so he could kiss her neck, turning her knees to jelly. His mouth was working its magic on her neck and she needed him to stop and kiss her properly already. Grabbing his hair, she pulled hard making him groan against her neck. The muffled sound vibrating against her throat as she felt herself getting wet - right there in the front doorway where anyone passing by could see them making out.

"I still have your present and I'm not sure you are gonna like it now." She said, trying to shift them into the house and find her balance. Denise had just gotten there and was going to need a few minutes before he could - as he had said earlier - *unwrap* his present. The idea that she was a present to be unwrapped just months ago would have brought on a fight, she wasn't some object, but he had actually made her feel more like a Goddess with the way he touched her. His eyes that once had held so much contempt, now held nothing but reverence, and it all made it seem like it was unreal. His pout at the idea of letting her go, made her bite her lip, his inability to be satiated was incorrigible and she was here for all the dirty things he loved to do.

Making their way into the living room, she saw that he had already lit a fire and still had the tree lights on - changing from colors to white - and she smiled to herself. He really was trying to be a great dad.

"The boys aren't here so you can change the lights. Colin told me all about how you had it programmed so they can both enjoy the lights. That is very sweet of you." She said, sitting down reaching for the mugs he had out for the two of them. Sweet was not how she would have described him a year ago, a pain in the ass, a dick, an asshole, sure those were definitely her favorite ways to describe him, but not who he was now.

"At this point my eyes don't even recognize that they change colors. Colin's funny -" he started with a light snicker, "he comes down after waking up and instantly plugs the tree in, he can't wait till the evening." He says and she watches his expression change and his eyes getting misty.

"God, I love that kid." A tear escaped his eye and he quickly brushed it away.

"He was the first one to forgive me." And then the second rolled down the other cheek.

"The seven-year-old forgave me without question or hesitation, simply because I was his dad and I told him I was sorry." He shook his head in disbelief, and now she was crying. "I could have been lying, I could have just said it and not meant it, but Collie was gonna forgive me regardless."

Denise watched as his chest rose quickly while he tried to control his emotions, but the tears just silently fell from his eyes. "He is the reason I go every week, every single session because he deserves the best dad, he deserves someone who is better than who I was."

As he looked up into her eyes, and every part of her heart broke for him as she saw, for the first time, a broken man who was just trying to be a better person for someone else. It wasn't the selfish person she had known for years; it was as if she was seeing the broken little boy who had been emotionally abused and abandoned by his parents. She saw the self-loathing that he had for himself, for years of neglect to his own children - children he should have been there for. But deep inside his baby blue's was hope, a desire to do better, to be there for those who depended on him. And all she wanted to do was wrap herself around him to make the pain go away. To ease and comfort this lost soul because she knew what it felt like, she was healing herself too. As the snow lightly started to fall outside, Denise wrapped her arms around the man in front of her and hugged him.

It wasn't sexual, it was to comfort, it was to let him know he wasn't alone and that he didn't have to do this by himself. Kissing his tear-stained cheeks, she would banish the years of hurt, pain and damage away - in her kisses he would be reborn to the man he was trying so desperately to be. The man she knew from the past was gone, this man in her arms melted in her embrace and he would know that he was loved. And there was that word again, it was a simple four-letter word that could destroy people, lives and worlds. She didn't want to say it out loud because then it would be real, but how could this emotion come on so quickly? To go from feeling complete loathing for so long, to suddenly feeling something so different. It scared her right down to her core.

She loved her father and daughter with all that she had, but could she love someone else as deeply? Could she finally have found the one person in this messed up world that was as much as a fuck up when it came to relationships as she was? Nothing could have prepared her for it to be him, to be the one to break down her walls by showing her that he had brought his down just to let her in.

Her heart swelled in her chest at the idea that someone would go through such lengths just for her, who was desperate for her, wanting to bring her joy and that was all she had ever wanted. Dusting her lips gingerly across his, she wanted to say the words, it was so simple. Yet so incredibly hard.

Taking in a deep breath she opened her eyes to see his closed, and gathered up all her strength as she whispered, "I love you."

CHAPTER NINETEEN

Hank

Hank's eyes flew open to Denise's hypnotic orbs staring back at him. He wasn't sure if he had dreamed what she had said, but he was sure she said something. Blinking at her, he still wasn't sure if what he heard was a reality or in his head, but her smiling eyes sent his heart into a stammer.

"I'm sorry, my head went somewhere else. Did you say something?" Hank asked pulling back from her delicious lips that were still distracting him as she sucked his bottom lip between her teeth. He held his breath and prayed he heard her correctly because if this was some cruel joke, it was the meanest thing anyone could say to him, he had been lied to about love before. But coming from her would be the cruelest thing he had ever experienced.

"I did say something." She paused and audibly swallowed. "I said, I love you." Her tone was even, but there was a bit of hesitancy, and his heart hammered in his chest.

"Denise," he got up from his seat and got down on his knees in front of her, "I am down on my knees, I am begging you," he grabbed her hands as her eyes widened, "please, please mean it." His heart wasn't sure if it was going to burst or implode in his chest and he felt a little lightheaded, that someone other than his boys loved him. "If you mean it, then say it again." He pleaded to her, and she smiled again bringing her face to his.

"I'm going to need you to say please again. Good boys say please." Denise said biting her lip, seeming to enjoy his groveling. And he would, he would grovel, plead or beg as long as she would say it again.

"Please Denise, tell me you love me. Tell me that as messed up of a human that I am, that you truly love ME." His heart was beating so fast that he could hear his own blood pumping through his veins - if that was even remotely possible. Pulling her hands from his, she gently held his face in her hands and brushed her lips across his. The world around him seemed to melt away, because all he could focus on was her eyes. Eyes that had carried anger, but now only showed love, he just needed her to say it one more time.

"I" she kissed his lips, "love" a kiss on the tip of his nose and then a long kiss on his lips, "you, only you" she whispered as she brushed her nose with his and the world around him disappeared. There was no one but this caramel-skinned Goddess, that he would worship day in and day out until she made him stop. Launching up from his spot on the floor he pinned her back against the couch and pressed his lips to hers as if they were the nectar of life. He would erect a temple to her if she wanted one and he would make offerings everyday if she asked, Gods help him he was a simp for this woman.

Pulling her up from off the couch, he bent over and hoisted her up over his shoulder.

"Oh my God, put me down! What are you doing? Where are you taking me?" She yelled, but he didn't say anything as he raced up the stairs with her over his shoulder. Only stopping for a few seconds to catch his breath on the landing, smack the ass she was wiggling around, and then carried her up the rest of the stairs to his bedroom, where he had set up a little surprise beforehand. Placing her down once they were in the room, he took another two seconds to catch his breath because he wasn't a young kid anymore and watched as she regained her balance looking around.

He watched as her eyes widened to see that he had set up the room with candles (the electronic ones), a tray of goodies and an ice bucket which didn't have any wine in it but had something else. He had also made sure that his new four poster bed had been delivered in time for Christmas and tied some silk scarves to the posts in advance, she was his present after all and he hadn't exactly said how he was going to wrap her up to begin with, only that he would.

Turning around, she threw herself into his arms and for the first time Denise seemed to be at a loss for words. He had finally made her speechless, and the devil in him knew that he would have her screaming by the end of the night. Slowly, he started undressing her as she pulled at his clothes. Unwilling to unlock her lips from his.

"Would you please stop rushing, we have all night." He said, as she was practically bruising his lips with hers, "and all morning." Her eyes shot open and then softened at the idea of having him all to herself for such a long time. They would steal hours at a time the past three weeks since they had started dating, little quickies here and there, but not a whole night since their first night together. They both knew they couldn't just leave Jodi or the boys to themselves or send them off to Grace or Nikki's just so they could spend the night together. But Phillipe was truly an amazing person since Hank and he had started chatting.

Taking a deep breath, she seemed to calm down long enough for him to guide her over to the bed and sit her down. Leaning over to the tray of goodies, he grabbed the plate of chocolate covered pineapple and had her open her mouth as he fed it to her, the soft sound of her gentle moan as she enjoyed it, had him straining against the confines of his pants. She then went to grab an orange and he pulled the plate away.

"Hey, I love oranges - they're my favorite." She pouted, slightly disappointed, and he simply grinned down at her as he took one of the slices putting it in his mouth and chewed.

"They aren't for you to eat; they are for me." He said, swallowing the last of the orange. He had been reading a magazine recently and had found a very interesting article that he wanted to try out.

"But I love oranges." Pouting like a little child which got him to smile and handed her another chocolate covered pineapple.

"My little brat will have to wait, now be a good girl and eat your pineapple." He whispered as he leaned down to kiss her jaw line near her ear causing her to shiver at his closeness. And like the good girl she was becoming, she took another bite of the piece of pineapple and ate it. Placing another orange in his mouth he sucked on this one and swirled the juices around his mouth praying that what he had read would work. Putting the plate down he stood in front of her first unbuttoning his shirt and pulling it from his waistband, and then slowly removed his belt. As her eyes tracked his movements, his heart leapt in his chest at the knowledge that someone was utterly enthralled by him.

She loved him and she was his. *Mine*, he thought. He felt as if he could take on a million men, knowing that this Goddess in front of him was his. He may have initially thought she was the gorgon Medusa, but if he would have envisioned her before Athena had turned her into the monster she became, then this Goddess in front of him was definitely the one who would have attracted Poseidon. She would be his Goddess, and no one would ever take her away from him.

Removing his pants and boxers at the same time, his erect cock sprung up and he heard her quick intake of breath as she watched his slow movements. There was a part of him that wanted to flex or something just to make her laugh, but then he knew the moment would be lost and he wouldn't be able to enjoy his Christmas dessert. Now completely naked, he walked over to her and pulled her up off the bed. He spun her around to unzip her dress, and as he worked, he placed tiny kisses down her spine – feeling the tiny goosebumps ripple across her bare skin as he helped her out of the dress to find she hadn't bothered to wear any underwear.

"Oh, my little brat remembered what I love so much about you. How desperate you are to be so free with me." Hank's words garnering a breathy sigh, and Denise was so close to melting right there in his arms as he lightly touched the skin from her hips up to her breasts. His lips setting tiny flames along her shoulders, up to the back of her neck, and then licked a stripe along the outer shell of her ear. Her knees buckled, and he couldn't help but love that he had this power over her. She was so strong, stoic and nothing but brute strength, but with him in his arms, she was the most tender thing he had ever held besides his boys. Releasing her he stepped away from her, earning himself one of her whimpers as he reached for the tray, and moved it over to his dresser. But not before grabbing another orange and putting it in his mouth as he brought over another pineapple to feed her.

Then, he scooped her up into his arms and placed her down on the bed as he stared at her for a few moments, wanting to take her in. She was almost not real. He expected that this was all some crazy dream and that he would wake up and none of this would be real, but as he opened the ice bucket and placed an ice cube in his mouth this was too cold not to be real.

Climbing up on the bed to lay next to her she reached out and pulled him down on top of her instead. But this was not his plan, and he rolled her on top of him as he reached for the ice again, crunching yet another cube between his teeth.

"What is with you, first the oranges and now the ice." Denise said trying to kiss his face, but he kept moving it away from her. He had a plan and she needed to give him a minute.

"I want to try something; I want you to put one more ice cube in my mouth and then you are going to use all those years of pilates and yoga and carefully sit on my face because I'm ready for my Christmas dessert." Her eyes widened as she looked at him like he had eighteen heads.

"I'm your dessert?"

"Yup, now be a good girl, give me an ice cube and sit on my face like I told you." He must have once again short-circuited Denise, because she was blinking non-stop as she realized what she was being asked to do.

Moving off of him, he laid down flat on his back and waited until she brought him over a piece of ice and placed it in his mouth, but not without dropping a bit of the water that was dripping from the cube onto his bare skin - and he flinched at the sensation. Then carefully grabbing the headboard, she lifted herself up and straddled his face, hesitantly lowering herself down as he allowed his cool breath to blow across her soft, wet mound. Holding the remaining piece of ice between his teeth, he ran it over her exposed, engorge clit and she pulled away squealing at the coolness. Locking eyes with her, he arched his brow silently commanding her to do what she was told, *and she did*. Running the tiny bit of ice through her slit, she let out a moan that came from deep in her throat and slowly, she settled on his tongue and mouth.

She was already as slick as a slip and slide, and he hadn't even started to lick her yet. Slowly sliding his tongue between her opening and the engorged bundle of nerves, she rocked back and forth to help guide him in which direction she wanted him. She seemed to enjoy the iciness of his tongue deep in her core as he tongue fucked her until she was a whimpering mess – only to pull his tongue out from between her folds and drag it over her clit. His tongue circled the sensitive bundle of nerves several times before he sucked it into his mouth pulsing his lips around it. Her moans had started off slow and soft, but the closer she got, the louder she became.

He then surprised her when his hands – that had been resting on her ass cheeks - moved towards her core, and she leaned forward for him to suck solely on her clit as he slid two fingers in. Her moans were now a loud wail, and he felt her deliciously sweet pussy pulsating around his fingers as her climax hit - squirting into his mouth, and he swallowed it down. This was the first time he had ever experienced it, and it took him by complete surprise – judging by her wide-eyed expression, she was just as stunned.

With her legs shaking she tried to climb down off of him, but exhaustion from the whole experience made her lose her balance, and Hank grabbed her in time before she smothered him - rolling her over onto his bed, leaving the two of them in a tangled heap. Still struggling to catch her breath, Hank rolled onto his side and got off the bed to grab the bottle of water out of the ice bucket that he had been taking ice cubes from and twisted the cap. Covered in sweat, hair stuck to her face he stood there beyond pleased with himself and he still hadn't made love to her yet. Taking a sip of water, he held it out to her.

"Need a sip?" He asked, and she lifted her head barely able to move as she nodded slowly. Climbing back onto the bed, he carefully brought the water over to her allowing tiny droplets of water to drip onto her skin, and she shrieked from the cold water.

"Sip now, please." Was all she could mutter as she grabbed the bottle, guzzling it down, and all he could do was laugh. "You, how" her mind still didn't seem to make sense, so he just laid next to her, brushing the stray hairs off her face as he bent down to kiss her blush infused cheeks. "Why did it tingle?" she asked, "Your tongue tingled, was it the ice?"

"I read an article that if you eat oranges and ice cubes, the acidity in the oranges causes a reaction and the ice cube makes a numbing sensation." She looked at Hank in disbelief.

"So that's why I couldn't eat the oranges, can I have one now, please?" She asked looking absolutely desperate, and he laughed getting up again to get her two pieces of the orange. He gave her one, letting her eat it as he placed the other in his mouth between his teeth, and she smiled, pulling him down to take it out of his mouth with a sweet acidic kiss. Pulling her close to him, the feel of her body made his dick twitch, and he was doing everything he could not to just have his way with her at this moment.

"Did I squirt, I've never done that before but everything was so intense, I thought I peed on you." Denise said, a blush blooming across her cheek.

"I've never experienced it myself, so I believe you did." Hank was rather proud of himself, the article had said that the orgasm may be intense and the doctor that had written it said that due to the intensity could possibly result in squirting, she had been right. He took the water bottle which was now empty and tossed it across the room, which resulted in her laughing at him for such a childish behavior. "I have another surprise, but I may need to warm it up hang on." He didn't want to leave her side, but he needed to check on something and she frowned as he rolled off the bed.

Walking into the bathroom, he checked the soaking tub and the water was still warm, making him thankful that they had invested in the heated model a few years back when they had remodeled the bathroom.

Stepping back into the bedroom, Denise was now sitting at the edge of the bed waiting for him. He held out his hand and brought her into the bathroom.

"You ran a bath already? Was there any part of this night you didn't plan?" She asked as he helped her into the massive tub, and she closed her eyes to the warmth as she lowered herself down into the water, moving over for him to join her. The warmth was as perfect as his bathing partner, who moved to lay her back against him so that she could lay in his arms.

"I wasn't expecting you to squirt, but other than that I planned this whole thing out." Hank said as he grabbed the lavender soap and started to lather it up in his hands as he started to wash her. Starting with her fingers, up her arms, over her shoulders and neck, down her back - and then, he moved to her chest. Lazily tracing his thumbs over each breast and nipple, he teased them before he grabbed the bar of soap, lathering his hands once more. Hank went to work washing her abs, finally working his way in the water, down to her over-stimulated quim. His dick throbbed with anticipation as she whimpered, shamelessly grinding against his fingers – her body wound just as tight as his – and he could feel his resolve beginning to crumble as his need to be in her grew.

Almost as if she could read his mind, she stopped his hand, shifted around and straddled him lining his hard cock up against her. Slowly lowering herself down onto him, the mixture of the water and her warmth with the scent of lavender was overwhelming to him as he tipped his head back, enjoying every last second of this. Despite wanting nothing more than for this to last, he knew this would be incredibly quick, because all of his senses were already overloaded. As she slid up and down his hard cock, he closed his eyes allowing her to take complete control and advantage of him.

Lifting his head back up he looked deep into those mesmerizing hazel-green eyes, and all he saw was love. He was loved by this woman, and she was making love to him. The idea of this running through his brain, and her riding him only brought his climax on faster as she bent down and kissed him. He wanted to get lost in her forever, and as he rutted up into her relentlessly, the exhilaration of his building climax washed over him. It came hard and fast, ripping a guttural moan from his throat – so loud it echoed off the tile walls, and he was sure it could be heard through the entire town. *But let them all know*, he was finally loved and he was all hers.

The phone buzzing on his nightstand woke him up and as Hank reached for it, his arm stopped short, just a few inches away being held back by the silk scarf that was still tied around his wrist from their mid-night tussle. Looking at the creature that was tangled up in his arms, legs and sheets he breathed in the scent of her as he kissed the top of her head. Despite wanting nothing more than to stay wrapped up in her, he still needed to check the phone that had stopped buzzing. Carefully rolling Denise over into the center of the bed to free himself, he untied the scarf, grabbed his phone and noticed that it was ten a.m. He had taken the day off, as he looked at the caller ID, he wasn't sure why Ginny had called him not once but several times, nothing at work could possibly be this important. Pulling out a pair of lounge pants and undershirt he threw them on and decided to make himself a cup of coffee.

With a spring in his step, he took two sets of stairs at a time as he smiled to himself at what a great day it was already. No matter how bad things could be at work, he was off and he planned on spending a few more times making Denise cry out his name. But first he definitely needed coffee. Grabbing the mugs from the living room – left behind from the night before – Hank went to work loading them into the dishwasher. He found it strange how he had become so domesticated since having to live on his own with the boys. Yet there were sweet moments when the boys would help, and even now when Denise would come over with Jodi, he would find those quiet moments to enjoy a simple life, happy for once.

Having made himself a fresh cup of coffee, Hank made his way to his home office to call Ginny back, even though every part of him just wanted to ignore the call. But if she had been calling so frequently something big must have been up.

"Morning Ginny, sorry I missed your calls. How was your Christmas?" He said, starting up his laptop to check his emails.

"It was lovely, thank you, it's just Mr. Nereid, I'm sorry, Hank, Mr. DuPree showed up this morning wanting to talk to you but I told him you were taking the day off to spend it with your family." Ginny's nervousness came through the phone and he knew that there was more to this. Sighing at the fact that Nick had traveled from the city just to talk to him in person at the office was not good. Hank still hadn't apologized for hitting him, but Nick had deserved it.

The past few weeks since the altercation he had insisted that Nick keep his conversations to business only with him if he needed to.

Fortunately, none of Hank's clients were in any way related to Nick's so there hadn't been a need to talk to him. Hank had also let his superiors know about the dinner and the results of their conversation, and despite their concerns, they understood that he hadn't started it and conducted himself in a way that was understandable.

"Okay, did he say what he wanted?" Hank asked but he knew. Nick had been bugging him, not to apologize for what he had said but to continue to harass him to the point that he had needed to have HR step in. He needed to grow up, Nick was still stuck in this childish behavior that Hank wanted nothing to do with it. If it didn't pertain to work he was not going to be interacting with him anymore because Nick was just a man-child who needed desperately to grow up.

"Um," Ginny started, "He left the office in quite the huff after Mr. Nero spoke with him. You may want to -" she said, as he heard a banging at the front door, and he didn't have to guess who it was. Regretting breaking the doorbell now, he sighed knowing that he would eventually have to face Nick.

"Thanks Ginny, he just showed up. I'll deal with this. Thank you." He said, as he rose from his seat but stopped before he left the office. Hank had been the one on the other side of the door once before, and he knew what state of mind Nick would be in. Taking extra precaution, he texted Denise to stay up in bed in case she heard the noise, and then another to George to ask him to come by. He didn't need another broken nose and since George lived a few blocks over he prayed he would be able to help him out. The muffled cursing coming from the front door reminded him of himself not too long ago, and all he could feel was utter shame in how he had behaved.

As he walked down the hallway, Nick saw him through the front door and flipped him off starting to curse at him. He could make out, *cocksucker, mother fucker,* all the good ones and he just stood there watching his former friend lose his mind. But then, he heard footsteps on the stairs and turned around to see Denise in his button down and a pair of his boxers, holding her phone in total shock. Then he heard Nick launching into an even louder tirade about Denise, and it was taking everything he had not to open the door and punch him in the throat.

"What the fuck is he doing here?" Denise asked in utter horror. Turning back to Nick who was now pounding on the glass, Hank was done. He needed to keep her safe, but he needed Nick to stop acting like an asshole.

"If you stop acting like a man-baby, I will talk to you, but back the fuck up." He yelled through the door, slipping on his shoes and grabbing his coat, he turned back to Denise. "You are going to lock this and call George, I texted him, but call him because this may get bad, but you are NOT to come outside do you understand me." Hank said, in a hushed tone and she blinked back at him. "You will not come outside." This was a command not a request, he was going to keep her safe at all costs.

CHAPTER TWENTY

George & Nikki

George

As George sat there eating the last of his breakfast, his phone went off next to him and he creased his brow at the message ID. It was Hank, despite the fact that he had essentially stolen his girlfriend away from him; George had actually become friends with the guy over the past couple of months. Seeing him in the gym and chatting about how therapy had been going, he found out he wasn't a terrible guy. Hank would meet him and Kevin at the gym, and talk about different books they had been reading, sports which Kevin would just sit and listen to because that was not his forte and music. And after Kevin and Nikki had talked about Nick, George was very interested in finding out a little bit more about this Nick person.

Hank had told them all about how the two of them had met while they were going to Rutgers University and had pledged to the same fraternity. It seemed that Hank really had no desire to go home or celebrate holidays with his mother, and as he never mentioned his dad George was left to assume he was either not in the picture or had died, Hank would spend time with Nick's family instead. The two of them would party and make finding women a conquest, which only made Kevin gag at the idea, but when Hank's mom died he was left with no one so Nick's family adopted him into their family.

But it seemed that he just wanted one of his own so when he met Grace, he thought he had a chance. Nick, however, was just trying to get him laid, and when Hank explained that he liked Grace, he would make fun of the fact that Grace was plus-sized and called Hank a chubby-chaser. George could remember Hank wincing at that thought because he himself had been awful to Grace about her weight and with hindsight being twenty-twenty, he knew just what a terrible notion it was now.

Explaining how Nicki was just a spoiled child who got whatever he wanted and that his parents really didn't give a crap about what he did, he had a very self-absorbed view on life. All Nick wanted to do was drink, have sex with women and then dispose of them once they had gotten too annoying. The last time they were in the gym, George had asked if he had ever heard the story about how Nick had dated Denise and he filled them in on what Nick had explained. He was not sure what Denise's side of things were but based on what he had learned about this Nick person George was sure that the break-up was well deserved.

Looking down at the text from Hank about Nick being there at his house, he knew this wasn't going to be good and he needed to get over there to help. As he leapt off the couch, Kevin looked up from one of Grace's books and furrowed his brow.

"What's going on?" Kevin asked, looking over the rim of his glasses.

"Nick showed up at Hank's house and was pounding on the door, he asked me to pop in to say hi." George was putting his shoes on when his phone began to ring and saw it was Denise. With his hands full he nodded over to Kevin to hit answer and put it on speaker.

"Merry Christmas, how was your supri-" George started to ask until Denise broke in.

"Nick's here, you need to get here now." Denise normally had a calm voice but her words had panic laced through it, and Kevin got up and started putting his shoes on as well.

"You're at Hank's, where is he now?" George asked as he threw on his coat rummaging through his pockets to make sure he had his keys and Kevin grabbed them from the spot on the couch table bringing them over to him.

"He just went outside and told me to lock the door and call you. Nick is furious, I don't know what happened but he just showed up banging on the door screaming and cursing." Denise recalled, and Kevin grabbed his coat and George's phone as they locked up the condo and ran to George's pick up.

"Alright, Babycakes, I need you to stay in that house, we are on the way over right now. Do not, I repeat, do not go outside that house." George said, as he looked at Kevin, knowing that he was texting Nikki and Grace to let them know what was going on. Mike was the closest out of all of them living just a few houses away, but with the snow the night before, the roads were a little slick and George needed to take precautions. It would take him less than five minutes to get there, and he hoped that Hank could keep Nick calm long enough for them to get there.

Nikki

"And this is why he needed to not destroy the doorbell! Fucking idiot." Nikki said, as she stood at the front door, trying to get a good view of what was going on over at Hank's as she slid on her outdoor slippers so she could stand on her front porch to hear what was going on.

Holding her phone up to her ear, she heard Grace telling Jim to get his boots on and walk over to make sure everything was okay. Since she was right across the street, Nikki knew it would take two seconds for Mike to run over there in order to keep the peace, but then he would have to get dressed. Sighing at the fact that she personally didn't like Hank and she really didn't want to help, Nikki thought of Denise, who could have handled anything, she was built to withstand a fight. But Kevin had said that she had sounded scared and if she was scared then it must be worse than she knew.

"Mike, get dressed and go help Hank." She yelled from the door pissed that the town had planted a tree right in her view at the curb next door making it impossible to see.

"Why, it didn't snow that bad last night." Mike called from the top of the stairs.

"I don't mean to shovel, go over and make sure he doesn't get his ass kicked, that dickhead friend of his showed up and Denise locked herself in the house." She said, as he walked down with a pair of socks in his hands. He already had on a pair of shorts and a t-shirt on, and considering he was only going to walk two houses over she knew he wasn't going to put on pants.

With the phone back up to her ear, Grace sighed on the other end and she heard her telling Calvin he couldn't go over. "Oh my God, why won't my children just listen to me?" Grace said and Nikki could hear the creaking of Grace's side door to the house closing behind Jim. "Alright Jim just left, but it's gonna take him a few minutes even if he runs. Any sign of George and Kevin?"

Nikki looked down the street and didn't see any cars or trucks coming, not even the plows had come through yet. "No not yet," she turned to look at Mike who seemed to have lost his other boot, rolling her eyes as she pointed under the stool he was sitting on, and he found it. "I love my husband but man is he a fucking kid, sometimes." Nikki said, just shaking her head at him. Grabbing his jacket and putting it on she walked him outside and stood on the top step and all she kept thinking was, Hank should have never broken that doorbell, because she would have had the cops called and her cute husband wouldn't have to go over there and break up some dumbass fight.

CHAPTER TWENTY-ONE

Hank

Hank walked out onto his porch, and the man standing in front of him was no longer his oldest friend, but a total stranger. This wasn't the Nick Dupree he had gone to college with; this was a sad man who needed to get a life. Watching as Nick clenched and un-clenched his fist, Hank could tell he wanted to take a swing but was waiting for Hank to say something.

"This couldn't wait till I got back in the office?"

"Fuck you asshole, you got me written up and they just told me that they are gonna be auditing all my accounts, claiming that someone said I was skimming money off my clients and I know it was you." Nick spat, his pupils were slightly dilated and he just kept sniffling as he was standing there in just his suit. Hank scanned over his once friend, and realized that he wasn't wearing boots, he wasn't even wearing a coat other than his suit jacket and he thought this was a bit odd. It was too cold out for him not to be wearing something as it had snowed the night before and there was snow on the ground. Always making sure that he was dressed to perfection and never wanting to ruin his expensive labeled clothing, Hank was a little shocked that Nick had not taken the time to at least toss on a coat or a pair of boots.

"Dude, first off I don't know what's going on with your accounts, alright. But yes, with what happened last year, I let them know that we had an altercation and that was it. I told them that it wouldn't affect our jobs because we don't even handle the same accounts. I was sure you were gonna throw me under the bus for punching you so I covered my ass but I didn't do it to get you in trouble." Hank explained.

Hank had been sure he was going to get in trouble for hitting another employee but he hadn't, they had been very understanding, which shocked him at first, but then he felt complete relief that he wouldn't be fired. As for Nick being audited, he knew it was a matter of time since they had asked Hank to look at them, and it had occurred to him that something was off. All of Nick's accounts were large companies based in the city - he had secured them over the years - but when a senior partner asked for Hank specifically to look at them, it had been very suspicious, even his own accounts had been audited but there had been no issue with his. In fact, his boss had given him a raise which was great right before the holidays.

Watching Nick's behavior, he knew something was wrong, he had noticed it at the dinner and now with the way his movements were just a little too erratic. The blown pupils, the sniffling, the over-confidence – he was high. Out of the almost thirty years he had known Nick, he had never seen him take drugs heavier than smoking a joint, although he had done a line or two of cocaine at his bachelor party, but Hank hadn't realized Nick must have been partaking it regularly. Nick was an ass, but now he was a doped-up idiot and he had shown up to Hank's home.

Then it hit him, if Nick had been told that he was home spending today with his family, that meant that Nick didn't care that he had gotten high and just showed up to his house. *Oh my God, what if the boys had been here instead of Denise, they would have been in danger,* his mind raced at the idea of something happening to them. Hank had been trying not to look at this shell of his friend, but now he forced himself to meet his gaze – to stare into the eyes of the man who hadn't just come to hurt him but put his loved ones in danger as well. Slowly lifted his head and then his eyes from the spot on the floor until he finally saw the pathetic human who no longer needed to be in his life. He didn't value the things that meant the most to him, his kids and Denise, and for Hank nothing else mattered in this world, and now he was the one feeling rage.

"I know it is you!" Nick screamed and shoved Hank on the shoulder, but he didn't react, his anger was building inside him and he just needed to keep it under control. "The sexual harassment complaint, the audit was all sparked out of your office so I know it's you. All because you are fucking jealous and you are being led around by your dick by that fucking bitch."

Taking a deep breath in, he thought of Dr. Mahoney and all the work he had been doing as he tried to stay calm. "I will ask you again, not to talk about Denise." His anger was hanging by a thread as he turned back to the door, and he could see her pacing and as she watched him. He saw the fear in her eyes, and it was not something he was used to seeing from her as she held her phone up to her ears talking on it. She had called someone, and he hoped it was George or the cops, because he wasn't sure if he was going to hold out much longer from hitting Nick right in the throat. Especially if he kept running his mouth.

"Shit man, she has you so pussy-whipped it isn't even funny. You think she loves you? She isn't capable of it. She's as fucked up as they come. I told you to run away from her and did you listen, no. You are what, trying to protect her? Let her out!" Nick yelled moving closer to the door, and Hank grabbed him by his arm to stop him from coming any closer to the house, but Nick wasn't drunk and unsteady on his feet this time. As he turned to Hank, his punch landed on his jaw knocking Hank back. The fall had been slightly broken by a chair and as Hank fell on top of it, years of being left out in all types of weather had weakened it, and it shattered into pieces splintering around him.

Rolling onto his side trying to get up, Nick leapt on top of him and continued his assault as he pinned Hank down onto the floor. A searing pain shot through Hank's side, and it seemed that a piece of the chair had penetrated his coat and shirt - lodging itself just under his rib cage. But his adrenaline was pumping too hard for him to care as he heard the front door open, and Denise came scrambling out trying to pull Nick off of him. With all his strength, Hank fought back as Nick kept punching his face, and his eyes started to cloud - but it was the moment of haze, he watched as Nick turned his anger on Denise - slapping her so hard she fell hitting her head on the ground with a sickening crack. As she lay motionless on his porch, in that spilt second he finally let his anger take hold of him.

With a guttural growled "NO!" Hank hoisted himself up to push Nick off, and watched as he tumbled off of him, clambering to reach for something on the floor. Now on his feet, Hank's right eye had swollen shut from the abuse from Nick's fist, he was only able to catch a brief glance of what he was reaching for - one of the arms of the chair that had broken. It looked like a wooden stake, and Hank knew Nick was going to use it as a weapon. Still reeling from the pain in his rib and face, he just shook his head.

"Don't do this! I know how this ends, you will go to jail, there is no turning back from this. You got your shots, now put it down Nick!" Hank wheezed, his breathing was labored and it took all of two seconds to determine that the piece of wood sticking in the side of his side was deeper than he anticipated.

"You don't get it! I'm going to jail either way and it's all your fault." Nick said, launching himself towards Hank. Putting his arm up to block Nick from striking, Hank lobbed a punch with his other hand to Nick's ribs. It had seemed that all those hours in the gym had paid off - if he was able to get a guy as big as Nick to double over. Blocking the stake, Hank threw another punch, but this one didn't have as much of an impact because it was the side where the wood was stuck in his side. He knew if he took it out he would bleed everywhere and make things worse, so until he could get medical attention it would have to stay.

Taking the opportunity to capitalize on the weak jab, Nick shoved Hank against one of the pillars on the front porch and he cried out in agony as the wood was driven deeper into his side -now finding it increasingly hard to breathe. With all his strength, Hank balled up his fist and flung it as hard as he could, landing a stunning punch to Nick's chin, but as he fell Nick pulled Hank to the floor with him. Hank wasn't sure how he was going to survive this but as they fell the look in Nick's eyes changed from utter rage to instantaneous shock as he loosed his grip on Hank - the wooden stake falling out of his hand and onto the porch floor. Rolling to his good side, Hank looked at the man who had once been his closest friend. The color was already draining from Nick's face, and a wet cough brought blood to the corner of his mouth. Hank's one good eye widened, his other so swollen it was sealed shut, as he took in the sight - Nick wasn't just injured, he was *really* hurt. More blood dripped down from his mouth, slow and steady, pooling onto the porch floorboards beneath them.

"Dude, Nick," he coughed out, crawling over to him. Hank just watched in horror as his friend started to go motionless, and then it dawned on him he must have fallen onto a part of the chair. Glancing down at Nick's chest, he saw blood seeping through his shirt and something odd bulging where his heart was. Then he noticed the shattered remains of the chair, and realization hit him like a punch to the gut – Nick had fallen right on top of it. Fear surged through him, sharp and cold, and he tightened his grip on Nick's jacket, refusing to let him go.

"Nick, come on man, don't do this." He cried as he heard the sound of feet crunching in the snow running towards them. Watching the life fade from his friend's eyes, he felt the sting of tears starting, and he couldn't breathe anymore as he tried to scream. As Mike approached the stairs his eyes went wide, and Hank started to cry. His longest friend and partner was dead. He couldn't hear anything after that, it was as if his hearing was lost as his head swirled at all that was going on. Denise was unconscious. Nick was dead, and he couldn't breathe anymore. As the pain took over him, he felt all his senses slipping and everything faded to black. The last thing he felt was falling onto the lifeless body of his friend.

CHAPTER TWENTY-TWO

Grace & Denise

Grace

The hospital was a flurry of activity that morning. With car accidents happening because of the snow, countless slip and fall injuries the hospital staff busier than ever. But the large group of people gathered in the triage weren't here for the routine emergencies – they were waiting to hear word about their loved ones, who had been rushed all the way up to the larger trauma center hospital just an hour ago. Jim and Mike had exchanged places with Phillipe and Grace, who had come together once they had gotten the call from George. He and Kevin had stayed behind at the scene. As witnesses, George informed Grace that now that he was officially back on duty they had assigned him the case to make sure that the investigation was going to be handled by someone they could trust and knew the details already.

She stood by Phillipe as they brought Denise back out from getting her CT-Scan and looked around the E.R., chills running down her spine. The nurses and doctors here were some of the best in New Jersey in her opinion. They had saved her life just a year and a half earlier after Liz had tried to kill her; and now here she was again, only instead of a car accident, that complete idiot Nick had shown up at Hank's to confront him.

"Where is Hank?" Denise asked with panic in her voice, now fully conscious and almost leaping off the gurney. Phillipe jumped up from the seat E.R. Nurse D. Slaughter had given him and was trying to get her to lay back.

"Mon Amor, please, we need you to sit back and relax." Phillipe said, kissing the top of her head as carefully as possible. Denise's scared eyes turned to Grace, and all she could do was sigh.

"He was just brought back to the O.R. to remove the pieces of the chair and repair any damage to his lung. I don't expect to hear anything for a while." Grace's concern riddled in her words, and she watched as Denise's brow creased in pain. Grace knew she needed to make sure that Denise stayed calm, she had just suffered a major blow to her head and she needed to make sure she took it easy.

"He's going to be okay, trust me. He is too stubborn and pigheaded not to." She said, with a slight smile and Denise blushed ever so slightly.

"Love is a great force to fight for, he will come back to you." Phillipe said, as Denise's eyes filled with tears. It had seemed that Grace had missed a lot, she knew they were dating and Hank had made a huge profession of love, but was the feeling mutual?

"Wait, I'm sorry, I know he told you that he loved you, but you told him that you loved him back? Why did no one tell me?" Grace asked.

"Because I only just told him last night. And I didn't know we needed to check in with you, you have your own husband." Denise said, her voice rising, and Grace quickly scanned the room for her nurse, seeing how agitated Denise was becoming. She was just about to call out for help when Denise's words fully registered.

"You don't have to check in with me, I just-" Grace thought about it for a second. "I don't know, I just figured that if you had such strong feelings and you wanted to talk, ex-husband status or not, I'm still your best friend. I love you and just want to see you happy." Sitting on the edge of Denise's gurney, Grace took her hand into her own and squeezed, "even if it is with someone like Hank who is annoying and a jerk but has a perfect ass." Grace said, with a wink and it got Denise to chuckle at her recalling their conversation from just a few months past.

Embracing each other, Grace knew that her friend understood that she would be there for her no matter what, or at least she hoped she did. But Grace wondered, when it had all happened, when the fighting and the hatred changed to passion and love. Ever the wordsmith she thought of the word 'passion', the mere definition is: *a strong and barely controllable emotion* and she thought that passion could be both negative and positive.

What if this hatred and anger had originally been a negative passion, the two of them both knowing how attractive the other was, but their overzealous personalities just got in the way. Their unwillingness to forgive was fueled by their passion to hate each other, but it had sparked this physical awakening in them. On numerous occasions Denise or Hank would complain how the other person could be so handsome or pretty, but be miserable, and awful and all the terrible things they would think about each other. It was very evident that they found the other person physically attractive, but they never acted on it. Perhaps, after all these years the passion of hatred between the two had shifted over subconsciously, after the divorce, to a more physical one. It had been as if a light switch had been turned on right after the wedding. OR maybe Grace was just thinking too much into all of it.

Fortunately, the same nurse that brought Phillipe the chair and had tended to her last year - Nurse D. who was a sweet short haired red-headed woman with warm blue eyes - was walking over to check on Denise bringing a large metal medicine cabinet with her. Watching Denise fidgeting with the blanket, Grace knew she wanted to ask about Hank but wasn't sure if the sweet nurse would be able to give them an update so soon. She figured it worth the ask if it would help calm Denise down.

"Another patient came in, my ex-husband Hank, I'm sorry Henry Nereid, is there any update on his surgery?" Grace said, and Denise just mouthed the words 'thank you' prompting a wink from Grace.

"I'm sorry, I don't think there is any status on that just yet, they did just take him in a half hour ago, unfortunately you will just have to check in with that nurse, he wasn't my patient." Nurse D. said, smiling at Denise as she passed her the pain medicine but must have noticed the anguished expression on their faces. Softening her face Nurse D. leaned in looking at both of them, "But let me see what I can find out for you." Giving them both a wink. "I can't have your blood pressure up, otherwise we can't discharge you and trust me you don't want to be sitting here much longer than you need to."

Grace knew this was going to be a very long day, and it would be even longer knowing that Denise was going stir crazy as she sat there waiting for test results and an update on Hank's surgery. But in the meantime, she had her dad there to keep her company. Excusing herself, Grace went out to sit with Jim.

An hour and a half later, Denise had been discharged and wrapped in her father's coat, she sat next to Grace holding her hand as they waited for the doctor to come out to give them any news. But instead, a warm surprise came out the E.R. door. Nurse D., whom Denise was now calling Momma D. came out the doors and waved to Grace.

"They just finished the surgery that is all I know, but I wanted to come out and let you know that the doctor should be coming out soon and I'm thinking about y'all." She said, with such a radiant smile that Grace's heart leapt with anticipation that everything had gone well. Overwhelmed with emotion, Grace embraced the nurse who squeezed her tightly back and smiled as she turned to return to work.

Turning to sit back with Denise, the doctor who had been treating Hank came out and pulled off his scrub cap. "Mrs. Nereid?" He called out, and Grace wasn't sure how she was supposed to respond, she wasn't a Nereid anymore, but then she saw he wasn't looking at her. Looking over her shoulder, she followed his gaze, and saw it was focused on Denise. Slowly getting up from her chair, Denise walked over and grabbed Grace's hand.

"I'm not Mrs. Nereid, but I'm Mr. Nereid's girlfriend and this is his ex-wife so please, what's going on." Denise squeezed Grace's hand and she felt her nose tingling, which only meant that the tears were bound to start. The doctor gave a puzzling glance as they just stood there and then proceeded.

"The surgery was successful; we were able to remove all the fragments of wood from his side and repair the puncture to his right lung. He is very lucky that it missed several other organs, but he is in recovery now. I can allow one of you to go back but only one." He said, as Grace and Denise gave a collective sigh. Looking up at her friend, Grace smiled at Denise, whose pain-streaked face melted in relief.

"Go, he needs the love of his life by his side, so get in there." Grace said, Denise's teary eyes widened, and then crushed her in an embrace with the force of two eighteen-wheel trucks ramming towards each other at full speed and Grace was sure she might have bruised a rib. Nodding to the doctor, she stood there watching her friend and the doctor walk through the door. She felt a complete sense of peace knowing that she hadn't made a bad decision and prayed that everything would be alright.

Denise

The walls seemed to shrink the closer Denise got to the recovery area she was being led towards. The steady sounds of the beeping monitors mixed with the sterile unsettling rhythm of the mechanical hiss of machines pumping air in and out of tubes for different patients had her feeling a sense of unease. Denise had been told he was fine, but she still found herself blinking back tears preparing herself for the worse. Rounding the corner of the nurses stations her heart skipped the second she caught sight of Hank laying slightly reclined with a nurse standing next to him, still trying to rouse him from the anesthesia. Her concern etched across her forehead as she gave a short smile to the nurse and walked up to place a gentle kiss on his bruised cheek.

"Hey asshole, you want to wake up, or do I have to smash your nuts in again in order to get you up?" She whispered in his ear, catching the odd look from the nurse, she bit the inside of her cheek to suppress the laugh bubbling in her throat.

"You would kick my perfect ass after I almost died for you?" His voice was gravely from having to be intubated, and Denise bent over to kiss him. Her heart fluttered hearing his voice, and the fact that he was poking fun meant he was feeling okay, or at least he was putting on a brave face just for her. Either way, he was alive and breathing, she could have lost him over some complete moron. Then it hit her, Nick was still out there. Panic struck her as she realized that she hadn't even bothered to find out what had happened, and if Nick was in custody?

"Oh my God, I just realized, I didn't ask anyone about Nick. I've been so worried about you, you jerk. I have to go find out -" fear coursing through her veins, all she could think of was that if Nick was still out there he would come and try and hurt Hank again. Pulling away, she made to leave and Hank instantly grabbed her wrist. His grasp was not as strong and dominant as it usually was, but it stopped her in her tracks and she looked into his bruised swollen face. In his good eye she saw shades of sadness, and she couldn't understand why.

"He's not going to bother us again." He said, still struggling to talk as he cleared his throat.

"George got there in time? Is he in custody, because he is gonna need protection from me if I get a hold of him. Look at you, you almost died!" she exclaimed, her voice getting louder, earning herself a stern look from a nurse passing by. "You could have died, he needs to be behind bars!"

Releasing his grip on her wrist, Denise looked at him as he took in a deep breath and it seemed to falter as his baby blue eye filled with tears. Reaching his hand up to graze her sore, reddened cheek, he brushed his thumb across her freckles and a tear fell from her eyes - one that she hadn't even realized had started to fall.

"I just found the other half of my heart, I can't imagine losing you already you stupid jerk." Denise said, as her heart pounded in her chest, in her whole life only two other people made her heart feel the way she felt right this second, her father and her daughter. But this man laying in this hospital bed, made her feel more complete than either one of those two, and she couldn't imagine losing him just as he had become hers. As more tears fell between the two of them, she twisted her face towards his inner palm and placed tiny kisses as she held his hand to her face.

"I'm the other half of your heart?" The words sounded almost stuck in his throat as he looked up at her, and Denise smiled.

"Yes, but don't let it go to your head and don't tell Jodi, she thinks she owns my whole heart, I mean she does, but -" she paused as the realization hit her, she wanted him, all of him. And she, for the first time in her life, wanted to give all of herself to someone else. Denise couldn't believe that out of all the people in the world, this human laying there; who had sacrificed himself to protect her and to keep her deepest secret, whom she had fought with for so long was the one she wanted to give her entire self to. The one person she felt safe to be herself, the good and the bad because she wouldn't be judged, they were a pair of messed up individuals that made a great one together as ludicrous as it may seem. "I can't lose you."

Considering that he had just had surgery and half his face was swollen Denise was shocked that Hank was trying to pull her onto the hospital bed. Shaking her head he just glared at her with his good eye. "Then be a good girl and lay with me." He demanded just as his nurse came over to check his saline bag and she shot Denise a shocked look.

"Mr. Hank, you can't be having your girlfriend hopping up into your bed, this is a hospital sir, not a hotel!" the petite Hispanic nurse said, shaking her head as she pursed her lips in disapproval which only made Denise laugh. "And you let him tell you to be a good girl? Girl, I would kick my husband's butt if he said that to me."

Denise had actually started liking this whole *'good girl'* thing that Hank did, and she bit her lip smiling at Hank, who seemed to be blushing - which was hard to see with all the bruising he had spread out across his face.

"I have kicked his ass, actually." She winked at Hank who furrowed his brow.

"She smashed my balls in with her head and slapped me to be correct, but you haven't kicked my ass, admired it yes, but not kicked it." Hank croaked as he shifted on the bed and it seemed he was trying to move so she could sit. The nurse just laughed at the two of them but then gave a slight frown as Hank patted the tiny spot on the bed so she could be next to him.

"Well, no hurting him this time, I think that dead guy banged you up enough." His nurse said, and Denise's head snapped up with her eyes wide, first looking at the nurse and then down at Hank, who seemed to know what she was talking about, "and not too much longer you two. He is gonna need some rest." She finished and walked back to the nurses station.

Slowly walking to the spot Hank had created for her, Denise didn't know what to do or say. She was lucky because she didn't need to say anything as Hank held out his hand to her and she took it. An electric shock ran through her fingers, like that time at the baseball game, and he looked up at her and said, "Please". This time it was him asking, and she slowly and carefully lowered herself down onto the bed, laying right next to him and rested her head on his shoulder.

"Did you kill him?" She wasn't sure where to start in this revelation. Nick was dead, according to the nurse, and Hank had said he wasn't going to hurt them anymore. Hank kissed the top of her head that was resting near his face, taking a deep inhale of her hair.

"No." She wasn't sure how a single syllable word could hold such remorse, but Hank just kept going. "You were knocked out and we were struggling and when he fell back he landed on the chair seat, it must have been broken in such a way that when he landed on it, it impaled him through the back." He said as tears fell from his eyes, carefully wiping them away Denise allowed her own tears to fall. How had this whole thing happened? What had triggered Nick to lose utter control of himself and his life that he thought that this was a good idea?

"The thing is, it is gonna be my word against a dead man, you were knocked out and it was just the two of us around. I heard someone come up the walkway just before I blacked out, Nick was already dead at that point so there are no witnesses." Hank said, as the heart rate and blood pressure monitors started beeping, giving away the fact that he must have been worried about a trial and possible jail. Not wanting his condition to worsen Denise made a shushing sound trying to calm him down.

"Will it make you feel better to know that it was all caught on camera?" Denise said, with a little smile as she lifted her head to look at him. His puzzled look was adorable to her and she kissed the tip of his nose which was all bandaged up.

"What do you mean it was caught on camera; I broke the doorbell." Hank questioned and she was rather pleased with herself for this surprise.

"I know, which is why before I knocked on the door last night I installed a new one and programmed it to my phone. We got so wrapped up in well – celebrating - that I didn't get a chance to give it to you, I just need to install it on your phone. But it's been up and running since last night and no Nikki will not have access to it."

She watched as relief washed over his face as he kissed her. "I love you." He whispered as she smiled against his lips.

"Say it again, please." She asked, he had called her my love, and she had heard that he loved her. But he had never actually said those words, and for once in her life she needed to hear them from someone other than her dad or her daughter. She wanted to hear it from him and only him.

"I love you, I don't know how or when this all changed for me, but I love you more than anyone in this whole world. I love you to the point that I would go to the depths of Hell and back for you. You drive me to the brink of insanity and if that is where you want me to stay, then God help me I will stay there, all you ever have to say is Please and I will go."

Denise's heart leapt in her chest and it took everything she had not to crush him against her, but with his injuries all she could do was kiss him as hard as she could and he let out a soft groan. A sharp clearing of someone's throat got their attention and the tiny nurse stood at the edge of his bed with her hands on her hips.

"Alright, you two love birds, I hate to break up this dramatic love confession, but he really needs to get some rest. We will let you know once he is in a room and then you guys can be that floor's problems." Denise just buried her head in Hank's shoulder and looked at him again before kissing him goodbye. Getting up from the bed, he squeezed her hand one more time before mouthing the words, *I love you*, and her heart fluttered - she was loved by the man that saved her life.

As she walked away the world seemed brighter, she was alive, Hank was alive and Nick was never going to bother them again. There was part of her that felt bad for Nick's family, no one should lose their loved one in such a way, but that other part of her was thinking good riddance. Finally making her way back to the waiting area, everyone got up and George had arrived as well. The bombardment of questions on how Hank was and what was going on with him warmed her heart, and she had only wished that Hank knew just how much so many people were worried about him. She hadn't really bothered to listen to the doctor as he was talking to her while they had walked back to see Hank, so trying to recall what he had said to let them all know was difficult.

Turning to George his face was a little too serious for her, and she was concerned for what the whole process was for the investigation.

"Not sure if Grace let you know that I'm the investigator on this case." He confessed and Denise hadn't been told yet, so *this was bound to get interesting*, she thought to herself. "So as much as I am your friend, I have to be thorough. Which also means that I am going to be asking questions that may make you uncomfortable, but you need to be okay with this." George said, and Denise knew that it was possible that he knew there was more to this story. Resigning herself to the facts that her past would need to be divulged, and it would come out that Nick was Jodi's dad. She had never met Nick's family, but at this point she wasn't even sure that Jodi would want to be a part of it. With a heavy sigh, she steeled herself to whatever questions George had.

He had been sweet not to make her go down to the station to make her statement, knowing that she was just waiting for Hank to be brought into a room. They went over the events of the day and how she knew Nick, Denise had been expecting some sort of reaction from George, but he hadn't even budged, he just kept taking notes and was just nodding to information that she provided. His face was stoic, not the warm person she knew him to be, tilting her head to the side, she looked at him as he made notes trying to get his attention. It seemed to work, causing him to stop writing, he looked up to her and she saw the concern in his eyes.

"I wish you would have told me about Nick and Jodi." He said, closing his eyes and shaking his head. "I would never judge you, that isn't my place. But I'm your friend, we all are." He looked around and pointed to their friends and her dad sitting there, waiting for more information about Hank. "We are here because we love you. We may not be blood, but we are your chosen family and I hope that you know that you can trust us with anything." He had reached over to grab her hand and squeezed it, it was such a little thing, but it was that tiny sensation that finally broke her resolve as the cascade of tears flowed. She knew that they all loved her, and there was nothing she needed to be ashamed of, but it had been years of not truly understanding how large cohesive families work. Families told each other things, they didn't keep big, massive secrets. Her mother had been a big, massive secret, she never spoke about her and then there was Nick, just yet another secret.

Dr. Mahoney had stressed that she needed to open up more, she needed to be honest with people and if it had to start today it would. As George held her in his arms, Grace joined them and took over hugging and supporting her. She didn't need a mother who would disappear on them from time to time, she didn't need some jerk who would gaslight her into thinking she was always wrong. What she did need was the people who were there with her right that second, the ones who had been there for all of her adult life, loving, supporting and caring about her. Never once leaving her, her true family. And then she remembered the first time she had met Grace. It had been at Kindergarten orientation thinking that she would feel left out, but then she and Nikki walked over and introduced themselves and hadn't left her side since. That was family and that was the first great decision she had made on a Monday.

EPILOGUE

Hank

May, 2025

Ginny walked into the newly painted calming blue office space that Hank had just moved into just a week prior. The office was still being set up and the smell of fresh paint hung in the air, and Hank took in a deep breath of relief as he looked over his new office on the second floor of the corner space on the main street, Maple Avenue in Toselle Park. With two young men on her heels, Ginny pointed to several filing cabinets along the wall, and they placed down the boxes they had been carrying and turned back to bring more in.

After a lengthy investigation into Nick's dealings with all his clients, it had turned out that he had been creating fake vendors in order to skim money off all the companies in his portfolio for years, leading to millions of dollars having to be paid back to them. It had been a major hit to the company which could have led to countless lawsuits but with the company willing to pay it all back they had avoided a massive scandal. It had been all this and wanting to put his past with Nick in his rear-view mirror; that Hank had decided to finally leave after the tax season and strike it out on his own.

He wanted to have complete control of his life and free of drama, he felt it necessary to find his peace. Finding out that Nick had been sending countless sexually harassing emails to Ginny, as well as other assistants, he felt like a failure to protect someone who had been a dedicated assistant to him for years. And the fact that she had complained directly to HR because of their friendship had made him sad. They had sat down and Hank let Ginny know that she should never have felt like she couldn't come to him to talk about the situation and that if he had known he would have put a stop to it immediately, but he understood why she went over his head and decided to go right to HR. What made him more upset was the fact that HR hadn't done anything serious about it until it was too late.

Despite the treatment that she had endured, Ginny shocked him by visiting him in the hospital with her fiancé, and it was then that after meeting him; Hank decided that he needed to protect her anyway that he could, and that meant getting her out of the corporate world and working with him. But he wanted to do something better than just get her out of there, she was an accountant and with all that she had done for him over the years, he wanted her to grow and succeed. Which was why, when he told her that he was leaving to start his own firm he asked her to come on board as his associate so that she could further her career.

"Hank, Denise wanted me to remind you that you still need to pack your bag for the competition this week." Ginny said, walking in handing him a cup of coffee from *PenStock Coffee Roasters* right down the block which he had developed a bit of an addiction to. The coffee was great and the pastries were delicious, but while he was overseeing the build out of the office he would make daily runs down to the shop which conveniently was right next to the gym that Denise had started going to and he enjoyed watching her working out. A tiny smile slid across his lips as he thought of how she smelt the other day after coming over from a training session, and all the sweat she had then worked up with him afterwards. Realizing that he needed to stop thinking of her writhing in his bed underneath him naked, he turned to look out the window that gave him the perfect view of the main roadway of Toselle Park.

He had never really thought too much about this town, it was tiny and close to bigger cities, but he had never truly felt like it was home. Until now. A house was just a structure, but home was a place that love resides. It is filled with warmth, laughter, joy, even sadness at times. This town was not just a place but a community of people who actively cared about each other as he watched people crossing the busy street going in and out of shops and the condos that were across from his new office.

Surveying all the different businesses, he saw Mrs. Locke coming out of *Just Jubilant* with a bag, probably filled with cards, and looked up towards his office window. Hank didn't realize that she saw him, and all she did was smile proudly up to him and wave. Such a tiny thing, that a smile and wave from his neighbor, someone he had known for twenty years would be proud of him was causing his nose to tingle and his eyes to tear. But then he realized that no one had ever looked at him like that before; his life may have started out a mess, and he might have made a complete wreck of it over the years, but that no matter at what age there was redemption. There was always a light at the end of that very dark tunnel.

Denise had been that fire burning brightly, challenging him, forcing him to reflect on his shortcomings, calling him out on countless occasions. He had thought that it was fueled by hate, but it had been hurt, and he would take years to make it up to her if he had to.

Her love had come as a surprise to both of them, but so had his, and there was nothing and no one that he wanted his heart to belong to more than her. Over the past few months his relationship with the boys had bloomed into something better than he could have ever hoped, and co-parenting with Grace and Jim had become actually enjoyable.

Always feeling like an outcast for years, Hank now found friends and loved ones who genuinely cared about him, what he did and thought, and at times he found himself lost in feelings bringing on tears of joy and appreciation. He never thought of himself as an emotional person, he lived for numbers because they were cold and concrete, yet he realized that his love of numbers stemmed from his mother's lack of affection towards him.

He was used to cold and calculated behavior from her, devoid of emotion and uncaring. Numbers were concrete but they were empty. Denise and the boys were none of those things, and he wanted the fire, love and warmth more than anything.

A slight tapping on his door brought his attention back into focus, as he whirled around to the door it seemed that he had a few more helpers bringing in furniture and boxes. Walking in with a smile on her face, Denise brought in a large pot with a snake plant in it and placed it in the corner of his office, but not before placing a quick peck on his lips.

"I thought you were told to go home and pack. We are leaving the high school at five a.m. tomorrow so no procrastinating." Denise said, taking a small box out of Colin's hands placing it on Hank's large white desk.

"Dad, you need to listen to Denise and go pack." Colin said, helping take out a picture the three of them had taken at Christmas dinner and placed it in between the two screens on his desk. Hank was sure that Colin had done that so he would always have them near him every second of the day.

"He only listens to her because she has him by the -" Calvin had started with a smile until Jim who was just walking into the office with a plant in his hand, clasped his other hand over his mouth stopping him from finishing that statement. Rolling his eyes, Jim looked at Hank and screwed up his face in dismay.

"I swear to God the hormones that this child has are insane." Jim said, as he slowly released Calvin from his grip. Hank just laughed because he had noticed that Calvin was just like him when it came to the hormones, all he had thought about back in high school was sex as well so he wasn't surprised. But he wasn't wrong, Denise could ask him to rob a bank for her and he would do it.

"Alright, well since you are all here, then I will leave and go pack so I am ready to leave bright and early." He said, as he walked up to Denise to kiss her quickly goodbye. Walking out the door of his office he was stunned to find that everyone else was there as well. Kevin, George, Mike and Jonathan, whom Kevin had gotten back together with, were bringing in a couch off of the elevator. It seemed they weren't the only ones there to help. All of their kids were here as well and listening to instructions from Ginny on filing paperwork. Nikki was working on setting up Ginny's computer and Grace was directing their brand-new assistants on how to set up the conference room with the chairs and table. He was shocked, as his eyes misted over and his nose started to run, he didn't even care that his emotions were getting the better of him. Catching Grace's eye in the conference room, he smiled at her and she finished her conversation with the assistants and walked up to him bringing him in for a hug.

"Go pack your bag, we've got you." Grace said, with a warm smile spread across her face, and he looked around wiping away the tears - and he knew that for the first time he was home, surrounded by those who loved him and the warmth he had always desired.

September 2025

"Alright, easy out!" Hank called standing up from behind home plate as Denise strode up and shot him a disapproving look as he lifted his catcher's mask placing it on top of his head. His heart fluttered, and he could feel a heat rising in him the closer she got. Her raised brow arched in displeasure just made his blood pressure rise even more, knowing what the outcome of this at-bat meant. The Marching Band Parent Softball Game was the second biggest fundraiser but last years had been the catalyst of his whole life changing for the better.

"You know Nereid, one of these days, you are gonna learn never to underestimate me and my bad decision-making processes." Denise said, before placing a quick peck on his lips, "one comment and you will push me to the point of me wearing orange and not having enough bail money." Denise winked at him and his stomach, which was already in knots, seemed to flip. After last years game, he had learned the best pitches for Denise to hit and which ones she loved to chase, so he had talked to Jack on what to pitch Denise for this particular at-bat.

"There you go always wanting to make bad decisions, last year it was you smashing my balls and now you want to beat me with a bat. George, if anything happens to me, you got your culprit right here." Hank said, as George just chuckled standing behind Hank.

"If you two weirdos can stop flirting long enough, we can get back to the game." George said, as he looked down at Hank and gave him a wink. George knew all about Hank's plan and he was just hoping that Denise would connect with the ball in order for this to work.

Watching her square up to the plate, he caught a whiff of that perfume of hers and he got slightly dizzy as his blood pressure was already up. The first ball had been a sinker right over the center of the plate, and it was strike one.

"You know if you just rest the bat on your shoulder, this will all be over and you can go sit back with Nikki and gossip some more." Hank quipped, he had made a comment similar to this and it had got her to hit the ball foul and he was hoping that it would work, either way he needed her to smash the ball again for all this to play out according to plan. Taking a deep breath in, she took a couple of practice swings and almost as if history enjoyed repeating itself she connected and sure enough it went foul.

"Oh, so close my love, but that's strike two, what are the odds of you actually hitting this one?" He loved riling her up, and she whipped her head around to him, pursing her lips with sheer determination etched into her gaze. He had her right where he wanted her. With a nod to Jack, he gave the sign for the pitch, and the ball flew to the plate. Denise's swing actually made a slight gust as she swung it as hard as she could, connecting with the ball. Dropping the bat, running to first he watched as the ball fell to Sheila who was terrible at baseball and completely dropped it. Grace, who knew what was going on, was trying to get the ball as well, and Hank watched as

Denise kept running while Grace argued with Sheila over the ball. As Mike made his way across home plate, he gave a quick pat onto Hank's shoulder.

With Grace's theatrics, she was able to act like she was messing up and it gave Denise time to think she had a chance to get to home. George had gone into the ball bag and handed Hank the item he had asked him to hide and stepped away. Tossing his mitt onto the ground, Hank got down on one knee so that he wasn't blocking the plate and as Denise rounded third and halfway down the baseline she came to a sudden halt, realizing what was happening. Hank watched as the whole crowd cheered and Denise finally started moving closer to him and stood on home plate.

"What are you doing?" Denise asked, her eyes filled with tears as she approached.

"Denise Gagnon, I have spent years of my life not sure who I was or what I wanted to be. I thought I was perfect, but you have challenged me from the very moment I met you. You have pushed me, you yelled at me, you hated me, but all of it was warranted. But then something happened, something I never expected ever in my life. You gave me the one thing I thought I could never find in a partner. Love. No one except my own boys has ever truly given that to me. You not only love me, but you showed me that I was worthy of it. That with all my darkness, all my insecurities I deserve love. And so do you. I don't want anyone else in this entire world but you. So, I am asking, *NO begging you*, in front of all our friends and family, I'm pleading for you to be my wife."

As the crowd around them roared, he watched as Denise scanned her view over all their friends and family who were standing and cheering from the stands and on the field, and then she turned her view back to Hank. His heart was racing, his knee was killing him, but then he saw it in her eyes and it looked like doubt. Bending over, she helped him to his feet and gathered his hands in hers, then brought her face to his gently rubbing her nose to his. The anticipation was killing him. She could say no. She could say sure but not mean it. She held his whole heart in her hands and just as he felt that tiny bit of doubt she lifted her gaze to his eyes.

"Say Please, good boys say please, Hank." Denise bit her lip, and he knew exactly what she was doing. As the world around them seemed to melt away, he looked deep into those hypnotic hazel green eyes and lost himself in them.

"Please, my love, marry me." Hank whispered against her lips that seemed to cause her to shiver. With the lightest of kisses, she stole his breath away, and he felt as if he were to die right this moment even without an answer he would die happy, but that kiss told him everything he needed to know.

"Since you asked so nicely, be a good boy, put the ring on my finger and smile and wave."

Hank didn't need to be told twice, sliding the ring on her finger he kissed her like she was the very life source he had been desperate for. His Goddess to bring him to life, to stun his heart, to make him at ease and hopefully to make some really great bad decisions with.

The End…

About the Author

G.M. Parrillo is the quintessential Generation X "Jersey Girl." Growing up in the Garden State, it is only natural that G.M. is happiest with dirt under her nails as she digs in her garden with her two boys and dachshund, Pennie, right by her side, or with her toes buried in the sand as she sits on the beach with her husband at the Jersey Shore.

As a child, struggling with a learning disability, her mother encouraged her to become a bookworm and, in doing so, she found herself inspired to write her own stories, but only for her own personal enjoyment, until now.

Bad Decisions is a love letter to her best friends who love making them. This is G.M. Parrillo's second published book. A Fall for Grace is the first book in the Toselle Park series. Bad Decisions is book two in the Toselle Park series and will be followed up with My Person, the third and final in the series coming soon.

The Toselle Park Series:

A Fall for Grace
Bad Decisions
My Person